A Winter Haven

Scottish Island Escapes
Book 1

MARGARET AMATT

Cover designed by Margaret Amatt
Map drawn by Margaret Amatt
ISBN: 978-1-914575-94-5
eBook available: 978-1-914575-98-3

LEANNAN
PRESS
INDEPENDENT PUBLISHER

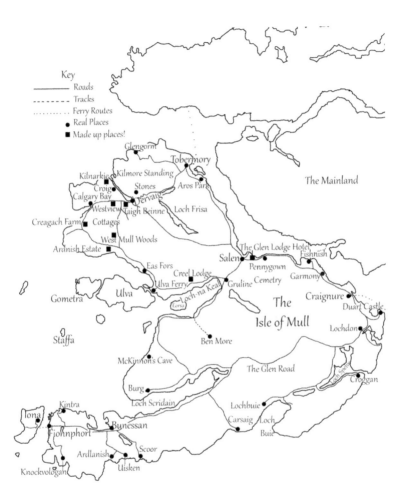

Key

— Roads
---- Tracks
.... Ferry Routes
● Real Places
■ Made up places!

Glengorm
Tobermory
Kilmore Standing
Kilnarkie
Stones
Aros Park
Croig
Calgary Bay
Jervaig
Westview Taigh Beinne
Loch Frisa
Creagach Farm
Cottages
West Mull Woods
The Glen Lodge Hotel
Ardnish Estate
Salen
Fishnish
Eas Fors
Creel Lodge
Pennygown
Garmony
Ulva Ferry
Loch-na Keal
Gruline
Cemetery
Loch

Gometra
Ulva
Craignure
Duart Castle

The Mainland

Staffa
Lochdon

Ben More
The Isle of Mull

McKinnon's Cave
The Glen Road
Croggan

Burg
Loch Scridain

Kintra
Lochbuie
Iona
Carsaig
Loch
Fionnphort
Bunessan
Buie

Ardlanish
Scoor
Knockvologan
Uisken

For Ian and Ossian

Prologue

12 years ago

Robyn stared into the night sky. Close by, the sea roared up, gushing and fizzing as it broke on the rocks. Settling her head on Carl's shoulder, she said, 'Are you serious?' The soft touch and the heat of his cheek on her forehead gave her the warm-and-fuzzies. She nuzzled closer, determined to preserve the feeling.

'Yes,' said Carl. 'I want to be with you forever.' He anchored his hands around her, holding her tight.

'But we're only eighteen.' A gentle laugh broke from her lips as she spoke. The devil's advocate talking. Carl was hers. She had no intention of letting him go.

'Yes, but I love you.' He tightened his hold.

Robyn stroked the silver pendant he'd given her and smiled.

'We're meant to be together,' he said, 'and there's nothing on earth that can tear us apart. Nothing.

Chapter One

Robyn

Dad died last night. Thought you'd like to know.

Though not unexpected, news like that was hard to take in, especially over Christmas dinner. Robyn ran her hand round the neckline of her black silk top. A chill slid up her spine. If ever she needed an excuse to leave, this was it.

'I really don't approve of phones at the table.' A shrill voice drilled into Robyn's head; Pete's mother, a short, ginger-haired woman, glared over her glasses. Robyn frowned at the message on the screen. What to make of this news? A loud tut. Pete's mother shook her head.

Robyn glanced across at Pete. His shrewd, dark eyes narrowed in return. 'Come on, Robyn,' he said. 'Mum's right. Put the phone away. It's Christmas Day. Who's going to need you? You can shut off your business head for one day, can't you?'

Robyn pulled in a deep breath and held it.

'How about more turkey?' A plate swished across the table. Pete's dad grinned with a twinkle almost as bright as his bald head. 'Have you had turkey before?'

Looking up from her phone, Robyn frowned. 'Pardon?'

'Turkey? Is it a new delicacy for you?'

'Why would it be? Of course I've had turkey before.' Her eyes flicked back to the phone. *Dad's dead.* Slowly the news took hold and a wave of memories and thoughts vied for contention.

'Really? Do they breed turkeys on that island you come from? We're big breeders down here; the Worcester turkeys are almost as famous as our sauce.'

Slowly Robyn closed her eyes. It was a struggle not to roll them. Fixing on the middle distance, she forced a calm tone and replied, 'Just because they don't breed them on Mull doesn't mean you can't buy them.'

The absurdity of the conversation. Why were they talking turkeys? The world had changed. Dad was gone. The Isle of Mull had lost Davie Sherratt. Robyn fiddled with her silver pendant. *How should I feel?* Normal people with happy family lives would know.

'I suppose not,' replied Pete's father. 'It must be a bizarre place to live though. I mean, they don't have proper roads, do they?' He chortled to himself. *Rude man.* Why did people assume life on the island was so primitive? Robyn focused on the ugly wired reindeer in the corner. Its red nose flashed intermittently. Pete snickered into his drink. What an unsupportive drip. So much for this test of their relationship.

'There are roads but mostly single track.' Robyn didn't make eye contact. Flash went the reindeer's nose. Feeling the sneer on Pete's dad's face, she balled her fists.

'Sounds like the dark ages.' He laughed into his wine. 'That's the Scots for you. No wonder you don't want to visit the place, son.'

'Oh, you mustn't,' said his mother, clutching her large bosom. 'What if you got stranded, or shipwrecked? And what about the children? You can't be that far away. It's bad enough you can't have them for Christmas.'

'It's not that bad.' Pete laughed. 'They're noisy little blighters, and the older they get, the cheekier. But don't worry, the only island I'm going to is Barbados. I think we'll book for this summer. Mull sounds worse than the back of beyond. I can't imagine how anyone can live without M&S.'

Robyn flicked her long blonde hair over her shoulders and drew in a deep breath. Her toe twitched and she felt the comfort of soft fur. Florrie, her little cairn terrier, rested her head on Robyn's foot and let out a sigh. Robyn slipped off her shoe and stroked her with her stocking sole. *Thank goodness for Florrie, my little rock.*

Pete threw back half a glass of wine. Robyn tilted her head. There was no question of him ever living on Mull or even visiting. With their current arrangement... little chance of him even visiting her house! She rubbed a dull ache low in her stomach.

'The problem with kids is the cost, my heavens.' Pete flung his hands high. 'That's the bit they don't tell you about. Honestly! Lessons for this, new kits, toys, electronics, it's ludicrous.'

'No patter of tiny feet for you then?' Pete's dad winked at Robyn.

'Robyn doesn't want kids.' Pete knocked back some more wine. 'She's a career woman. Thank god. Three is enough for me. Couldn't be doing with the baby stage again. Nightmare.'

Edging on her shoe, Robyn pushed back the chair. 'I have to go.'

'Go?' She wasn't sure who said it; she didn't care either. Three incredulous faces gaped.

'It's Christmas dinner,' said Pete. 'Where are you going?'

'My dad just died.'

Ignoring the stares, she stood. Florrie chased her out of the room.

Robyn had almost packed when Pete arrived at the bedroom door. He leaned on the frame.

'Hey, I'm sorry about your dad. But,' he frowned, 'I thought you didn't get on?'

'We didn't. But I have to go.'

'Go where? Robyn, it's Christmas Day. There won't be ferries or whatever.'

Pulling in a deep breath, she slammed her case shut. 'I know. I know all about the ways of the Hebrides. A lot more than you ever will. I didn't say I was going back. What I'm doing is leaving this house. And you.'

Pete shook his head. 'Why?'

'The arrangement isn't working.' Talk about the understatement of the decade.

'Oh, come on. What's wrong with it?'

'Don't get me started. Now let me pass. And enjoy life with M&S. I hope you don't choke on their range of speciality turkeys.'

In the driveway, she loaded the car. Pete followed, scuffing his feet, hands in his pockets. 'Come on, Robyn. Come back in.' Too late. He could save his crocodile tears. She rammed the boot shut and glanced up just in time to catch his angry scowl. 'So, eh... Where does this leave us with work?'

'Well, you're not fired. Yet.' She tugged up the collar of her long grey coat. 'I guess having a rude family isn't grounds for dismissal.'

'It was just a joke, Robyn. They were ribbing you. You can't take it. You're so cold. Lighten up, have a laugh.'

Have a laugh? The joke was on her, all right, for having stayed with him for so long. The car door slammed. The engine revved. Pete jumped out of the way. A screech of BMW wheels and she was gone.

*

Throughout December, the need to escape had increased every morning until Robyn's head throbbed at just the thought of work. She'd made it to the Christmas break at a crawl. January brought new beginnings – and a funeral – still, where better to be than back home. A chance to heal.

Robyn boarded the ferry, carrying Florrie upstairs from the car deck. The wild beauty of the sea and the darkening sky tugged her chest, her breathing slowed. Serenity. But the island's proximity was unsettling. A queasy sensation bubbled inside. In fifty minutes, she'd be back on old territory. Fidgeting with the clip on her bag, she tried to put away the car keys. Despite not being prone to panic attacks or seasickness, she had a burning need to find a dark room and a brown paper bag.

Slumping on a soft seat, she took Florrie on her knee and patted her. 'This isn't going to be pretty.' Robyn pulled down her thick camel scarf and muttered into the soft hairs on Florrie's neck. How to face up after all these years? She didn't expect to be welcomed with open arms – the opposite. Her mum blamed her for so many things. It stung. Mum knew exactly why she hadn't been back and chose to forget. Flattening her lips, Robyn stroked Florrie. 'When I left I missed it so badly. But I couldn't go back. Maybe things will be different now.'

The need to put distance between her and Pete burned strong. A few weeks of sea air and rest would do her the world of good. A phantom pain pricked her stomach. She held her breath as a warm tear trickled onto Florrie's nose. Florrie spun around and licked Robyn up the side of the cheek. Laughing with watery eyes, Robyn held her close.

Chapter Two

Carl

The bike tyre clipped the edge of a rock on the track. Carl lifted the handlebars and jumped, pedalling faster. A surge of adrenaline pumped through him. The Glen Lodge Hotel loomed. He was almost at the back door. Spinning around, he freewheeled towards a little wooden cabin. Home.

Icy wind clipped his face. He lifted his arms and stretched as though he'd won the Tour de France, not just completed a few miles across the island. No better way to start the year. Pulling off his helmet, he freed his wild curls and dismounted, propping the bike to the cabin side. He ran his finger across the bike's shiny paintwork and smiled. A work of art – unique. Possibly his finest creation.

A warm shower called, and a beer. He glanced up at the sound of voices and saw some familiar faces. The trees in the wood behind the cabin swayed in the breeze as the figures approached. Carl flipped his hair. A chocolate Labrador lumbered up, wagging its tail.

Maureen, the hotel owner, pulled tight the collar of her navy parka and gave a weak smile. Carl returned it with a wave and stooped to pat the dog. When he straightened up, Maureen drew close; her bony hand stretched out and tapped him on the arm. 'You should have come with us.' Her lined, taut face brightened.

'Another time, maybe. You're staying for a few days, aren't you?' He flicked a glance at the hunched man beside Maureen, her son, Liam. He stooped over a three-wheeler baby buggy, fussing over the wrapped-up bundle inside. His wife, Elsa, watched, hands in her pockets.

'Yeah, a few.'

'Come over later.' Maureen rubbed at her red eyes and ruffled her white spiky hair. 'You can have dinner with us.'

'That's kind.' Flexing his neck, Carl smiled. 'But I don't want to intrude on your family time. Not with the funeral tomorrow.'

'It isn't a problem.' Liam thrust his hands in his pockets and quirked a grin. 'You're like family to us. And one of Harris's toys got broken. You can help me fix it.'

'Sure.' Carl's chest tightened, and he rubbed his cheek. Family. At what cost? He forced a smile. 'No bother. I'll come round later.'

The shower and the beer lost their appeal. Carl lifted his bike into the wooden lean-to beside his cabin, taking care not to knock over any of his tools or works in progress. Pulling off his gloves, he saw the group at the back door of the hotel. Liam's limp was so pronounced as he spun the buggy to pull it inside. Carl swallowed. *I did that. It should have been me. Yet, here I am.* His cheeks burned. He dug his thumb hard into a sharp splinter in the wooden doorframe and held his breath.

*

It was after six when Carl headed up for dinner. The path was dim; only a few spotlights still worked, casting a faint glow onto the darkened lawn. Carl stopped, making a mental note of the ones that needed fixed. The Glen Lodge's grey stone walls loomed two stories high, dark against the purplish velvet sky. Shutters were drawn across all the upstairs windows, it looked abandoned.

An arctic wind bit Carl's cheeks. He rubbed his hands over his blue fleece. The moon reflected in the sea beyond and beamed twinkling rays onto his little boat. It bobbed up and down close to the rickety old pier. Utterly quiet, peaceful perfection. If only it could be bottled – he would drink the lot.

In the family kitchen round the back of the main building, a light shone from the window. Up above too, there were signs of life. Carl heard the faint cries of a baby. Pushing open the creaky backdoor, the scent of spices and fried onion filled his lungs. Maureen spun around and Chewie, the Labrador, looked up from nibbling his back paw.

'It's you.' Maureen put her hand to her chest.

'Yeah. Is that still ok?'

'Of course. I thought it might be… Well, never mind.' Maureen turned back to her sizzling pan.

Carl took off his hat and ruffled his curls. 'Hi, Chewie.' The dog wagged his tail. His paw tread on a crack in the vinyl. Carl's gaze followed the crack line the length of the kitchen. What a state.

With slightly narrowed eyes, Maureen dialled down the heat on the stove and glanced at Carl. 'I know, the place is falling apart.' She took off her apron and sat at the table, tenting her hands at her chin. 'Despite everything I do, it's never enough. We had the hall redecorated, I bought new fittings for the bathrooms, but I've never had time to do any of it. All my time was taken up nursing Davie and now he's gone and I'm here with nothing.'

'Things will get better. Don't worry about the hotel just now. You're too raw. I could fix these cracks.' He tapped the ugly brown floor with his thick-gripped shoes. 'It wouldn't be perfect, but I could get it so you wouldn't notice unless you were really looking.'

'I've been so preoccupied, I've let everything slip. Now Davie's gone, I can't see the way forward. This is my life. I sacrificed everything for this place. I didn't ask for it. It was Davie's place. He inherited it from his parents, but he didn't have business sense. It was all left to me. I don't think I can cope any more, but I have nothing else. Nothing.'

Carl glanced at her and frowned. 'You have Liam, and Elsa, and your grandson.' And Robyn, your daughter. Carl hadn't heard her name mentioned in the nine months he'd been back. Was that good or bad? A numb sensation deadened his thought process where Robyn was concerned, otherwise his head thumped as curiosity battled with the need to forget.

'That's not what I meant. They won't be here forever. Liam can't stay. His life isn't here. After the funeral, he'll leave. I'll be stuck here, alone.'

'Look, I could do some repairs.' Carl flipped his hair and sighed. Maybe on a small scale, but the hotel needed a professional. He wasn't qualified for a task of this magnitude.

'You're so good at fixing things. That's why everyone on the island calls you The Fixer.' Maureen looked up, blinking. 'I meant to ask before, but other things took over, how's the cabin? Did you manage to sort the problem with the door? Now the festive season's over, I'll be able to get a new one.'

'Look, don't worry about it. I sorted it.'

'And what about the washing machine? Is it still playing up? I'm sure I could stretch to that.'

'I fixed that too. It's the funeral in the morning. Don't worry about anything else.'

'How can I?' Maureen stood up and her expression turned grave. 'I worry all the time, Carl. I worry I'm not doing enough.'

'For me? You've done enough for me. And I'd like to repay you, but you need a cash injection. I don't have any of that.' Carl tried a smile, but what was remotely funny about his inability to make money? 'My work doesn't exactly pay big bucks.'

Maureen's lips curled down. 'I know, Carl. And I hoped the cabin would help, but I see you're struggling.'

'The cabin's fine.' His chest burned with guilt. Maureen had given him it rent-free for several months now. He owed her some repayment, even if she wouldn't take a penny. It came at a cost, however. Being this close to the hotel kept all the old memories fresh. No escape, day or night. *Not how I planned my return.*

'I'll help if I can. But I'm not good at project managing.' He checked around, his mind ticked over a list: eight en suite guest bedrooms, a lounge, a dining room, an industrial kitchen and family quarters. Rubbing the back of his hand, he let out a sigh. Outside it was a beautiful highland lodge with an extensive lawn that opened straight onto the beach. A stunning spot, but the renovations would also include a patio, a vegetable garden, woodland paths and the jetty. Far too much for one person.

Maureen pressed her hand to her lips. 'Oh, thank you. People send you all sorts of precious treasures. You've never failed to fix them. I'm sure you can do the same for us.'

'But that's not—'

'Gillian told me,' Maureen cut in, 'I had to stop trying to do everything by myself and accept help. She's such a good friend. She understands. She lost her husband some years back.' Maureen covered her eyes and let out a sob.

Carl hesitated, biting hard on the inside of his lip before stepping behind and putting his hand on her shoulder. 'Maybe you should rest.'

The door opened. 'Hey.' Liam limped forward and clapped Carl on the back. 'Aw, Mum.'

'Maybe I should go.' Carl backed off, but Liam fixed him with a smile.

'No way. Mum's just worried about tomorrow.'

'It's not just that,' said Maureen.

Liam sighed and rubbed his forehead. 'There was some bad news.' He sifted through a pile of letters on the table. 'Mum got this, before Christmas. She wasn't going to tell me.'

A bank logo emblazoned the page thrust into Carl's hand. He read. His heart sank. That bad? He handed the letter back to Liam. 'I said I'd help but... well, this is out of my depth.'

Liam beckoned him into the far corner, next to a cluttered jumble of brushes and mops. 'You know what's really bothering her?'

'What?' Carl glanced back at Maureen. She must still be able to hear.

'Robyn,' whispered Liam.

Carl's stomach contracted. He pulled back. Robyn. The name did so many things to his head. Thoughts pushed through the numbing vines that had strangled his feelings for so long. The woods, the kisses, the accident. The girl that got away. And moreover, he knew Liam harboured a deep dislike for her – *also my fault.* 'What about her?' Carl pushed the words through his teeth.

'We thought she'd at least come back for the funeral. But the last boat came in hours ago and she hasn't shown up.'

Bracing himself on the tiny space on the worktop between a clutter of crockery, utensils and papers, Carl experienced an unexpected release of tension in his shoulders. Perhaps her no-show was a good thing, especially with Liam back on the island. Carl's eyes slipped out of focus. Sometimes the memories were so strong, he could almost touch her. Other times, her face was beyond his recall. 'What does she do these days? No one talks about her.'

Liam raised his eyebrows and tapped his finger. 'You don't know what she does?'

A lot of effort had gone into not finding out. He wasn't a stalker. Curiosity burned deep, but dredging up old memories didn't help anyone. Exactly the reason standing in this kitchen was a bad idea.

'She runs a business in Manchester. Mum gets messages now and then. We got the impression she was coming home for this. Has she never contacted you?'

'No.' Carl looked at his feet. In the early days, he wished she had. But after twelve years, hope had long died.

'Probably best,' Liam said. 'She wasn't right for you. She's toxic.'

Clearing his throat, Carl glanced at Maureen. If she could hear, she was doing a very good impression of playing deaf. 'Robyn didn't do anything.' Except leave. 'I don't know what you have against her,' he whispered.

'She ruined this family.'

Carl rubbed his brow. Liam's memories – always tainted – were now warped into a tangled mass of hatred. Because of the accident... *and me*. It had damaged so many things. Liam's body, family relations, *my life*.

Contemplating Liam's face, Carl's mind slipped back twelve years. He'd never forget that day – the horror. He'd only meant to catch Liam to explain. Yes, he'd been seeing

Robyn, but it was ok. Sure, she was Liam's older sister, but it wasn't as if he'd crossed lines. Liam had spotted them. Fury etched into every feature as he ran into the woods. Carl vowed to sort him out, chasing after him until they'd reached the tumbledown folly in the woods.

'That was gross, you and my sister.' Liam had said, his eyes checking out the dilapidated building. Carl protested only to have it thrown back in his face. 'You're supposed to be my friend.'

'I am.'

'Then how come you go off with my sister and call me a coward?'

'I didn't…'

'I'll show you. I'm not a coward. *You* are! You only go out with my sister 'cause you're not brave enough to ask anyone cool.'

'That's stupid.'

'Look, I'm going up here.' Liam found a foothold and dragged himself up.

'No, Liam, don't. I didn't say you were a coward. I just told you to stop whining and grow up. And that's exactly what you need to do.'

'Oh yeah. Who's chicken now?'

'Liam.' Carl folded his arms. 'Just come down.'

'You should stay away from my sister. She's a little liar. Didn't Dad tell you? She lied to a guest saying I'd been peeking through keyholes. Now they want their money back. As if I would. You can't trust her.' He dragged himself up further, fingers scrabbling on the bricks. 'She's only with you to make me feel left out. She's so jealous because she has no friends.'

'This is exactly what I mean. Stop being such a moany baby and come down. What exactly are you trying to prove? You're a terrible climber. Get down!' Carl took a step back and made a run for it, jumping up the wall after Liam. Liam's foot slipped just out of Carl's reach. Regaining his balance, he hauled himself to the top, Carl just behind. The roof had caved long ago and lay crumpled inside with broken beams and splintered timbers. Stinging nettles tangled through it.

Back in the cold, cluttered kitchen, Carl's insides turned over as the memory played out. He observed Liam's stooped figure and held his breath. The vision of him splayed on the ground, sprawled over the splintered beams would never leave. Carl had been sure he was dead. Robyn had come running. Her face white, eyes aghast. 'Is this how you sorted him out?'

'Get help.' The only two words he could squeeze out. They echoed in his head even now – *get help*. He rubbed his throat; it was tight, constricted. He glanced from Liam to Maureen. Liam stared ahead, picking his thumb.

Maureen looked up. 'I knew Robyn wouldn't come. Her messages were always brief and cold. She doesn't care about us. And now it's too late.'

Digging his short nails hard into his hand, Carl breathed slowly and didn't reply. She'd cared – back then. Her face after the accident spoke a thousand words – shock, pain, blazing white anger. *She blamed me*, of course she did. Carl was three years older, he should have done more to stop Liam. Maureen had arrived on the scene and been overcome with grief, but Davie... Carl was never sure what Davie had thought of him after that. For the man who'd been happy to teach them sea fishing and how to identify fungi, he'd gone cold.

When Carl had returned to the island the previous February, Davie was diagnosed with cancer just weeks later. Within a few short months, he was a shadow of the man who'd shown Carl how to whittle a flute and catch lobsters.

A hand waved in his face. Carl blinked. 'Earth to Carl. Are you thinking about the hotel?' said Liam. 'I didn't know it was in so much trouble.'

Carl looked away. It wasn't hard to miss. After having covered all sorts of shifts, he knew something was up – apart from the obvious – no one could miss the outward signs. Guests certainly didn't. It had been one long bad-review-fest for months. Using his skills, he'd fixed everything he could, but it was like sticking a plaster on a shotgun wound.

Maureen couldn't afford staff. She used him to fill in. He needed the money, so didn't turn it down. He didn't mind helping, but there was a limit.

Liam rested his hands on his hips. 'My life is on the mainland; I can't move back. I'm tied to my job because of my injuries. The company I work for are really progressive. They've adapted my desk and everything.' He rubbed his left shoulder – the slight deformation particularly clear. Carl bit the inside of his lip. 'I like it there. Plus, I have a wife and a baby to consider.' His eyes lingered on Carl. 'You don't have any ties. It's hard to explain.'

'I understand,' Carl said, digging his nail into his palm, it deadened the impact of Liam's words. 'Just because I'm happy on my own doesn't mean I don't get family commitments.' After he'd given up searching for a job to help his dad last year, he knew very well.

'Exactly. So you get my problem. Mum doesn't want to sell. We have to help her.'

'I'm in the room.' Maureen leapt up and grabbed her apron, tying the strap around her skinny form with a snappy flourish. 'I don't want to sell. But that Calum Matheson has been sniffing around. No chance will I sell this place to the likes of him. This has been my life for over thirty years. Selling it won't cover all the debts and leave me enough to buy a place of my own. We've spent so much money over the years making sure Liam got the care he needed. And I don't grudge you a penny, son. It's just…' Maureen pressed her palm into her forehead.

Carl's chest tightened. He felt like stabbing it. Always it fell back on him, if he could just have prevented it, grabbed Liam or fallen in his place.

'That's why we need you.' Liam clapped Carl on the back. 'You're The Fixer. You can fix anything.'

'Practical stuff.' Carl raked back his long curls. 'But I'm not a businessman.' Didn't they know how he'd lost his job?

Liam smiled, pulling out some plates from the dresser. 'You'll manage. You did it for your dad. Do it for us. And while you're here, can you help me with Harris's broken toy?'

Carl's jaw hardened as Maureen dolloped out the dinner. What did they expect? A magic rabbit. And what if he failed, damn it, he *would* fail! Fixing clocks, jewellery, fences, bikes and other oddments was fine, but a hotel on the verge of liquidation? Did he have a choice? No! The Sherratts had him neatly placed over a barrel and he couldn't get away. Now, he not only had a lack of income, but a wrecked hotel to save, and not the faintest clue where to start.

Chapter Three

Robyn

Dropping her head against the rain, Robyn pushed a wet strand of hair behind her ear. A thump of soil hit the coffin in the ground.

'Earth to earth.'

She shivered, her hands raw, her teeth chattering. Beside her, Maureen stirred. Robyn glanced sideways. Under a large black umbrella, Liam's thick hand clamped around Maureen's tiny shoulder. Robyn looked into the grave. There lay her father. She wrapped her arms around herself and rubbed them. Lifting her eyes, she glimpsed so many familiar faces. Memories rushed back. Her heel sunk into the turf. Isle of Mull ground. She hadn't set foot on it for twelve years.

Mist hung low, obscuring the sea view beyond the wall of Pennygown cemetery. It was bleak and exposed to the elements. Robyn's gaze travelled over the assembled mourners to rows of weather-worn headstones before landing on a young man at the edge of the crowd. Spiral curls fell around his face. He stooped under a pink spotty umbrella with an older man and woman. Was that Carl Hansen? Why had he travelled for the funeral? Did he care that much for Davie? *More than he did for me.* Robyn shuddered, ducking her head low into the collar of her grey wool coat. Carl's eyes wandered up, meeting hers. Frozen, she stared back, then blinked and dropped her gaze. Sickening bile rose in her stomach.

It was a relief when the minister concluded. As the assembled crowd moved off, well-wishers surrounded Maureen.

'Come back to the hotel for the wake,' she insisted as she shook hands with everyone.

Fixing her eyes on the ground, Robyn hovered as people dispersed. No one would approach her. They probably didn't know who she was. She'd been away a long time.

*

Heat radiated from the dining room at the Glen Lodge Hotel along with a slightly smoky, cooking smell. Robyn sidled in. Groups lingered, chatting quietly. Cups chinked as Maureen's friend, Gillian McGregor, served up coffee and tea. A large crowd gathered around a board covered in photographs, The Life of Davie Sherratt. And what a life it had been. Maureen dabbed at her eyes as a group of friends chatted to her nearby. The tartan carpet deadened the impact of Robyn's heels. She squinted between two people close to the board. Picture after picture of her portly dad with his shaggy beard, ranging from black, through shades of grey, to white. So, that's what he was like at the last, a frail old man, much older than his years. Casting her eye across the board, Robyn raised her eyebrow. There was Davie with Liam as a baby, with Liam on the beach. Liam and his friends. Maureen and Davie at their wedding. More of Liam – in a wheelchair after the accident, with Davie pushing. *But none of me.*

A sniff. Consoling voices. Maureen hung her head as two of her oldest friends stood by; Gillian McGregor, holding a tray of teacups, and Fenella Hansen, Carl's mum. Fenella laughed, sweeping back her brown bob. A few strands of silver glinted in the light. Robyn remembered Fenella as the sort of mum every kid dreamed of – the one who did crafts, made costumes for every event, and always had a kind word. Unlike Maureen. Maureen was always busy, she was more likely to bake cakes for other people's kids than her own. Robyn had spent many an afternoon sitting at the kitchen table with her craft kit, waiting for Maureen to stop being 'too busy just now'.

One last look at the board and Robyn turned, coming face to face with Fenella. 'Hello!' Fenella beamed. 'I hardly recognised you. Only when Maureen said who you were.' She clapped her hands on either side of Robyn. 'You look fabulous. How are you?'

'I'm ok. Thank you.'

'It's a sad day, but Maureen's done so well.' Fenella scanned round. 'I love the picture board. Full of nice memories. Some gorgeous ones of my boys. The one of Carl in his shorts, bless. And, do you remember Jakob, my middle boy? Look.' Fenella pulled out a phone. 'That's him; he's had all his curls cut off. Can you believe it? My boys have such beautiful hair. Jakob couldn't come because his wife, Livvi, just had baby Polly, and she's too little to travel. Isn't she the cutest? Our first grandchild.'

The pink bundle gazed from the screen. Robyn forced a smile. 'Very nice.' She blinked and unconsciously stroked her hand across her lower midriff.

'It's lovely to see you here.' Fenella beamed. 'It's been such a long time. Carl's here somewhere. And Magnus, my eldest. There he is, with his girlfriend.'

Robyn's eyes lifted, and she pressed her lips together. Magnus Hansen was easily recognisable. All the Hansen boys looked alike. But his girlfriend. Blood boiled in Robyn's ears. 'Is that Julie McNabb?' She knew it was, but felt the need to have it confirmed. Julie's eyebrows drew together as she took a gander in Robyn's direction.

'Yes, you must have been at school with her. She's the same age as you and Carl.'

'Yes.' Humiliation pierced like a knife in the ribs. Julie had bullied and teased Robyn mercilessly at school. And Carl had played his part as well.

'Magnus is back living with us,' Fenella said. 'Only temporarily. He's a pilot. He's been working the long-haul flights, but he's changing jobs, and Julie's hoping he'll settle back here. She can be a bit full on. In fact, I've had a right full on year. Carl lost his job last March. Then a couple of weeks later, Per, my husband, slipped and broke his femur.' Fenella pressed her fingertips to her forehead. 'You might remember we run the forestry plantation. Well, he couldn't do that with a broken leg. He was stuck in hospital in Oban. I had to dot back and forward, which wasn't easy. My Aunt Jean lives with us. She's completely cuckoo, and she keeps me on my toes. I can't leave her for too long. Thank goodness for Carl. He came home and rose to the challenge magnificently.' Glancing around, Fenella leaned in. 'Between you and me, I wish he'd stayed, but Maureen offered him the cabin. I don't think he could wait to get away from Aunt Jean. Just as well he did because lo and behold Magnus decided to come back too. It's only a small house. It was fine when the boys were little, but now they take up so much room.'

'Sounds busy.' Where were the words? At work, Robyn was fluent in jargon, but private conversations were a different ball game. She fingered her pendant, trying to summon some magic to get her through.

'Very busy. You know, Robyn, it's lovely to see you again. Are you staying for a bit?'

'No.' Originally she'd thought maybe a few days, even a week. But after the frosty reception, she'd seen enough to be sure nothing much had changed.

'That's a pity.' A hand tapped Fenella on the shoulder. She spun around and greeted someone else.

Robyn took the opportunity to sidle off. Hovering close to the swing doors leading into the corridor, she cast her eyes around. No one would miss her. Backing through the doors, Robyn spun around only to crash straight into a man. She bounced back, froze, and stared. Carl Hansen. A nervous tingle spread from her shoulders, down her arms to her fingertips.

Curls of sandy hair fell across his forehead. Was he a surfer these days? Or a skier forced into a shirt. His tie was squint and his collar sat open, leaving a scruffy gap at his Adam's apple. Dropping his gaze to Robyn, he stiffened. Her heartbeat picked up. Memories stirred. Dusty boxes in her brain waiting to be opened. She had to keep the lids firmly on. His eyes twinkled grey-blue. *Oh no. Where do I look?* It had been a long time. The last time she'd seen him, the circumstances had been fraught. How could she forget what he'd done?

'Hey.' He ruffled the curls behind his ear. His woody aftershave drifted around, enticing Robyn forward. 'I, um, you made it,' he said.

She drew back, breaking away from the scent. No need to be so close. Those fleeting days were long gone.

'Indeed.' She peered sideways at the tartan carpet, so many bare patches.

'So, how are you?'

'Fine.'

'It's good to see you.' His words fell softly.

Robyn blinked and breathed deeply. That smell – so warm and natural. Her gaze levelled on his. She raised her pendant unconsciously to her chin.

His eyes narrowed. He opened his mouth, closed it again, then said, 'So, what is it you do these days?'

'I'm in marketing. How about you?'

Carl's eyebrows flickered up. 'This and that. Sometimes, I do shifts here. I help my dad at the plantation. And I have a small online business fixing broken things.'

'Oh, I thought you'd gone into IT.'

'I did. I fixed computers. That's how it all started. The company I worked for went under. I came back here to slow the pace, you know.'

Robyn took a deep breath. 'Not really. My life is manic.' Sometimes she dreamed of slow, quiet moments. In those dreams, she would walk here, back on Mull, the wind in her hair, but it was a fantasy. Her life was in Manchester now, with Pete, even if he wasn't her partner, he still worked for her. What would he be doing? Sitting at her desk, chairing her meetings, securing her deals? Her tummy squirmed. She dropped her hand to it. Pete wouldn't be in any rush to have her back. He liked power. Here was his chance to seize authority.

'Well, I guess I'll see you around.' Carl's gaze wavered. Laughter echoed as it had done from the concrete school walls. It rung in Robyn's ears. She squinted at Carl's pensive face – no longer a teenage boy – his rugged skin creased across his forehead. For a few days, twelve years ago, she'd mistaken his smile, believed it was real. Liam had too and look what happened to him.

'I'm leaving tomorrow.' Robyn's ears grew warm. She pulled her blazer tightly across her chest. Heartache burned even now. Carl had slashed her foolish ideals. He'd been her first boyfriend; so good, kind, and caring. Until Liam had seen them together. Revealing his true colours, Carl had goaded Liam into a dangerous stunt after vowing to sort him out. So much for the gentle Carl. Then, adding insult to injury, he'd told her dad she'd put him up to it. Davie had never had a better opportunity to tear a few more strips off her.

'Well, I eh, hope you have a good trip.' Carl unbuttoned his cuff and rolled up his sleeve, revealing a muscular forearm. Robyn chewed the inside of her lower lip as he started on his left. Heat crept up her neck. Scrapes and scratches covered his bare skin like he'd been attacked by an angry cat. Robyn winced. How had he done that?

'Thanks.'

With a brief nod, Carl joined Fenella at a table. She stretched up and ruffled his head, and he gave her a one-armed hug. Such warmth. Robyn flattened her lips and stared. That feeling had been hers for five short weeks. After all the pain and the bullying, he'd stepped up and asked her out. Yes, Carl! The carefree boy with the broad grin and the floppy hair had asked *her*. The boy she'd watched at school and on the beach. He'd sent her heart skipping. Her fingers trailed across her neckline. The warmth of his touch had been so real, the plans they made, foolproof, and the connection they had, unbreakable. It had been a dream come true. Now it was just a fragment of a nightmare.

Robyn left through the swing doors into the corridor, passed the ancient MDF doors to the bathrooms and the side stairs, into the chilly kitchen. A faint snuffling revealed Florrie and Chewie half-heartedly looking up from Chewie's fleece-lined bed. Florrie had wasted no time moving in. 'Don't get too comfy though, we're not sticking around,' Robyn warned her.

An official-looking letter on the table caught her eye. Both dogs put their heads down. Robyn picked it up and read. *So this is what it's all about.* Earlier, this room had been the scene of a family quarrel. How many over the years had played out here? She'd only been back on the island a few hours and her family were furious with her. Why had she expected anything else? For a fleeting moment, she'd thought with her father gone, things would be different. Wrong again.

The letter confirmed the vague suspicions that had been growing all day. Not just bad reviews, but bankruptcy. Phone in hand, she tapped open Trip Advisor and scrolled down. No getting away from it – the reviews were terrible. Nothing better than three-stars for almost a year. Pulling a pout, she had to agree with the one calling it unclean and outdated. It looked like it hadn't been properly cleaned since she was last here. You just had to look around. Leaks in the ceiling, peeling paintwork, threadbare carpets. The restaurant kitchen was like something from 'Gordon Ramsay's Kitchen Nightmares'. Why had they let it get so bad?

Dad had been ill. That was a factor. But things must have been bad even before Dad's diagnosis. This was years of neglect. It would take more than a few weeks to sort it out. *Not my place.* Robyn put her phone down and considered. *They don't want my help.*

Maybe it wasn't about what they *wanted*. Maureen *needed* help. Robyn had the management skills. She was used to coordinating projects bigger than this. Dad was dead. He couldn't remind her of her failings or blame her for things now. *Maybe this is the chance I need.* If she could showcase her skills, prove her worth, she could rebuild the bridges. It would take her mind off other things and she could stay away from Pete just a little longer.

Running her hands up and down her arms, she shivered. All her warm clothes were in her case. She could nip up and get something, no one would even notice she'd gone.

Upstairs, the door to Maureen's room was open. Robyn entered, drawn by the view. An impressive vista of sea and sand sprawled beyond the long rolling lawn. Twilight was creeping in on the back of darkening clouds. The trees loomed like silhouettes of giants.

Robyn closed her eyes, cherishing a moment of peace. Years ago, in those woods, she'd kissed Carl Hansen. The pinnacle of all her teenage desires had come true. Twenty minutes later, she'd found him standing over her brother's broken body. Opening her eyes, she squinted. The cabin was barely visible in the fast dimming light. He lived there? How desperate was he? Why cling to this place?

With a sigh, she glanced around. Some medical equipment stacked in the corner loomed. She recoiled. Those machines had kept her father alive in his last few weeks. She didn't want to see them – it was easier not to know. Her own recent stint in hospital jumped the memory queue. Her throat felt thick, she wanted to run from the place. Hoisting up the creaky sash, she breathed the fresh, icy air. Leaves rustled in the blocked gutters. She flicked a piece of chipped paint on the windowsill. *It's here or Pete.* A melting pot of excitement, fear and uncertainty churned inside.

Closing the window, she shuddered. Decision time had arrived.

Chapter Four

Robyn

Robyn opened the kitchen blind and knocked over a flowerpot. Soil splattered into the sink below. 'Seriously!' She jumped back, checking none had landed on her pink cashmere sweater. Chewie looked up from his slumber. Sweeping her hair behind her ear, Robyn searched for something to clean up the mess. But removing the muck from the sink would barely make a dent in the midden. Throwing the soiled cloth into the washing machine, she stepped back and sighed, just avoiding knocking over a pile of plates. She steadied them before they toppled. Cluttered was an understatement. Maureen was verging on being the next candidate for one of those dreadful TV shows about hoarders.

Robyn pulled a letter from the stash of papers behind the microwave, a bill from eight years ago. 'And I bet it still hasn't been paid,' she muttered, throwing it back into the heap. Chewie rolled lazily back into his basket. Florrie dotted about, sniffing the kitchen. Robyn let her out. With one eye open, Chewie considered. 'It isn't compulsory,' Robyn said. His look clearly said, *I am right in the middle of my sleep, thank you very much!* With a reluctant sigh, he heaved himself out of his basket.

Shaking her head at the precariously balanced dishes, Robyn opened the dishwasher. With a jolt, she withdrew.

What a disgusting smell. She'd suggested the night before they cleared up straight away, but no. Liam had rounded on her.

'Since when did you have the right to give orders? Where were you all afternoon, anyway?'

'It was just a suggestion. I went to my room.'

'Exactly. You show up in the middle of the night, right before the funeral, and spend half the wake hiding in your room. It's a poor show. We're exhausted. If you want to clear up, do it yourself.'

She hadn't, but she supposed she should make a start now, otherwise, she'd get another earful. Some things never changed. Opening the door, she called the dogs back in. 'I'll take you for a walk later.'

After spraying the dishwasher with half a bottle of bleach, she clinked plates into it. How had Maureen endured her life chained to the sink, living with the tyrant? This room was like Maureen's base, she'd set up camp here and only seemed to leave it to go to bed. Robyn lined up the cups on the top tray. If they could just reconcile, she could help give Mum a fresh start. Right now, she needed a mum, someone who cared, who understood. Maureen had never been that. After the operation, Robyn had wanted to confide in someone, but there was no one. Chewie flopped into his basket with a groaning sigh.

The door opened and Robyn shuddered at the sudden blast of cold air. Walking forward to slam it shut, she stopped as a man entered. He stamped his feet on the doormat and clapped his thickly gloved hands. Robyn squinted. Who was under the layers, the thick scarf, and the beanie pulled low? A twinkle of grey-blue eyes gave it away. Carl pulled off his beanie, unleashing a tangle of curls.

'What are you doing here?' Robyn fiddled with her cuff. Did he always wander in uninvited? He lived in the cabin.

Did he come over for breakfast every day? Were he and Liam still close? She'd always assumed their friendship had ended after the near-fatal fall, but here he was.

Swinging his tail from side to side, Chewie heaved himself from his basket and loped over to Carl.

'Hiya, pal.' Carl ruffled Chewie's broad jowls. 'Maureen asked if I could walk Chewie this morning. She thought she might not sleep well and didn't want to have to get up early.'

Robyn raised her eyebrows. 'Wow. She's got you well-trained.'

'I just help out, if I can.' Chewie leaned in his head for more pats.

Robyn stroked the neck of her pastel pink jumper, watching as Carl's hands massaged Chewie's withers. Long ago, Carl had used those hands to rub Robyn's back, teasing out all the tension and helping her to live in the moment. And what a beautiful moment it had been. The stress in her shoulders released momentarily.

'And who's this?' asked Carl. Florrie skittered over and leapt about, caught between nerves and excitement.

'Her name's Florrie. She's mine.'

'She's cute.' Carl looked up from tickling her chin and smiled.

Robyn turned away, her legs slightly wobbly. *Don't do that. Do not smile at me.* Picking up the teapot, it slipped and shattered.

'Oh, no.' Her hands leapt to her face.

'What is going on?' Maureen came in, pulling a fluffy purple dressing gown around her.

Robyn stared at the china fragments scattered across the stained, cracked floor.

'Good morning, Carl. Robyn.' Maureen frowned and shook her head. 'What have you done?'

'I smashed a teapot.'

'Not my grandmother's pot. That's been in my family forever.'

'Don't worry.' Carl bent down at Robyn's feet and picked up the pieces. 'I can fix it. Just put all the bits in a box.'

Robyn held her palm to her forehead. How Maureen could class anything in here as valuable, she couldn't quite fathom. It resembled a junk shop forgotten for about fifty years.

'What are you doing anyway? I hope you're not clearing up. Just leave it,' Maureen said. 'I'm so used to doing it all.'

You are? It was a struggle not to say the words aloud. Mum the martyr. Same as always.

'You've got a long journey later. Have a rest while you can,' said Maureen, filling the kettle and frowning at the bleached sink.

'I'm not going back today.'

Carl stood up, holding the smashed teapot pieces. Robyn blinked. *Why is he staring?* She had things to discuss with Maureen and didn't want an audience.

'Oh?' said Maureen. 'I thought you were booked on the boat this afternoon.'

'That was my original plan, but—'

'Thank you, Carl. If you can fix it that would be brilliant.' Maureen passed a cardboard box to Carl. He carefully put the shards of china into it. 'But Robyn. Pardon?'

'Listen, can you leave us, please.' Robyn blinked at Carl. Eye contact was hard. 'I have some things to say to my mother. I'd rather do it in private.' Her chest tightened.

'Robyn, honestly.' Maureen frowned at her. 'Carl is always welcome here.'

'Hey, it's ok,' Carl said. 'I'll take this and get Chewie for his walk. You'll want space to talk about things.' He looked between the two of them. Robyn tried to nod her appreciation. Had her head moved? Her body was in some kind of grip-lock. Florrie pattered across the room and leapt at Carl's ankles. With a grin, he bent down to scratch her shoulder. 'Maybe another time, little one.'

'There's nothing to talk about.' Maureen picked up a cloth and turned on the tap. Water gushed, splashing across her dressing gown. 'For heaven's sake,' she muttered, slowing the flow.

'Actually,' said Robyn, 'we need to talk.'

'If you want to stay another few days, that's fine.' Maureen scrubbed at the work surface. 'It's not as if I need your room.'

'It's going to be longer than a few days. There's a lot of work to be done.'

'What do you mean?' Maureen put down the cloth and faced Robyn.

'This is why I want to talk to you.'

'I'll duck out,' said Carl. 'Come on, Chewie.'

'No, stay.' Maureen picked up the cloth and restarted her scrub. 'Just get on with it, Robyn.'

Robyn took a deep breath and bit on her lower lip. Carl rubbed the bristly stubble on his cheek and gave her a vague smile. She didn't return it. The words needed to come out. 'Well, in short, the hotel is failing. I'm going to stay and sort it out.'

Maureen leaned back on the worktop and folded her arms. She threw an almost amused glance at Carl. He shuffled his feet and rubbed his eyebrow. 'Yes. I thought that's what you would say. But no thank you.'

'Pardon?'

'You heard me,' Maureen said. 'We don't need your help. I'm not daft. I know things are bad. They've been bad for a while. But where were you then? Where were you when your father was ill? When I was juggling that, the business, and everything else?'

Robyn bit her lip. An honest answer? 'I didn't realise just how much help you needed. I wrongly assumed you were managing fine. You never communicated about any trouble.'

'Oh, that's a good one.' Maureen's lips tightened. Staring at the window, she shook her head. 'You accuse me of telling you nothing? What about you? You haven't been here for twelve years. If you cared, you'd have come sooner.' Maureen flapped a tea towel with a snap and hung it on the oven door. 'I don't need your help. Carl has already offered.'

'But I don't—'

Robyn didn't allow him to finish. 'This is family business.' Carl wouldn't be *sorting* anything. Not after the last time.

'Family business?' Maureen's lips quirked up. She gaped. Robyn couldn't see anything funny. 'What do you know about family? You didn't even come home in time to say goodbye to your father.'

'You know my reasons.' Robyn tapped her thigh, not making eye contact, her throat uncomfortably dry.

Maureen pressed her hand to quivering lips and shook her head. 'I don't want to talk about this any more.' Without looking at either of them, she hurried from the room.

Robyn focused on Carl. He eased around and slipped Chewie's lead from a hook by the door. Chewie's tail slapped his leg excitedly. Florrie yapped hopefully and dotted in and out of Chewie's legs.

'This is why I wanted to talk to her alone,' said Robyn. 'It's a sensitive subject.'

'It certainly is. But it's not an easy time for her.' Carl raised his eyebrows towards the window.

'I'm well aware of that. But it has to be said. She might go bankrupt.'

'Yes, but maybe just tread softly. You've been away for a long time. People need time.'

Robyn's stare hardened. Who was he to tell her what to do? 'The last thing I need is you standing in judgement. My reasons for coming back now are my own.'

Carl's brows met in a deep furrow and he tilted his head. 'I'm not judging. You know better than anyone, I lost that right long ago. Your life is yours to do as you please.' It was. And she knew better than to trust him. 'For the record.' Carl pulled on his hat. 'I agree with you. Maureen needs help.' He clipped Chewie onto the lead. 'She asked me to do it and I said I'd try. I guess we could work together.'

Robyn closed her eyes slowly and let out a long breath. 'I'm not sure we can.' She felt her cheeks warm.

'Why not?'

'Because I know what you did, Carl.' She bit the inside of her lip. 'There's no point pretending. It's not like I'm going to forget. You almost killed my brother.'

Carl's jaw tensed. 'I know.' His voice rasped. 'Do you think I could forget?'

'No, but you could blame it on someone else.'

Narrowing his eyes, he rubbed his forehead. 'What? Everyone knows what I did. Maureen's helped me despite that. That's why I have to help. I owe her.'

Robyn frowned and drew her head back. 'You're accepting the blame now?'

'Of course.'

'Then why did you tell my father it was all my idea? Apparently, you only did it because I made you.'

'Made me?' His voice was indignant. 'How could you make me do it? I didn't tell him anything like that.'

Robyn backed off. 'Funny, how short people's memories are when it comes to things like that.'

'I remember it perfectly. I never said a thing to Davie about you. Ever.' Chewie tugged towards the door. 'Look, I have to go.' Florrie stood alert, her tail sinking slowly as the door snapped shut.

Robyn lifted her hand to her chest and breathed slowly. Was it true? Was Carl blameless, or full of lies? No going back. She'd lost all faith in him. After giving him her soul, he'd run off, almost killed her brother and laid the blame on her. If that wasn't bad enough, Julie McNabb had taken great pleasure in telling her Carl's interest had all been a set-up. They wanted to see who was brave enough to *crack the ice queen*. Step up, cocky Carl. Well, he could step right out. Hot blood rushed to Robyn's fingertips and pounded in her ears. The five weeks of bliss she'd known were a neatly packaged dream that couldn't be opened again. She was used to unforeseen hitches in business and Carl Hansen was just one minor hitch.

Chapter Five

Carl

It was when Carl opened the letter, he remembered his dream. Reading over the latest rejection from the bank, he tossed it aside and pinched his lips together. Dreams didn't come true. Well, only the bad ones. Unravelling what they meant sometimes led into the realms of fantasy, but the meaning of last night's needed no interpretation.

Carl gazed from the window over the lawn to a long, low sandy shore. Grey waves rushed to it. He'd dreamed he and his brothers were back playing there, carefree kids. They'd cycled through the woods to see Liam, just as they always did. Robyn was nearby, watching; hovering on the fringe, tall and gangling. The dream had rambled away from the open sea to the concrete walls of Tobermory High School. Carl and his friends were talking. Julie McNabb and her gang sidled up. 'I dare one of you to ask out Robyn Sherratt. Who's brave enough to melt the Ice Queen?'

Carl had done it. Why not? It was a good excuse. Julie's dare, spurred on by jealousy – Robyn was much prettier and beat her in every test – was intended to hurt. Carl was supposed to laugh and tell her there was no way he'd ask her for real. Doing it for a dare kept his status amongst his friends and got him what he wanted. Robyn had been worth it. Not weird like everyone thought. Her funny, intelligent, and sweet side shone through. They'd forged a bond that seemed unbreakable and planned their whole lives together – a cottage in a remote part of the island, three kids and six dogs – what could possibly go wrong? He'd woken up before the answer could play out.

Forgetting was never going to be an option, and having both Liam and Robyn so close was a nonstop reminder, pounding his head like a hammer on a spring. Carl leaned forward and pinched the bridge of his nose. *Who cares?* It was years ago. The few weeks he'd shared with Robyn were a sweet memory in amongst a black hole of horrors.

The Glen Lodge Hotel wasn't the only thing in dire straights. The official letter loomed on the table like a warning to anyone who might feel inclined to help him out. Here lives Carl Hansen, lenders and investors approach at your peril. Almost every email, letter, and text he received was a bank notice, a loan refusal, or an unpaid bill. Where could he get the money to move on? His limited income from his online business barely brought enough to survive day to day. And he wasn't going to scrounge.

The shattered teapot fragments waited on his table by the window. Another job to do – for free. Not that he grudged it. Well, he didn't usually, but certain people asked him once too often. Easing into a chair, Carl prised the lid from a bottle of superglue. Bit by bit, he stuck the pieces back. If fixing the Glen Lodge Hotel was this easy, he'd have it sorted by the end of the week.

In the bedroom was a box with other items needing to be fixed. He could do the lot. Shuffling around the bed covered with his giant wolf-print fur, he inched between it and the wall. 'For crying out loud.' He tripped over his slippers. Picking them up, he launched them across the tiny room. The lack of floor space made everything he laid down a hazard. He frowned. Someday, he might have a house where he could walk across rooms without feeling like he'd completed a special forces assault course. Yeah, right! How could that ever happen? His savings didn't amount to enough to buy a property. He couldn't even cover the rent of a tiny room on his earnings.

A shiny silver BMW twinkled in the winter sun. Carl raised his hands to shield his eyes as he looked out at it. Robyn's car. She could afford that? All he could afford was a fifteen-year-old bashed up pickup that used to belong to his dad. He ran his hand through his tangled curls. A dull ache thudded in his chest. Her words from earlier had thrown him. How had she somehow been implicated in Liam's accident? And did she think he'd done it on purpose?

A sharp blast of wind hit the cabin; the walls shuddered. How had things gone so pear-shaped? He was living here, a penniless wastrel, while Liam had a wife and family and Robyn drove a BMW. Curiosity fired in his stomach. He reached for his phone. What exactly did Robyn do now? It had taken years to realise she wasn't coming back for him. How stupid he'd been. His eyes narrowed as he read through the search results. 'Seriously?'

With a sigh, he glanced out the window. A flash caught his eye. A small blue car glinted into view, snaking down the driveway, taking the icy bends slowly. He squinted; it was coming his way. Damn it. It parked next to the pickup and a young woman got out. Her long dark hair swirled in the wind. Kirsten McGregor, a long-term acquaintance. *What does she want?* Carl spread out his fingers and looked around. What a mess. Grabbing a pile of clothes from the living area, he chucked them through the bi-fold doors onto the bed. Quickly he straightened the cushions. It made no difference. Nothing could change the fact that he lived in a glorified shed.

A knock. 'Come in,' yelled Carl.

The door opened and smacked off the wall. Kirsten blew in. Shoving the door against the fierce wind, her cheeks reddened in the sudden heat. 'Wow, it's cosy in here.' She fanned her face and shook her wavy mane. 'How are you?' Plonking herself in a chair in front of the crackling stove, she smiled

'Fine. What brings you here?'

'I wonder if you could help me.' Kirsten leaned over the chair arm and rested her chin on her hands. 'I have this old brooch of my grandmother's. Do you think you could reset it? I bought new fittings, but I can't see how best to do it.'

'I guess. Do you have it?'

'I do.' Kirsten rummaged in her handbag. Her eyes darted back and forward. Passing him a small gauze purse, she beamed. Carl took it to the window and examined the pieces in the light.

'I'm sure it's possible.'

Kirsten clapped her hands. 'I'm so glad you're my friend. You're like the ultimate DIY Encyclopaedia. You always have a solution.'

He threw an eyebrow-raise in her direction. Seriously? He couldn't see a solution to any of *his* problems. Perhaps winning the lottery? Though he didn't even have a spare pound to enter.

'How're things at the hotel?' Kirsten asked. 'I can't believe Robyn came back for the funeral. I haven't seen her for years.' She looked up, wide-eyed.

'Yeah, it's been a long time.'

Kirsten pulled her legs up onto the seat and swivelled to face him. 'Is everything ok? How's it going with Liam?'

'Fine.' Carl sighed and rubbed his forehead. 'They've roped me into helping up there. I'm sweating it because I haven't a clue where to start. I mean, how many workers do you need? Where do you find them? How do you pay them? Do you need warrants and planning permission? It's like Maureen and Liam just expect me to wave a magic wand. I owe them. They keep reminding me how much of this is my fault and I can't get away. I can't afford to go anywhere else.'

Kirsten's frown had an edge of pity. 'Carl, you don't owe them. You didn't cause the accident. We all know that.'

'It should've been me. Liam was never cut out for it.'

'Liam is the same age as me, he was always a wimp. But all things considered, he's done ok for himself. He got married. They have a baby. It could have been a lot worse. At least you were there to get help.'

Carl couldn't argue with that, but he knew what a struggle it had been. 'If something isn't done, the hotel will get repossessed. It won't reopen in the spring. If Maureen loses her livelihood, I lose this place.'

'And would that be a bad thing? Why not cut loose? I'm sure there are other places you could stay.'

'I feel I have to repay them. I've caused so much pain.' He closed his eyes and shook his head. 'And I have nowhere else to go.'

'What about your parents?'

'I can't live with them forever. A few months last year was enough. Aunt Jean drives me round the twist. And Magnus is staying there.'

'But he'll be away soon.'

Yes, he would. Pilot Magnus would jet off any day. Their other brother Jakob was a top computer programmer. Carl, the baby, would muddle along fixing broken ornaments in his cabin.

'I can't move back there. I need my own place.' Last year, he'd had a flat in Edinburgh, a great job, even a relationship that had gone further than usual. How quickly things changed. He'd botched a deal, his boss committed suicide, the company folded. Carl was suddenly jobless. When his girlfriend ran off with his flatmate, it was the last straw.

Kirsten rested her chin on her hands and gazed. Carl ran his hand around his neckline. The staring was unsettling. 'I need that too.' Kirsten sighed. 'I'm hoping to move this year. Maybe we could house share?'

'What?' Carl rolled his shoulders. 'I don't know. Right now, I have to find a way to keep the hotel open. Then I can stay here and hopefully get my business off the ground. Now let me take a look at this.'

Sitting by the window, Carl put on his headlamp, feeling like a mad scientist. Was that why Kirsten was scrutinising him? Concentrating on the piece of jewellery, he prised the purple gem from the centre with his tweezers. Kirsten joined him at the table. Her fingers brushed his as she showed him how she wanted the new fitting to look. He moved his hand away. Her stare was blinding. He felt compelled to work quickly, but it wasn't a job that leant itself to speed. Carefully and painstakingly, he manoeuvred the jewel into the new housing.

'What time is it?' Kirsten checked her phone, after what felt like several hours. 'Only two, it's getting dark already. And it looks stormy.'

Carl held up her reset brooch. It now hung on a chain and looked quite pretty. Kirsten opened the clasp and looped it around her neck.

'Can you fasten it?' Swinging her hair to the side, she held the two ends, waiting. Carl stepped forward. Something about her stance caused his ribs to tighten. He wanted to draw back. Quickly, he fixed the clasp and walked away. Taking his jacket from the hook on the back of the outside door, he swung it on. 'I might go for some air. It helps me think.'

'I'm going to pay you for this,' Kirsten said, admiring the necklace. 'Send me an invoice.'

'Don't worry,' said Carl. 'I don't mind.' Pushing open the door, he blew out a misty breath and clapped his hands. Kirsten followed him, shivering. A dark shape loped out from behind her car, Carl grinned. 'Hey, Chewie.' The dog plodded towards Carl, tail swinging. 'Where did you come from?' Carl looked up from patting Chewie's head to see Robyn striding across the lawn, Florrie at her side.

'Chewie! Chewie, come here!' Robyn quickened her pace.

'Come on.' Carl took hold of his collar. 'I think you're going for a walk. And not with me.'

Kirsten stepped away from her car, toying with her keys. Robyn stopped level with the headlights. 'Come on, Chewie. He wasn't meant to come out. He doesn't really know me.' Robyn kept her eyes on the dog.

'It's ok. He's a good dog, he won't run away.' Carl led him to Robyn. 'He just recognised me, that's all.'

'I have a message for you.' Robyn's gaze trained on the sea behind Carl.

'Oh?'

'Liam wants to see you.'

'About what?' His heart sank into his boots.

'He's leaving tomorrow, and he has all sorts of things to show you.' Her voice held a note of sarcasm. Her eyes lingered on his face. Carl pulled his zip tight. Was she giving him the once over? No luck. She'd had her chance and thrown it away. Now, he wasn't available.

'What things?'

Kirsten edged closer. 'Can't he come down?'

A small frown crept across Robyn's forehead. She skimmed over Kirsten. 'No idea. He told me to ask Carl to come and see him. I said no, but as Carl's here, I might as well. I expect Liam has a list of things needing to be done. He's been scribbling notes all day.'

'Ok, I'll go see.'

'You don't have to,' muttered Kirsten, taking Carl's arm. 'He could come to you.'

'It's fine.' Carl pulled away from her.

Robyn clipped Chewie onto a lead and he stared sadly as Carl shoved his hands into his pockets. With a cool flick of the back of her glove, Robyn cast her eyes over Carl and Kirsten, tugged on Chewie's leash, and strode towards the beach.

'Still as unsociable as ever,' said Kirsten.

Carl kept his eyes on her back. 'I don't know.'

Kirsten flattened her lips and sighed. 'Why didn't she come back when her dad was on his deathbed?'

'They didn't get on.'

'I know. My mum said something about it, but she wouldn't go into details. What happened? Did he, you know, do something to her?'

Carl stared towards the beach. 'I don't think so. He favoured Liam because he was a boy. Davie was old-fashioned. Girls should be cooking and that kind of thing. But nothing sinister.'

'Ridiculous,' said Kirsten. 'I hate men like that.'

Carl fished in the dark chasms of his memory, trying to pull up anything odd. Many things about Davie were unusual: the bird's nest beard; the camouflage shirt, Bermuda shorts and long socks combo; his crazy ex-army tales. Nothing to set alarm bells ringing. 'He was an eccentric sort of guy.'

'I always thought he was a weirdo.'

'He taught us about stuff. My brothers, Liam, and I went places with him. If he'd been creepy, I'd remember. My mum wouldn't have let us anywhere near him.'

'I guess. We never really came here. Mum's always been friends with Maureen, but we mostly stayed home and played on the farm. Oh, well. I best get on.' Flashing a bright grin, Kirsten patted Carl on the arm and headed for her car. 'And thanks, Carl. You're great.'

'Right. Bye.' With a frown, he watched her drive away. Then, drawing in a large breath, he faced the hotel. Once more unto the breach. His feet wouldn't move straight away. For a long time, he gazed at Robyn walking along the beach. From what he'd read earlier, she'd made a big success. Obviously, the cool demeanour worked well in business. She walked slowly, head down, hands in the pockets of her long, elegant coat. Even with all her money and accomplishments, she looked just as sad and lost as ever. The urge to run to her burned perilously strong, but what would he say? What was there to talk about? The dreams they'd shared had washed up years ago like an old bit of bladderwrack.

Chapter Six

Robyn

'Don't you go poking your nose in where it's not needed. You lost the right to be part of this family long ago.' Liam glared across the kitchen table at Robyn.

Robyn stepped back almost tripping over Chewie's water bowl. 'Excuse me? I'm offering to help Mum. What's wrong with that? And how did I lose my right to be part of the family?'

'Because of this.' Liam gestured at his shoulder, running his hand down the left side of his hunched frame.

Robyn shook her head. 'That wasn't my fault. Dad blamed me, but he blamed me for everything. When you smashed the shed window with your football – my fault. When you rode across the vegetable garden and ruined the plants – my fault. Everything! Always blamed on me. You just had to say "da-ad" in that whiny little voice and he'd come yelling at me.'

'Oh stop it, you're embarrassing yourself.'

'No, I'm telling it like it was. I had nothing to do with your accident. It was your own stupidity. That and trusting Carl Hansen.' Just as she'd done, and he'd betrayed her. 'How can you forgive him? Why do you blame me when you know it was him?'

'Dad told me what you did.'

'I didn't do anything, Liam.' Robyn placed her hand on her forehead. What new lies? Dad! Always so quick to turn everything against her – even from beyond the grave.

'You paraded yourself on the beach. Hung about in skimpy clothes, making eyes at Carl. He was a stupid hormonal boy who couldn't resist. Dad was furious with you.'

Robyn shook her head and placed her hand on her mouth. Nothing she said could change things. Liam had learned to despise her at their father's lap. An ear-splitting cry made her jump. Elsa marched into the room, with baby Harris bawling.

'Take him.' Thrusting him at Liam, Elsa flung herself into a seat. 'I can't get him to calm down.'

Robyn backed towards the door. Only a couple of months ago, she could have walked past babies and not batted an eyelid. Now, she couldn't look at them without a prick of pain, striking high and ending low. *Let me out.* Despite his fall, his broken body and all the rehabilitation he'd attended to help him walk again, Liam had found someone, got married and had a child. Robyn stared at the red-faced bundle. His sobs were soul-wrenching. She gently rubbed her midriff and bit her lip.

'What's going on?' Elsa looked between her and Liam.

'The usual.' Liam bounced the baby on his good hip.

'The usual for you, anyway,' said Robyn. 'Whining and blaming me for something I had nothing to do with.' Snatching the door handle, Robyn pulled it. It slipped clean off. 'Seriously?' Before she could begin to work out where it went, the door flew open and Carl walked in. Not again!

'We really must stop meeting like this,' he said, wiping his feet on the mat. Sleety rain dripped from the gutters above. Harris let out another earth-shattering scream. Carl raised his eyebrows and frowned. Robyn sighed and pinched the bridge of her nose, gaping at the broken door handle.

'Hi, Carl.' Liam swayed Harris gently from side to side. 'It's quite the party here.'

'So I see. I came to say goodbye.'

'What time is it? Holy moly.' Elsa jumped to her feet. 'I need to finish packing my stuff. Harris kicked off, and I gave up.'

With fumbling fingers, Robyn attempted to shove the handle back on.

'Did you check out my list of things to do?' said Liam. 'I think it's fairly simple.'

'I had a look.' Carl took off his beanie and ran his hand through his hair. His eyes fell on Robyn. 'Here, let me do that.' Carl's hand brushed over hers as she passed him the handle. The bolt of electricity made her smart. 'It always does this. I need to remember to bring up the tools and fix it properly.'

'But what about my list?' Liam's whiny tone grated in Robyn's ears.

'Well, I'm sure the ideas are good, but how are you going to finance it?' Carl finished attaching the handle and straightened up.

'Oh,' said Liam, 'I expect Mum has a budget.'

'I'm not sure she does. Is she planning on selling off part of the grounds, or something?'

'No, she doesn't want to sell.'

'What do you think?' Carl glanced at Robyn.

Robyn tilted her head and narrowed her eyes. 'I can't answer for Mum, but unless she's hiding a fortune under her mattress, I'd say there's no money to do anything.'

'So, what are you saying?' said Liam. 'You'd rather she sold up or let this place go under? You just don't give a monkey's about your family, do you? You're cold and thoughtless.'

How could he say that? What did he know? She pressed her lips together. Maybe she was. Maybe that was why she didn't deserve a family of her own. Her middle finger lingered on her midriff.

'Liam,' Carl frowned, 'that's a bit harsh and pretty unfair.'

Liam patted Harris on the back. 'Don't turn on me, Carl. I can't believe you'd take her side. She already abandoned Mum once in a time of need.'

'Excuse me?' Robyn threw out her arms. 'I left to go to college. You did exactly the same. The only difference is, you were welcomed back with open arms. I didn't come back because no one wanted me here.'

'Oh, boohoo. And I wonder why that was?' said Liam.

'Because of your lies.'

'Stop shouting, you're upsetting Harris.'

'I'm not shouting,' said Robyn. 'You're the one yelling.'

'Hey, let's just calm down.' Carl stepped beside Liam. 'Come on. Take it easy.'

Robyn took a deep breath and leaned on the table. 'So, who's going to finance the project? You?'

Liam rolled his eyes.

'Or you?' She stared at Carl. He held her gaze for a few seconds before looking at his feet.

'Carl will do it. He already promised Mum.'

Carl shook his head. 'I can help out. But Liam, I don't have a pot of gold. I can't make money out of straw.' He faced Robyn and sighed. 'I googled you.'

Robyn raised her eyebrows. 'Why?'

'You're a big success,' said Carl. 'Out of all of us, if anyone could turn this place around, it's you. But the best thing would be if we all work together.'

'Mum won't allow it.' Liam walked to the window, stroking Harris as his sobs quietened. 'She doesn't trust her.' He glared at Robyn. 'You abandoned her before, there's no saying you won't do it again.'

'Why do you keep saying I abandoned her? I left home at eighteen. It's what happens.'

'She needed you here. She had to take me to lots of appointments on the mainland. You chose some crazy job and didn't lift a finger. You never did. When she needed help during the season, where were you? Parading yourself on the beach for *him*.'

'Liam, that's not what happened,' said Carl.

'And did *you* ever help out?' Robyn folded her arms.

'How could I? I was in a wheelchair.'

'Not all the time.'

The door burst open. Elsa dumped two cases and a baby bag on the floor. Maureen came in behind and scanned around. 'What is all the shouting?'

'Robyn,' muttered Liam.

'Seriously?' Robyn glowered. His attitude stank. As immature and whiny as ever.

'Things are a bit fraught,' said Carl.

'Here, can you hold Harris a minute?' Liam offered him to Carl. 'I need to take stuff to the car.'

Like lightning, Carl's hands shot up. 'Not me. I'm not good with babies. He's just calmed down. You keep him. I'll take the cases.'

Robyn threw herself into a chair and put her head in her hands. Chaos ensued. A carry-on film of slip-ups and crashes, bumps and clatters played out as they loaded Liam's car and left. *Maybe I should go too.* Leave the carnage. Switch off to the hotel and detach from it again. Return to Pete and the office. Her eyes strayed across the scratched table. She and Pete had unfinished business. Should she tell him what had happened? Was there any point in him knowing? She dreaded his reaction.

A noise at the door drew her attention. Carl leaned on the frame. 'I'd like to hear your ideas about the hotel. If you have any.'

Her brow furrowed. 'Several.'

'Liam's list was a bit vague, especially regarding finance.'

'I bet it was.'

Maureen stepped in and threw off her boots. 'Oh dear, it'll be so quiet without them. I'll make you a coffee, Carl.'

'No, I'm ok, thanks.'

Robyn let out a long sigh, at least with Liam gone she could attempt the impossible. She banged her palm on the table. Both Maureen and Carl stared. Honestly, the opinionated men in her life. So pigheaded. So full of their own importance. First her father, then Pete, now Liam. Nothing could ever be said against him. Not now. After the accident, he'd become a saint. Anything he wanted, he got. She'd been sent to college to do a business-training course despite having grades enough to go to university, but Dad had decided it wasn't right for her and refused to pay. Liam got into Strathclyde University after three years of intensive tutoring alongside his rehab. Robyn ground her teeth. None of it mattered now. She'd used her training as a springboard to better things. Liam may have a steady job, but he hadn't made a success like her. *One to me!* Her head dropped. It didn't have to be a competition. Why did it always feel like one? Liam didn't want her help with the hotel in case she succeeded. Surely that was it? He'd rather Mum sank than allow Robyn the credit or satisfaction.

She opened the hotel ideas page on her iPad. Maureen sat down opposite with a loud sigh and cradled her mug. 'I thought you'd at least come and say goodbye to your brother.'

'I think you know as well as I do, he didn't want me there.'

Maureen folded her arms and flattened her lips. Carl gave a little cough, edging towards the door.

'I know I'll never be as good as him,' said Robyn. 'I left the island and never came back. He's the dutiful son who comes back just enough to keep everyone happy. But you know my reasons for staying away. Even if you choose to ignore them.'

Raising a mug of coffee to her lips, Maureen shook her head. Her eyes darted to Carl. She lifted her brows. Denial. Always the same. Before the accident, there were times when Robyn had connected with her, but more often, Mum sided with Davie. Never brave enough to step out from his shadow. With a deep breath, Robyn slid her iPad across the table. 'I've drawn up some plans. What do you think?'

Maureen pushed back the iPad and sipped her coffee. 'I don't need them. I can handle things.'

'I'm offering to help,' said Robyn. 'Can't you even look? I can start the ball rolling straightaway.'

'I'd like to see them,' said Carl.

Robyn held the iPad behind her shoulder for him to take. An electric shock shot up her arm as his rough, calloused hand brushed against hers. He still made her heart race, even when driving her mad.

'I'll look later,' said Maureen, 'I need to chat about it with Gillian. She's having some renovations done at the farm. We can find out who's doing the work. I want to make sure we use local trade.'

'It might be more cost effective to contract in some mainland companies. I've worked with some that I think will do it, especially if we provide accommodation.'

'No thanks.' Maureen got up and slung her cup under the gushing tap. 'I'm staying local. Now, I need to get on. I have Liam's room to clean.'

Robyn lowered her head with a bitter smile. No point in pushing things. Carl placed the iPad on the table. 'I think she'll come round,' he said. 'These plans are really good, but I don't think she can afford them.'

'Well, she's dead set on you doing it, she obviously thinks you have hidden cash.' Standing up, Robyn scanned around the room, trying not to connect her eyes to Carl's. His powerful presence seeped into her skin. The memory of days gone by; kisses in the woods, hugs on the beach. His arms hadn't been as muscular back then, but they'd given her sustenance in barren times.

'Not me. I don't have a penny to my name.' He ruffled his hair.

'Well, I don't know what you're going to do then.' Robyn stood up and grabbed her tweed coat and cashmere scarf from the utility room. She threw them on the table and gathered her keys and her bag. 'Come on, Florrie.' Florrie followed as Robyn opened the door. Chewie peered up with a half-asleep look, obviously hopeful she wouldn't shout for him too.

Carl followed her outside, looking like a lumberjack in his thick fleece jacket and jeans. 'Where are you off to?'

Robyn settled Florrie in the passenger seat. 'To the nearest shop, I need strong gin and chocolate.' She tried to rub a view hole in the windscreen with her gloved finger, but the ice was solid. *Where's the scraper?* Looking around and clapping her hands, she averted her eyes from Carl.

'Good plan. Here, I'll get you my scraper.' Carl headed towards his pickup, winding a soft woollen scarf up to his stubbly chin.

'It'll be clear in a minute once I get the engine started.' She got in, shoved the keys in the ignition and turned them. By the time she looked up, Carl had disappeared. Robyn threw her head back, waiting for the window to clear. Moments later, Carl jogged up and started to scratch off the ice.

'I can do it myself,' said Robyn, flinging open the door and jumping out. 'I'm not some helpless girl.'

'I didn't think you were.'

Snatching the scraper, she leaned over trying to get the middle bit. A pain smarted in her lower tummy. 'Ow.' She straightened up.'

'Is everything ok?'

'Fine.' She thrust the scraper back at Carl and jumped in the driver's seat, rubbing her tummy. Now and then, it gave her little reminders. Before she could let down the handbrake, the passenger door opened, and Carl leapt in. 'What are you doing?'

'Can I tag along? I need some things too. And we need to talk.' He pulled the seatbelt across and clipped it.

'You're kidding, right?' This was more than she'd bargained for. She wanted time to gather her thoughts, not add to them. And to walk Florrie after her shopping, somewhere wild and free – not with Carl.

'It'll be kinder to the environment than me going myself.'

'Environment! Fiddlesticks! Honestly, this is ridiculous.'

Florrie jumped onto his knee. 'Hello.' Carl laughed and rubbed her all over. She wriggled about, panting and nuzzling.

Robyn narrowed her eyes. *Get your hands off my dog.* But Florrie was in a particularly treacherous mood, lapping up the attention. With a screech, Robyn pulled off. 'This better be good,' she said. 'Whatever it is you want to say.'

Carl let out a little laugh as Florrie nuzzled further into his thick fleece. Ignoring them, Robyn drove along the track to the exit. Grit lay across the empty main road. Turning right, she headed towards Salen.

Carl nosed around. 'Nice motor,' he said, his eyes lingering on Robyn. Her hands clenched the wheel. *Is he critiquing my driving?* Should she follow the Highway Code to the letter? Or was that Miss Goody-two-shoes Robyn? The one he'd duped into dating him twelve years ago. Conned her into believing he liked her.

'So, what is it you want to talk about?' she asked.

He rubbed his chin. 'The hotel… and Liam's accident.'

'Why? That's not exactly my favourite subject.'

'You said some stuff yesterday that confused me. I want to clear things up. What do you think I did to Liam and why do you think Davie blamed you?'

She glared at him. His curls hung down as he fussed Florrie. 'Because he blamed me for everything. He thought I'd put you up to… pushing Liam.'

'I didn't push him.'

Robyn blinked and flattened her lips. 'You said you were going to sort him out.'

'I meant to talk to him. We'd already fallen out because I'd said he needed to grow up. When I caught up with him at the folly, I said it again. He was angry and determined to do something stupid. I couldn't stop him. I guess I didn't try hard enough. But I didn't push him.'

Staring forward, Robyn took a deep breath. Could she believe him? 'It doesn't explain why Dad blamed me. What did you say to him?'

'Nothing. I swear. When you said that yesterday, I didn't understand why. I know I was to blame. I'd never have pretended it was you. I… I really cared about you. I never wanted to hurt you.' His eyes pierced her skin.

'Oh, please.' Heat rose in her cheeks. She couldn't look at him.

'I mean it, Robyn. You were… special.'

Her lips curled up. She wasn't sure why because she didn't feel amused. 'Is that why you asked me out? I was special? That was the reason you spent those weeks with me?'

He frowned. 'Yes.'

Gripping the wheel tightly, she controlled her breathing. Florrie nuzzled into Carl. Robyn's blood pressure spiked. 'No. You asked me because Julie McNabb and crew dared you to do it. It was all a big fat lie.'

Carl drew in a sharp breath and stared. 'You know about that?'

'Yes, I do.' She rounded the car into the parking area in front of the shop, almost knocking over the sign for the cash machine.

Chapter Seven

Carl

Carl followed Robyn into the shop. She hadn't given him a chance to explain. He pulled his scarf high on his neck and waved to Florrie's sad puppy dog eyes watching from the passenger seat. From the shop door, Robyn zapped the car lock and marched inside.

'Robyn. Can we talk—'

'There's your girlfriend,' she said. 'You can get a lift back with her and save me the bother.'

'What girlfriend?' Carl saw Kirsten McGregor waving from across the chest freezer. Trying to catch Robyn, he pushed forward, almost knocking over an old lady with a basket. A tin rolled across the floor. Carl picked it up. 'Sorry.'

'Hi, Carl,' said Kirsten. Spinning around, he noticed she wasn't alone. Two other women stood beside her, her sister, Beth, and their friend, Georgia Rose, a local artist and photographer.

Kirsten waved, pulling a long wavy lock of brown hair behind her ear. Her cheeks glowed pink. Carl held back. He flicked his eyes around for the exit but a queue had formed, blocking the route to the door.

'Hi,' he said.

Georgia's bright red grin was enormous – too bright to be allowed. Amongst the locals, she looked like a film star.

Robyn slipped past on the other side of the shelf. Beth, the older sister, peered through the gap. Carl rubbed his chin. Beth would remember Robyn. They were all in the same year at school.

'Listen, I need to…' He had to get to Robyn and tell her the truth.

Kirsten fiddled with her collar and bit her lip. 'How are you?' she asked.

'Fine. Yeah. Good. You?'

'Still quiet. It's always the same in the winter. We did a few tours over the festive season, but the demand isn't there. Look, the pendant's nice, isn't it?' She pulled down her jacket to reveal the sparkling purple gem.

'Yeah. Very nice.'

'We were talking about having a party on Saturday.' Georgia ran her hands through her tousled blonde bob. 'It'll break up January, such a long month.'

'We'll host it at the farmhouse,' said Kirsten. 'Anyone who comes can bunk overnight.'

'You in?' asked Georgia.

Carl's eyes snapped back to the row of expectant faces. Kirsten beamed. He breathed in. 'What? I might, I don't know.'

Georgia put her hands on her hips. 'I thought you liked a party.'

'That's Robyn Sherratt, right?' Beth watched Robyn in the far corner. Carl could see Beth's mind ticking over. 'Wow.' Her mouth dropped open. 'She looks amazing. I feel a bit pathetic now.'

'Come and say hi. I need to speak to her.'

'No.' Beth glanced at her mucky wellies. 'We didn't really know each other. She was always…' she searched for the word with her palms up. '… quiet.'

'Yeah,' muttered Carl.

'Didn't you go out with her?' Beth asked.

'Did you?' Kirsten stared.

Georgia's eyes widened. 'You kept that quiet.'

Just why he would have told her, he wasn't sure. He didn't make a habit of discussing his teenage romances with nosy-parkers. The glint in her eye gave him a sinking sensation. Was she about to add matchmaker to her list of talents? He could see her mind working. But she could forget it. His days with Robyn were a blissful memory. Reality could never live up. He was on a solo path, and that was that. Marriage, kids, and all that jazz were not his thing. He couldn't be trusted to look after himself, never mind anyone else. His relationships had been short and anything but sweet, they barely counted as relationships at all.

'It was just a few weeks,' he said. The most perfect of his life. How was that possible? In a whole thirty years to have had just five perfect weeks.

'She's coming over,' said Georgia through her grin like a ventriloquist.

'Good,' said Carl. 'I need to…' He swallowed as she approached. Her elegance took his breath. For someone slumming it at the local convenience store, Robyn looked totally out of place. Her slick coat was set for London fashion week rather than the grocery aisle.

'I'm done,' she said. 'Are you coming back with me? Or will one of your girlfriends give you a lift?'

'I'm coming.'

'You can come back with us,' said Kirsten, 'we don't mind dropping you off.'

'No, I—'

'What a good plan. Then I'm free to walk Florrie.' Robyn headed to the till without a backward glance.

Moving was impossible. Kirsten blocked the aisle. Robyn paid and left. Carl had no choice.

Georgia took hold of his arm and pulled him aside before he got into the McGregor's Land Rover. Her left eyebrow almost lifted off her forehead. 'You used to date her?'

'Years ago. It was nothing.'

'Nothing? A nothing you can't take your eyes off.' Georgia poked him in the tummy.

'Listen.' Carl stepped away from the car and ran his fingers through his hair, trying to untangle some stubborn curls. 'Don't go getting any ideas. It was twelve years ago. It's complicated.'

Georgia pulled a side pout. 'She didn't seem very happy. What happened to the two of you?'

'Nothing. We split after the accident. It was a bad time.'

'Carl, hurry up,' shouted Kirsten, drawing down the passenger window.

'Better go,' said Georgia, 'and have fun.' She winked and nodded at Kirsten.

Jumping into the Land Rover's backseat, Carl felt like an animal trapped in a cage as they sped off towards the hotel. Robyn had obviously gone elsewhere. He didn't see her car until much later and when he called at the hotel, Maureen didn't know where she was.

For another two days, he watched for her. Calling on Maureen every few hours wasn't something he relished. She ensnared him into long conversations about how they could afford repairs.

Feeling hot under the collar, Carl left after his umpteenth failed attempt to see Robyn. Maureen was still talking as though she expected him to raise thousands of pounds in a couple of weeks, plus carry out all the repairs before the reopening in late March. Well, she'd picked the wrong man.

On the upside, Kirsten's party was cancelled. Carl didn't have the chance to jump for joy however when he discovered the reason. It was Maureen's birthday. Gillian McGregor, Beth and Kirsten's mum, decided a party at the hotel for Maureen would be much better than a drinking fest in her farmhouse.

Carl found himself roped into putting together a mini-concert to entertain the guests. After Maureen mooted it as a quiet affair, Carl discovered half the island was invited.

Robyn was as elusive as the winter sun. If he hadn't seen her car parked in the front driveway, he'd have thought she'd left. She must have started driving somewhere to walk Florrie because he hadn't seen her about, and he'd given up asking Maureen if she was in. Her questioning looks were too probing.

Certain Robyn would be at the party, Carl spent a large part of the day setting up. The dining room had space for big events – bags of it. An empty waste ground losing money by the hour. Moving tables and setting up was his domain; if this was all he had to do, he could have the place up and running by the end of the week. He fixed in the last section of the portable stage and sat on it. In the hotel's heyday, the room would have been buzzing. Even in the winter, it had attracted enough visitors to make it viable. That wasn't an option now. The winter season was repair time. But reopening in the spring looked impossible. The amount of upgrading was too much. And no one could agree on how to finance it. They needed a miracle. The looks Maureen gave him convinced Carl she expected him to work it.

Where was Robyn? He'd been sure she'd appear to lend a hand. The repertoire of songs he'd put together for the evening were heavily inspired by memories of their short weeks together. It was like a woodpecker was chapping at his chest, poking holes in the fences he'd constructed round his heart.

He rested his forehead in his hands. His life was going precisely nowhere. Fixing things earned nothing – most people expected him to do it for free. He subsidised it with any work he could get. A far cry from a year ago when he'd been a top technician in an IT company. How quickly life could turn around, usually for the worse.

Standing up, he lifted a heavy box and pulled out the sound-system. His music had gone down well in reviews last year. One of the few things that had. On the occasions he'd done shifts, he'd entertained the guests. The boyhood dream of being in a band. He smiled and plugged in the sound-box.

'Oh, goodness me.' Maureen pushed through the swing doors from the industrial kitchen, holding her hand to her forehead. A strong smell of burning wafted in. 'I think the oven has packed in. I'm not sure what to do. Maybe I should do batches in my own kitchen.' She checked her watch. 'I'm not sure I have time.'

'I thought Gillian was bringing food.'

'Oh, she is. I thought I'd do something though. I hate leaving it all to her. Also, I want to show Robyn I can cook perfectly well. Apparently, I cook with too much fat and the kitchen smells like a roadside diner.'

'Did she say that?' Carl gave himself an internal slap. He almost laughed. Robyn had a point. Judging from the smell, she was right. Maureen's cooking was hit or miss and recently there was a lot more missing.

'No. But she oh so kindly read out the worst reviews to me.' Maureen sounded like she was covering anger with sarcasm, but her eyes looked red.

'Well, do you have a budget yet?' Carl fixed up the microphone stand. 'Maybe starting small like replacing the oven would help?'

'Oh, Robyn's drawn up lots of big plans. And she wants to hire some fancy people she's worked with before. Anything to make me look small.'

'I don't think that's why she's doing it.' Carl jumped off the stage and shoved the empty boxes behind. 'She wants to help. Though I'm not sure how hiring mainland companies will work. Local businesses might be easier if they're available.'

'Thank you, Carl. That is exactly what I said. But she will not listen. I won't change my mind. I don't care what she says. I'm not having anyone from off-island doing the work unless there's no one here who can. And that's final.'

The swing doors to the hallway creaked. Robyn stood in the entrance. How long had she been there? She folded her arms and stood straight and tall, like a company director in a boardroom. Intimidating. Super-hot. Carl stepped back, sensing the heat from the radiator, but it wasn't that making his palms sweat. He tugged the neck of his jumper. Desire surged through him at the raw power emitting from Robyn's eyes. What wouldn't he like to do with her? Grabbing his hand, he dug his nails into his skin. Why such inappropriate thoughts?

'If I'm financing the work, I'll employ the best value option. That's using sense, not sentimentality,' said Robyn.

Maureen's white face reddened. She balled her fists and gritted her teeth.

'You're financing it?' Carl moved closer. 'How?' She couldn't possibly have that much cash lying about. Carl felt a queasy wave. Almost jealousy.

Maureen narrowed her eyes. Robyn raised her head. 'I don't think that's your concern.'

'Maybe not. But can I just remind you, you've not lived on the island for twelve years.' Both women looked at him. Maureen triumphant, Robyn unreadable. 'Maybe, you don't remember what it's like to live here. What if your contractors get held up because boats don't run? Supplies don't come in? There are all sorts of problems. If we stay with island trade, we get people who are used to this. My dad's worked with island tradesmen all his life. He can ship supplies here and miss out the ferries. Your solutions might work in the city, but it's different here.'

Robyn's gaze hardened. Maureen smiled and nodded. Carl swallowed and dropped his eyes. Now he'd said his piece, he wanted to curl up in a corner and die.

'You have nothing to do with any of this.' Robyn's cool tone made him shiver.

'Yes, he does.' Maureen stood up straight. 'He's like part of this family.'

'Well, that's not much then, is it? I'm part of your family and look at how you treat me.'

'You never wanted to be part of this family. You were always running off, refusing to help. Why come back now? Why not when your father was still alive? Cowardly and shameful.'

'Maureen, please,' said Carl. 'She's not—'

'Yes, she is. I don't know what her motives are for coming back now, but I don't trust them.'

Robyn breathed deeply and looked at Maureen, her piercing eyes burned with blue fire. 'You know exactly why I didn't come back sooner. You pretend not to. You've hidden it all these years. Covered up, blamed me, twisted the facts. Why don't you tell Carl the truth? Tell him why I never got on with my father. And why mistrust my motives? Is it wrong for a daughter to want to help her mother?' With a flick of her long hair, she walked out. The double doors swung behind her.

Carl wanted to follow. Stepping towards the door, he made to push it when Maureen said, 'I'll explain.'

She slumped into a chair. Carl turned, still eyeing the door, and folded his arms. 'Go on.'

'As a girl, Robyn was so quiet around people, you might remember. Sometimes it was so awkward, especially when we were out. But it all came out at home. It's still the same. She spoke barely a word to anyone at the funeral, yet she's happy to tear lumps out of me and Liam.' Maureen stood up and stared out the wide glass-fronted room.

'I saw her giving as good as she got with Liam,' said Carl. 'He was just as quick to jibe her.'

'She drives people away. She never had friends. You were her only boyfriend, and that was a farce.'

'Why?' Heat prickled in his neck.

'Oh, no offence,' said Maureen. 'We all understand what happened. Maybe I should have sent her to therapy, but it was never easy to access things like that here.'

'Why did she need therapy for going out with me?' A sickening sensation rose in his stomach. Maureen's ruthlessness and complete misunderstanding stung. His heart ached to hug Robyn, to show her she wasn't alone. A flood of desire surged within. He wanted to help her.

'It wasn't that. It was her complete lack of social skills. Utterly impossible when we were trying to run a hotel. She wouldn't help, she skulked about, and as soon as we were in private, it was like she was possessed. I'm not denying her achievements, she's always been strong and had big ideas.' Maureen steeled herself against the glass, then returned to her seat. 'Davie wasn't an easy man to live with. He and Robyn could be as bad as each other. They both had to win at everything, no matter what. He took it bad when Robyn got older because she was more intelligent than him, and he knew it.' Maureen looked into the distance as though watching something from those days and shook her head.

'That wasn't her fault.' Carl slumped down opposite Maureen. All Robyn needed was some concern. Some love. Instead, her parents had cut her loose. 'But why?' His words got lost. Why hadn't her family helped her? Why had they abandoned her?

'Instead of letting go, Robyn would go on and on. Davie never laid a finger on her, of that I swear, but what he did was almost as bad.' Maureen's face crumpled.

Carl swallowed and looked away. Davie had liked control. Carl and his brothers had been like pupils, they'd done as he said, no question. If Robyn hadn't complied that would have irritated him.

'Davie was harsh. He shouldn't have said the things he did. He would tell her she was worthless, useless, that she'd never amount to anything. And the names he called her, I won't repeat them. It upset me so much. Robyn sometimes found me crying. She thought it was his fault. It wasn't. Both of them upset me. She never understood why I stayed with him. She still doesn't. She can't see she was part of the problem.'

'Was she?'

'Yes, Carl. She should have backed down. There was no need to provoke him. Then when Liam—'

'Look, that wasn't her fault.'

'I know that.' Maureen buried her head in her hands. Her shoulders shook with emotion.

Carl let out a sigh. His head reeled. 'I need to talk to her.'

Maureen shook her head. 'Leave her. She's better off without me. I'm a terrible mother. I heard her talking to someone at her work yesterday. She's heading back. There's a man she spent Christmas with. Pete, I think his name was. I remember her sending me a message at the time. She wants to get back to him. I'd rather she didn't start all her fancy plans, only to leave us in the lurch.'

Carl lost the thread. Robyn had a man in Manchester. The words pricked him in the ribs. It had always been a possibility. A probability even. Carl bowed his head. His limbs grew heavy. Somewhere deep inside, the secret flame flickered and died.

Chapter Eight

Robyn

Robyn abandoned her car on the island's west side and walked for hours, trying to clear her head. Darkness crawled over the western sky. The view towards Coll and Tiree vanished into pitch black. Robyn fumbled across the rocks until she felt grass underfoot. Imprinted memory led her back.

Lifting an exhausted Florrie into the car, Robyn took her seat and rested her head. Opening the window to the night, a sharp cold breeze touched her cheek. The sea crashed beyond, mesmerising and soothing her. Her eyes accustomed to the darkness. An edge of white horses hit the rocks.

'Maybe coming back was a mistake,' she told Florrie with a sigh. 'When I was young, I never wanted to leave here, I loved it so much.' Words failed, she bit back a tear. It was rare for her to cry, but recently she'd been so weepy. Her hand fell to her midriff. She rubbed the tiny scar. It didn't hurt any more. No sensation at all. Just emptiness. 'Do you know, I once thought I'd marry Carl.' Her vision blurred. 'We had such silly plans. But I couldn't stay. He betrayed me. Dad made my life a living hell. Mum always took his side. The kids at school were just as bad. I didn't fit. I still don't. What am I actually fit for?'

She started the engine and pulled off into the darkness. 'I can't even face work any more,' she whispered as she drove slowly around a corner. 'Not with Pete.' If she wanted, she could leave the island. A lingering air of unfinished business pricked at her chest. Whether it related to Pete or Carl, she couldn't tell.

She could always fire Pete. But he was so self-absorbed, she could trust him to run the business as if it was his own, usually he acted like it was. Raising her chin, she groaned. *Pete never wanted me, just the business.* Letting out a sigh, she could see plain as day, she was nothing but a stepping-stone in his career.

Approaching one of the island's wildest parts, she drove around the twisting hill road to the south of Loch-na-Keal. Conditions could be treacherous at the best of times. Pitch-blackness shrouded around. No streetlamps, headlights, even houses. An occasional warm glow twinkled in a far-flung window. The remote cosiness tugged her heart. Once she'd dreamed of a cottage here; with Carl, three kids, and six dogs.

'Oh no.' She emergency stopped and fake bashed her head on the steering wheel. 'The party. I forgot. I was so mad, I stormed out. Mum will kill me. It'll be almost over and I'm miles away.'

It was after eleven when she finally returned. Florrie was famished. Several cars were parked outside. Lights in the main rooms were on, and a couple of upstairs windows glowed. Was Maureen letting the guests use the back bedrooms? They were barely fit for purpose and it was hardly a way to make money. Unlike the sea view rooms, they didn't have shutters, and they were so grim inside. What an embarrassment, but best not say a word. It would just cause more falling out. The kitchen door was open. No one ever bothered locking their doors. She could have walked into any house on the island. Muffled sounds of chatter and laughter from the dining-room door carried through as Robyn fixed Florrie some food. Chewie nosed into her leg. How could she refuse those big brown eyes? She passed him a snack.

Her clothes were covered in mud. Would she have time to run up and change before the party finished? The door opened, a young woman with a wavy blonde bob burst in, rubbing her hand. Robyn blinked; the woman's bright red dress was dazzling.

'Oh, hello.' The woman jumped in surprise. 'I didn't know anyone was here. Are you Robyn?'

'Yes.' Robyn squirmed at the sight of blood seeping from the woman's finger. 'What happened?

'One of the tables split. I got a bit of a scratch from a loose nail.' She ran her hand under the tap. 'I've heard about you, but we haven't met. I'm Georgia Rose. I'm a photographer. And an artist… and well, a sort of will-try-anything-crafty-type.'

'A table split?'

'The edge broke off. Carl can fix it.'

Robyn took a deep breath. Great. More disasters. 'I hope you're ok.'

'It's just a scratch. I didn't want Maureen to see. That's why I snuck in here. It's the nearest sink. Maureen was wondering where you were.'

'Was she?' Robyn fiddled with the sleeve of her jumper. 'I, eh, had to go out.'

'Well, if you come in just now, Carl's doing a concert. He's such a good singer, I'm really jealous. I love singing, but I don't have the nerve to do it in front of anyone.' Georgia clamped a bit of kitchen roll to her hand.

Robyn tried to smile. 'Sounds nice.'

'He's normally quite upbeat with his music, but he's been so sappy tonight. I don't know what's got into him.' Georgia examined her finger.

No blood. Robyn breathed a sigh.

'Everyone goes gooey-eyed over him, especially Kirsten McGregor,' continued Georgia.

'Are they together then?' Robyn walked to the fridge and took out a drink.

Georgia laughed. 'No. Carl doesn't do relationships – so he says.' Pausing, she eyed the door. 'I wonder. Maybe he's changed his mind and that's what's inspired all the romantic tunes. Kirsten will be thrilled.'

Robyn furrowed her brow. Carl didn't do relationships? Nothing had changed. Poor Kirsten. Robyn had been that girl; the one who set her hopes on Carl, believed the plans they'd made together could come true only to discover it was all fake. Was he still playing? Toying with people's souls? His games had broken her heart and her brother's body.

'I better get back in. I don't want to miss "You're Beautiful". I know it'll make me cry, but I'm a sucker for it.' Georgia slipped through the door, and Robyn caught a lilt of music. With a slight tremor in her hand, she headed out the side door. Was there time to change? Another door led off the back corridor into the dining room. Curiosity tugged at her. She pushed it open and leant on the frame.

Sitting on a stool, Carl caressed his guitar, a microphone perched in front of him. He plucked a few strings in preparation. With lithe fingers, he gently strummed the opening bars. Goosebumps erupted over Robyn's arms. "You're Beautiful" was *their* song. Why had he chosen to sing it now? Had he forgotten? Did it mean nothing to him any more? Well, why would it? Everything about that time had been a lie.

His voice – mellow, soft, strong, and fluid – moulded the words perfectly. A rough edge added depth. Not a hint of a crack. He rose and fell through the notes. Lost in the melody, Robyn put her hand to her nose. Tiny beads of moisture crowded her eyes. Spellbound, she studied his face. Once she'd loved him with all her heart, in the days when a fresh-faced boy had sung her those words and meant them. Or so she'd thought. Carl closed his eyes as he sang. When he opened them, he looked directly at her, like he knew she was there. 'You're beautiful, it's true.' His gaze lingered over her before he closed them again.

Robyn stood rooted to the spot. Had he meant the words for her? She shook her hair and took a sip of wine. Only a naïve child would believe that, she'd been there and she wasn't going down that road. Not again. Twelve years ago was bad enough. She shut the door and headed upstairs. Must keep the music from her head. Tears pricked. Just to feel those arms again would help. No! It wasn't real, it never had been.

Faint notes echoed in the dull silence of her bedroom. She'd reached the unspoken deadline, she had to decide. To stay or go? After getting ready for bed, she downed her remaining wine, jumped under the covers and pulled the duvet tight. It shrouded her like a warm hug. An imprint of Carl's grey-blue eyes burned into her eyelids.

*

Robyn had taken a long time to fall asleep. The darkness on the island in winter was as absolute at eight in the morning as it was at midnight. She didn't wake until almost ten. *So unlike me.* She liked to rise early, get things done. Hopefully, someone had let Florrie out and given her some breakfast.

Opening the curtains, Robyn looked down to the shore, pulling her robe tight. Carl and Georgia were on the beach, throwing stones and laughing. Poor Kirsten. Had Carl shaken off her advances for a fling with the beautiful artist? Perhaps the romantic music selection was never meant for Kirsten. Robyn lowered her head and pressed her lips tight. She'd been easily led by his gentle words, long ago. How many others had followed?

Robyn picked up her make-up bag from the dressing table and dropped it into her suitcase. She might as well pack up. This venture had yielded nothing but pain. Back in her real life, she was someone. She had staff, people to manage – not friends, but people – people who respected and admired her. The opposite of what she had here. Even facing Pete would be worth it to get back that respect.

The figures on the beach drew her eye again. Wait. *Is that…?* Chewie and Florrie leapt around on the sand, rushing in and out of the water. Robyn crushed a bottle of moisturiser in her palm. *They took my dog?* She breathed deeply and counted to ten, reminding herself they were just being kind, that was all. But it set her teeth on edge, seeing them like a happy couple, chucking stones in the water for the dogs to chase.

Over an hour later, she went downstairs for whatever meal it was – breakfast, lunch, brunch? It was all party leftovers anyway, so it resembled nothing normal. Now to face Mum. Hearing a clattering, Robyn poked her head around. Maureen was hunched over something in the corner, silhouetted by the light from the expansive windows. *Maybe I should back off.* Maureen was likely to be furious. Or was she crying?

'Are you all right, Mum?'

'What? Oh, it's you.' Maureen looked up, the old industrial hoover in pieces below. 'Just this damned old thing. It's always blocking. There's something stuck right inside it.' She fished about, her arm so far in it might never come out. 'There!' She pulled out a giant hairy lump. Robyn screwed up her nose.

'So, you decided to show your face,' said Maureen. 'What happened to you yesterday? You missed my party.'

'Well, you haven't been especially kind to me. I needed to clear my head.'

'Right. You couldn't even make an allowance for one day.'

'I don't particularly like parties. How about I take you to lunch, or something like that instead?'

Maureen stood up and folded her arms. 'Not today, I'm still full from yesterday. Robyn, you have a good job and a life in Manchester. Why don't you go home? Don't feel you have to stay. This place will get sorted one way or another. I've been slaving here for the best part of thirty years and I haven't failed yet. Go home to where you're happy.'

Robyn teased out some hair at the back of her neck. 'I have expertise… and money. If you would let me show you.'

Maureen tilted her head to the side. 'I don't need a display of your wealth and talents. If you want to make me look rubbish, you already have.'

'That is not what I'm trying to do.' Robyn put her hands on her hips and glared. Maureen shook her head and returned to the hoover. 'I want to help you because you're my mother and I… care about you.' She swallowed. The words came out faster than her thoughts, something she never allowed. Maureen looked up and gaped. Robyn steadied her breathing. 'I never forgave Dad, but I forgive you because I know what you went through.'

'Forgive me for what?' Maureen's brows lined and her eyes narrowed.

'For standing back and letting Dad strip me down with his words until I was like raw flesh being beaten by a stick.'

79

Robyn side-eyed Maureen. Maureen's brow grooved into a sharp V. 'You never stood up for me,' continued Robyn. 'Sometimes you shouted at me too, told me not to provoke him. Jeez.' She turned away and held her forehead. 'I wasn't provoking him. I was defending myself.'

Silence. Robyn didn't make eye contact until Maureen spoke again. 'I don't want to start another fight. But there were times when you did provoke him. Times when you should have walked away.'

'But you can't live your life like that. Under someone's thumb, always doing their bidding and acting like it doesn't bother you.'

'If I disagreed with Davie, we talked. We compromised. I knew certain things angered him, but I picked my battles. You never stopped to think, you just burst in all guns blazing.'

'So, you condone what he did?'

Maureen shook her head. 'You both played a part.'

Robyn let out a disgruntled breath. There was just no getting through.

'You know what hurts me now though?' said Maureen.

'What?' Robyn dropped her head to the side and folded her arms.

'The fact it'll never be resolved because you didn't come back in time.'

Robyn shook her head. 'It's not as if he couldn't have approached me at any point in the twelve years I was off the island. He never visited me once.'

'He wasn't a good traveller.'

'He knew I couldn't forgive him. He couldn't face seeing me again either.'

'He was dying, Robyn. He wanted to see you. He knew he'd made mistakes. But out of all of us, you're the one that made money and a name for yourself, so it's not like it's done you any harm.'

Robyn bit the nail on her thumb and stared at Maureen. 'Yes, I've done all that. But it did me harm. How could it not have harmed me? Dad even pinned Liam's accident on me. People around here still think I had something to do with it.'

'Davie needed to blame someone.'

'And I was easy prey?' Her father's poisonous words had crushed her confidence, leaving her cold and dead. She struggled to make friends, trust people. Walls came up. She steered clear of relationships. That was the harm. Learning to deal with it had been her life's mission. At times, the need for human contact burned deep, but where to find it? She'd built a relationship with Pete because it was safe and had well-defined boundaries. Her fingers grazed her lower midriff, coming to rest on her punishment. She'd broken the rules.

'Let's not talk about this,' said Maureen, 'we just end up arguing. Carl called round. He wanted to talk to you.'

'I'd rather not.'

Maureen shrugged and started putting the hoover back together. 'Well, suit yourself.'

What did Carl want? There was only one way to find out. Robyn grabbed warm clothes, and set off for the cabin. She fidgeted with her scarf. Was he cross she'd missed the party too? Maybe he'd wanted her to hear his songs, tug her heart, remind her of the love he'd once faked. Straightening herself out and adjusting her coat several times, she decided it best to treat it like a meeting with an employee; cool and professional. Knocking on the door, she waited, holding her head high and her back straight. *I've got this.*

'Hey.' Carl opened the door and stepped aside to let her in.

Instant warmth hit her, along with a dreamy scent that was either him or a particularly pleasant scented candle, perhaps a combination of both. Although shabby from the outside, the cabin was welcoming. Robyn loosened her coat as she admired the quirky homely style; a cross between the *Ikea Catalogue* and a yurt retreat, full of furry blankets, logs, driftwood and several odd knickknacks, presumably things he'd rescued and fixed.

'You wanted to see me?' Robyn propped herself on the arm of a chair and crossed her legs. Her eyes lingered on a set of painted stones near the wood-burning stove. Each one was a quaint little cottage. One of them stood out clearly. She remembered him painting it exactly the way she'd described. A perfect image of what one day they'd planned to live in. Their own little cottage by the sea.

'Do you want a coffee or anything?'

'No, thank you.' Robyn smoothed her jeans and pressed her lips together.

Carl flopped into the opposite armchair and stretched his arms behind his head before settling. 'I am knackered. I tried to better my speed, cycling to the village and back. I think I've killed my legs.'

Robyn folded her arms. 'Is that what you wanted to tell me?'

'No.' Carl laughed. He had even teeth and cheeky dimples. Maintaining eye contact became difficult. When he looked at her, a tremor ran down her spine. 'I just wanted to say sorry.'

'I see.' Robyn tilted her chin and turned towards the window. Easier than focusing on him, but her eyes drifted back.

'Yeah. About yesterday. I wanted to avert the argument. I think I made it worse.' He pulled his curls tight on the top of his head. 'You and I want the same thing. We just have different ways of getting there.' His hands clasped behind his head and he leaned back.

'And what is it we both want?'

'To fix up the hotel.' He stared into the crackling fire in the stove.

'And how do you propose to do it?'

He dropped his arms and glanced up. His eyes made her shiver. 'That's what I don't know. At the end of the day, it's Maureen's hotel. She should make the decisions. But you're the one with the experience.'

'And the money.'

'That too.' Carl gave a nod of acknowledgement. 'I said I would help, but I don't have a clue. It's like asking me to man a solo rocket to the moon.'

'So your point is?'

He shook his head and held his palms to the ceiling. 'I'm not sure I have a point. I'm just waffling. But if you say hiring outside contractors is the way forward, I think we have to suck it up and go with it.'

Their eyes locked for a moment. Blood rushed to Robyn's head. She couldn't look away. Did those grey-blue orbs hold more secrets? More games? Or was he an innocent ensnared by her family? His lips quirked up. Oh, to touch them.

'Well,' Robyn folded her arms, 'as you've been so thorough in your reflection, I'll tell you, I've been thinking about what you said. There may be some merit in using local trade.' This was true. She waited for the smugness to creep into his face. It didn't. She inclined her head. He was smart enough to have planned this all along, behind the *I'm just waffling*, façade. 'The availability at this time of year is a big consideration. As you said yesterday, I haven't lived here for a long time and I overlooked things like that. I'll fathom it all into my calculations.' She took a deep breath and folded her hand on her lap. Should she close her eyes while he gloated?

'Really? Wow, that's great,' said Carl.

She frowned, was that it? *You've won!* He wasn't reacting properly. He just kept on smiling and waggling his woolly socks in front of the stove.

'Well, I should go. I have work to do,' she said.

'I, eh.' He stood up. 'There's something else from back then I need to tell you—'

'Let's not discuss that. I can't face it.'

'But it's important.' He swallowed.

'No. I don't want to talk about it.'

His wide shoulders dropped. He nodded and opened the door. She inhaled the heavenly scent again, keeping her eyes averted.

As she made her way back to the hotel, a flutter of nervous energy ran through her. It didn't feel like she'd lost anything, despite conceding one of her objectives. Her shoulders hung light and free. Even the thought of Carl jumping in the air and clicking his heels in a victory dance didn't bother her. She grinned at the idea. Whatever he'd been about to dig up from the past, she'd brushed off. Best let it stay there. Dragging it up couldn't change anything. The air had cleared. She and Carl could now meet as people doing business together – cool and detached. Just as it should be.

Chapter Nine

Carl

Carl looked out on Wednesday morning to see a team of builders pulling up. And snow! Boyish excitement tickled him. Snow! Although it barely covered the path, it was a cause for celebration. And builders too. Robyn was a fast worker. He'd seen her efficiency when she'd called at the cabin. An intimidating boss. His office days were over, thank god. Never again did he want to return to cut-throat boardrooms, but he could see Robyn thriving there, she had the poker face, the jargon and the grit.

Rubbing away the condensation, Carl watched Maureen step out tentatively to greet the builders. No one slipped, and everyone looked happy. Donning his jacket, Carl went outside to the lean-to. His thoughts lingered back to Robyn. She'd cut him down when he'd tried to tell her how things had been. Maybe she didn't care. She was in a relationship now; it was water under the bridge. Just as it should be for him. But she still wore the pendant. At least it looked like the one he'd given her. Why? Shaking the thought from his head, he turned to the task in hand.

A commission to fix an intricate pendulum clock had come in, now was the time to start. With jobs like this it was easy to get engrossed and Carl spent three days working on it before he ventured up to the hotel. If anything practical needed doing, he was willing to give it a go now Robyn had found a way to finance the project.

The snow had melted away, along with any hopes of a sledging trip when Carl finally crossed the bleak-looking lawn, breathing in the chilled salty air, and clapping his hands to keep warm. He poked his head around the backdoor to find Maureen in the kitchen. A cloud of steam fizzed up from a pan.

Maureen jumped back, rolling her eyes as a loud banging and clattering shook the ceiling. 'They're ripping out the old bathrooms. Robyn is supervising. She's quite the bulldog.' Maureen raised her eyebrows. 'She's found an outlet for that temper of hers. Making sure they do as they're told. Poor Bill, I've known him for years. I doubt he's ever had a tougher job with her standing on guard.'

Carl smirked, what a shock to their systems. Bill was old-school and well known for his delight in tea breaks and rain checks, especially if they brought opportunities to sample home baking and have a good chinwag. 'So, you don't need me to do anything. I'm sure I could be quite handy with a crowbar.'

Maureen pulled on her cow-print oven gloves and opened the oven door. 'I think we have enough men with crowbars here already. But I do have an idea.'

She pulled a steaming roast out of the oven and placed it on the table. If sampling was the task, Carl was definitely up for the job. It looked like Maureen's most successful dish for months. Even if it was a bribe, he'd take it.

'I was thinking about organising some kind of fundraiser. Robyn has decided to finance this project, but I feel bad. I don't like handouts. I thought if we did something simple and charged folks. Nothing too big. I'm not sure I can handle anything on a grand scale. Especially with all this going on.' She pointed to the ceiling as a heavy drill vibrated above.

'What sort of thing?' Carl inhaled wafts of deliciousness.

'Maybe a quiz night? Everyone enjoys them. You could make some flyers. We could sell tickets to teams, get a prize and maybe a buffet.'

'Sure, I can do the flyers and tickets. No problem.' His stomach rumbled.

'Would you like some of this for lunch?'

He let out a laugh. 'It does smell good.'

'You should find a wife and settle down, young man. That's my advice.' Maureen carved a slice from the chicken. 'Kirsten McGregor, she's the one, I reckon. Give her a chance, she's a good lass.'

'What?' Carl gaped. The chicken looked less appetising. Carl rolled his eyes at the plate as he set it in front of him. So, that was Kirsten's game. He lowered his head with a sigh. Well, he'd have to disappoint her. 'That's pretty shocking, Maureen.' He tried to laugh it off. 'You're not seriously suggesting I get a wife just to cook me nice lunches. That's a bit old-fashioned. I don't think Kirsten would thank you for that remark either.'

'Well, I am old-fashioned. Even in my day, it was expected. Wives cooked. And it wasn't that long ago. Times change so fast. But as for Kirsten, I'm serious, don't dismiss her.'

Carl stabbed the chicken. 'I'm not looking for anyone, Maureen. I'm better on my own.'

'Oh dear. That's a terrible waste. You and Kirsten would make a lovely pair.'

The food couldn't go in quick enough. Carl wanted out. Not only had Maureen decided on Kirsten, she now had them married off. Excusing himself to make a start on the flyers, he filled his lungs with fresh sea air. He'd love to move to a bigger house, do it up, make it his own. But there would be no wife. No family. If he'd known that was what Kirsten was after, he'd have steered well clear. He was bad news. Inflicting himself on a girl like her wasn't fair.

Flyers done, he left to drive around the island and stick them up. He couldn't help glancing up to the window above the hotel kitchen. Robyn's room was there somewhere. What was she doing? He hadn't seen her for days, not even walking the dogs. It was like school all over again. Hanging about, desperate to see her. Nothing he did could truly rid her from his mind.

He handed flyers into every shop and pub he could think of. In Salen, he stopped to shove one through Georgia's letterbox. For an artist, she had terrible taste in houses – a dull semi with the most boring view on the island. Still, she could afford bricks and mortar, unlike him. Her door opened.

'What are you doing?' She frowned and read the flyer. 'Why not just knock? Oh, this looks fun.'

'I'm delivering them.'

'Are you going west?'

'I am.'

'Oh good. Could you drop me at the McGregors' farm? And get me after? I want to get some shots at the cove there.'

'Fine, but I'm not coming in. I don't want to see Kirsten. Have you been trying to set me up with her?'

'No. But you've finally worked out she likes you, have you?'

Carl rubbed his forehead. 'I don't want to hurt her. It isn't her fault.'

'Yeah, I know.'

He remembered Maureen's words. 'I don't need anyone. I'm fine.'

'But you had a girlfriend before you came here, didn't you?'

'You mean the one that ran off with my flatmate?'

Georgia tilted her head. 'Oh.'

'Yeah. That's the kind of girl I usually end up with. You see why I'd rather not bother.'

'You've just had really bad luck.' She patted his arm. 'Not everyone's like that.'

'I just want a simple life.' He shook his head. 'But that hasn't worked out either.'

'I think you need a complete change. Get out the cabin and do something else. Go and sing in a band, invent bikes, be an outdoor adventure instructor. Live your dreams. Who cares about the money? Look at me. I don't have a clue where my next paycheck is coming from, but so what? I could fall off a cliff or be hit by a bus. Just live the life you want, Carl.'

His lips curled up. 'You're such an optimist.' But he was trapped. Caged in by the memory of his failure. If only Liam hadn't fallen.

Pulling up at Creagach Farm, some miles south of Calgary, Carl stopped at the track end, well away from the door, and drove off quickly. The afternoon frittered away. He enjoyed the rugged coasts and blustery hillsides as he delivered the flyers and pinned a couple of laminated ones to fence posts. Years ago, he'd wanted to get married, have kids, and be a family. He knew what an amazing place this was to grow up in. But how could he be trusted? Robyn's face fractured the temporary peace in his head. *Why won't she leave me alone?* He sighed, she'd found someone, he should be happy for her. He braved the notifications on his phone to see about fifty new messages from his brother, Jakob, all with pictures of his new baby. That's what the model family looked like. His new niece had a father with a steady job who could put a roof over her head and could be trusted not to mess up at the first sign of trouble.

He returned to the farm to get Georgia. She wasn't back. Carl had little choice but to accept the invite into the beautiful old stone farmhouse. Kirsten smiled and tugged a strand of hair around her chin. If only he could reciprocate her loving glances. Instead, he wanted to run a mile.

'We'll come to the quiz night,' she said. 'Georgia thought the four of us could be a team. You, me, her, and Beth.'

'Yeah. Sure.' Carl hoped it sounded enthusiastic.

When Georgia finally returned, her cheeks were rosy. She pulled an apologetic face as she spied Carl and Kirsten sitting opposite each other at the farmhouse table.

As soon as they got into the car he said, 'I hope you weren't late on purpose. I told you—'

'I wasn't. Sorry, I didn't realise the time.'

'You know, maybe I should try setting you up with someone, then you'd know how it feels. There's a nice builder at the hotel who wears Bart Simpson boxers he shows off every time he bends down. He'd be right up your street.'

'Oh, shut up.' Georgia threw a scrunched-up flyer at him.

An hour later, he dropped her off and returned to the hotel. A shape on the path drew nearer. He squinted as the darkness rolled in. Robyn's figure drew closer, she pulled her coat tight against the wind. Carl jumped out of the car, shoved his hands in his pockets and strolled towards her.

'Hey. How are the builders getting on? It was great you found some at such short notice.'

Robyn looked around. 'Yes, but they're not the most efficient group.' In the light from the lantern above the door, her icy blue eyes sparkled. 'I needed to get out for a bit. They've ripped out a couple of old bathrooms. It's so dusty in there, and the old hoover has packed in. It'll take a month for them to deliver a new one, even with some ridiculous delivery charge.'

'Ah, the island curse,' said Carl. 'I'll have a look if you like.'

'Mum's in the kitchen, you can ask her.'

'Here,' he pulled a flyer from his pocket. 'You'd be good at this.'

She studied it.

'Your mum's idea to raise a bit of cash. I was just delivering them around and about. It isn't the best time of year for this kind of thing, but it's worth a try. It'll probably drum up some local interest.' He scraped back his hair. 'It took me ages to get back. I had Georgia with me. She's always late.'

'Why don't you move in with her instead of staying at the cabin? Or does she not have a house either?'

'What? Why would I move in with her? She isn't my girlfriend if that's what you mean.'

'Isn't she?' Robyn blinked. 'So, is it Kirsten?'

'No. Neither.'

Absently rubbing her arms, Robyn looked away. Carl felt a compulsion to explain. 'They're both my friends, but that's all.' Carl's gaze travelled over Robyn's face. She bit on her lower lip as she looked back. Carl held the door, Robyn stopped in the doorway. Only a few centimetres of air drifted between them. They were almost eye to eye; he was just a few inches taller. Holding his shoulders against

91

the frame, he leaned forward, a subliminal force pulling him. 'Robyn, I need to explain about something.' Her proximity sent his brain spiralling. His eyes searched hers. She was so beautiful. Once he'd kissed those lips. An electric current hit him in the gut. He wanted to kiss her again. Just once, for old times' sake. He bent forward a fraction. She stared, frozen still.

'About what?'

An almighty crash from inside made them both jump.

'What was that?' Carl gaped. His heart thumped ten times its normal rhythm. Memories of Liam crashing through the derelict roof flashed before him.

Robyn ran across the kitchen to the door opposite and up the back stairs. Carl followed. At the top, they darted along the corridor, past the family rooms and through the door into the guest section. Two men covered in white dust emerged. Maureen appeared in the corridor from the other direction.

'Is everyone all right?' asked Robyn.

'What happened?' Maureen gripped her white cheeks. 'Is anyone hurt?'

'We're ok.' Bill, the building foreman, stepped forward, stroking dust from his hair. 'There was damp in one of the partition walls and it caved.'

Robyn pushed her way into the room. Her eyes widened. With a deep breath, she shook her head. 'This could put us back weeks,' she muttered.

'It wasn't our fault,' said Bill. 'We can't work miracles.'

Carl's pulse returned to normal. 'At least everyone's ok.' Bill's mutinous expression held. 'No one's blaming you. It was an accident.'

Bill stared with blunt indignation. 'She is.'

'Me?' Robyn's voice pierced the dusty air. 'I'm not blaming you for this. I just don't like the lack of progress.'

'That's not our fault either,' said Bill. 'We can only work with what we have.'

'Yes,' said Maureen. 'Come on guys, I'll fix you a drink.'

'Let's take a breather. Coming?' Carl asked Robyn.

'No. I have work to do. I have my own job plus all this. And so far, the island contractors have done nothing but cause more problems. They used the wrong insulation, they put the wiring in the wrong place, they haven't sealed the windows properly, and that's just a few things. Money and time are being wasted, and it's all thanks to you.'

She stalked past him towards the family corridor and slammed the door hard. Carl watched in total disbelief. His fault again? Whether she wanted to hear it or not, he had to tell her the truth about twelve years ago. He just had to find a way to make her listen.

Chapter Ten

Robyn

Robyn spent a day in her room – self-inflicted. She was just through the door from Bill smashing down walls. Dropping in on him now and then kept him on his toes. It wasn't his fault the wall had fallen down. But the other things were. She created a job folio full of schedules and specifications, surely that would keep them on track.

'Aye, whatever,' said Bill, when she handed it to him. 'I've been in the business for over thirty years, I know how to do my job.'

'Well, I'd still like you to refer to it.'

Robyn didn't get her hopes too high. She was surprised the following day when one of the young apprentices beckoned her into a guest room. Holding her hand over her mouth, trying not to cough with all the dust, her eyes widened as he said, 'That folder is the best thing we've ever had. We need one for every job. I know Bill moaned about it, but he's been looking at it ever since you gave him it.'

'Has he?' With a little spring in her step, she returned to her room and her regular job. Earlier, she'd had a video-conference with Pete to check-in. He had it all under control – exactly what Pete did best – control. They'd kept it professional, which suited her. They'd been like that most of the time anyway. Dating a colleague had never been her smartest move. The set-up always made her uneasy. At the beginning of December, it had landed her in hospital. Pete still believed she'd been to an urgent meeting with a client in London. He probably didn't even know what an ectopic pregnancy was. The idea that life for him just went on as normal grated on her. Why should he get off scot-free? But would he even care? How would he react? Fury? Relief? No more kids for him. His three with his previous partner were enough, and he was on a waiting list for the snip. Robyn had never meant it to happen; kids hadn't been on her radar either. Just as she'd come to terms with the idea and seen it as a new chapter, the chance was ripped from her. Her punishment. How to raise a child with a man who didn't want one? She'd been that child. Caressing her midriff, she let out a sigh. *You were saved,* she told the void.

Facing Pete on the video link had renewed her confidence. Seeing him wasn't so terrifying. She was still the boss in her world. Keeping to her room meant no time to socialise. The geometric wallpaper was like a stress reliever as she tried to work out all its intricacies. In the evenings, the warm glow from the somewhat retro glass-and-brass lamp was quite cosy. Despite not being able to see the sea in the darkness, its presence was reassuring.

She and Maureen had come to an unspoken agreement not to discuss the past. Or anything. An unresolved air lingered. A quiver in Robyn's stomach jabbed at the temporary bubble of peace.

From her makeshift desk at the dressing table by the window, Carl's cabin loomed under a grey mist. Robyn's neck stretched almost to snapping point as she craned it, following Carl's progress along the path to the woods. Where was he going? *Why do I care?*

If he was out, she wondered where he was. If he was in, she pondered over what he was doing. Often he'd be wrapped up to the nines, working in his little lean-to or fixing fences by the woods. Georgia called a few times as did Kirsten. Friends as he said? Or was he a player? Robyn squirmed. *What am I doing?* Exactly what she'd done twelve years ago, obsessed over him until her dream had come true for a fleeting moment.

The desk was stuck in place. It wouldn't budge. *Why can't I stop looking?* Knowing where he was meant she could miss meeting him in the flesh. That was her real motive. Avoiding him. Yes, that was it. Lowering her head to her iPad, she continued her work.

On quiz day, she intended staying in her room, well away from the action but Maureen had other ideas.

'I need you on my team this evening,' she said.

'Aren't you asking the questions?'

'No.' Maureen lifted a batch of shortbread out of the oven. 'Per Hansen is doing it. He has the banter. I can't do that kind of thing. I need one more person with me. So far I have Fenella and Gillian.'

Robyn wanted to say no, but Maureen had already decided. No escape. After showering, Robyn dressed up in a short black dress and heels, put some sparkle on her ears, neck and wrist, and tossed her hair into a messy up-do. It worked at the corporate events, so why not here?

'Oh, you look nice.' Maureen ran her eyes up and down as Robyn arrived downstairs. 'Though you might be a little overdressed.'

'Seriously?' Robyn smoothed out the dress. 'Should I change?' Her stomach had tangled in enough knots as it was. Now, she was overdressed? She never got it right.

'No time,' said Maureen, 'that's people coming now.'

Robyn claimed her seat at a table in the dining room with a strong gin. Fenella Hansen joined her. The resemblance to Carl was strong in the eyes and the dimples. Robyn took a long sip.

'Hello.' Fenella shoved a large handbag under the table. 'Gosh, what fun.' She took off her scarf and hung it on the seat back. 'I'm terrible at quizzes but I love them. How are you?'

'Fine, thank you.' Robyn brushed her dress and blinked.

'You look stunning. What a beautiful dress.'

Running her hand along the heart-shaped neckline, heat flushed in Robyn's face. 'Thanks.'

'Oh, here's my boy. I'll just be a minute.' Fenella ran across the room and hugged the golden-haired bear that was Carl. Robyn sipped her drink, trying not to look or listen, but their voices were clear over the muffled chat and clinking glasses. Carl returned Fenella's hug and laughed. The emptiness consuming Robyn multiplied. He looked gorgeous in his crisp white shirt – slightly open – and tight jeans that fitted perfectly.

'Where's Aunt Jean?' He stepped back from his mum.

'Oh, she's not up for things like this. I've left her with a sack of knitting wool. She'll have knitted a life-size Eiffel tower by the time we get back.'

'Shame. I'll miss her.' He clapped Fenella on the back.

'Oh, you cheeky boy.' She smacked him carelessly. 'Come, sit for a minute until the others arrive. Your dad's getting all the stuff out of the car.'

'Should I help him?'

'No,' said Fenella, 'he likes doing it all himself. Then he can moan, no one else ever does anything.'

Robyn gripped her glass, trying to keep her hand steady as Carl and Fenella sat down.

'Isn't Robyn's dress gorgeous,' said Fenella, 'and her hair too.'

Carl scrutinised her as he sat. Robyn attempted a smile, but her face reddened, burning like sunburn. 'Beautiful.' He blinked.

Where to look? Her cheeks must be beyond beetroot by now.

'And you're very intelligent too, I haven't forgotten.' Fenella patted Robyn's hand. 'Carl always told me you got the best grades in class. Which will help.'

'Mum, you're great at quizzes. What are you on about?'

Robyn sat back, trying to hide as they talked. But with Carl so close, her pulse raced. The warm scent of musk and oriental spices tickled her senses. And his smile. She gulped her gin.

'Ooh, look at you.' Kirsten appeared behind Carl and put her hands on his shoulders. He spun around. 'You look super nice.'

'Eh, thanks, Kirsten.' He casually extricated himself from her grip. *Because he doesn't like it? Or because he doesn't want everyone to see?* Robyn sipped and considered.

'So where are we going to sit, shall we get a table over there?' Kirsten beamed.

'Sure. See you later, folks.' Carl's eyes lingered on Robyn. She fingered her pendant. 'When we're holding the prize.' He winked at his mum.

Gillian McGregor, Beth and Kirsten's mum, joined them. She scouted around before sitting down and anchoring her iron-grey hair atop her head with her glasses. 'A very good crowd.' She observed Robyn with a brief nod of recognition.

'Excellent,' said Fenella.

Robyn kept quiet and watched Carl taking his seat with the sisters. They chatted and laughed. Kirsten's eyes never left Carl's face. Moments later, a flustered looking Georgia arrived in a bright red coat and flopped down beside them, unravelling a long scarf.

'How are you?' Gillian turned her attention to Robyn. 'It's been years since I've seen you.'

'I'm fine.'

Gillian raised her eyebrows. 'And how are the repair works? Don't they interfere with your job?'

'Not really.'

'What is it you do again?'

'I'm the director of Creative Genius. It's an online marketing agency. I can run it from here, thanks to the wonders of technology.' She gulped more gin.

Gillian glanced at Fenella and raised her eyebrows.

'Oh, there's my other lad. He had to pick up Julie otherwise we could have brought him. He's staying with us just now.' Fenella waved at her eldest son, Magnus. He looked like a taller, better-groomed version of Carl. Tension gripped Robyn's shoulders. Heat flushed up her neck, and she flattened her lips at the woman on his arm. Julie McNabb. Since seeing her at the funeral, Robyn had avoided contact. *Do not let her come over here.* Fire simmered low in Robyn's stomach. Julie wore a sophisticated top, tight jeans and heels. Robyn knew not to trust her. Even being in the same room as her, set Robyn's teeth on edge. Names reeled through her as if Julie's voice was shouting them from far away. *Ice Witch! Virgin Queen! White Nun! Twiglet!* Maybe Carl had joined in. *Let me show you how I melt the Ice Queen.*

Julie glanced over, giving Fenella a broad grin and whispered something to Magnus. Clenching her teeth, Robyn looked away, she didn't need to care. Just a few hours and this would be over. More school memories nudged her. Recollections that hadn't surfaced for a long time.

She remembered entering classes, checking the clock and reminding herself how many minutes she had to get through. Not long in the grand scheme of life. Here she was again, counting seconds, wishing her life away.

Fenella leaned across the table and smiled. Robyn listened as she and Gillian chatted. Maureen joined them and took her seat. Her bright red lipstick made a shocking contrast against her pale skin and hair. Puffing out the shoulders on her top, she beamed around.

'You're looking good, Maureen,' said Fenella. 'Nice to see you smiling.'

Per Hansen tapped the microphone, ready to begin. It squeaked, and he gave it a funny look before welcoming them all. He was an older version of Carl, except his hair was thinner and Carl was much broader across the chest and shoulders. Per's large sweater hung loose on his wiry frame as he gesticulated to the guests. As he read the questions, he interspersed them with anecdotes and jokes. Even Robyn smiled, Per was quite a character. But a neighbouring table distracted her. She sensed Julie's eyes boring through her.

'You're very knowledgeable,' said Fenella, scribbling down answers.

'Though not so good on film and TV.' Gillian cast her a superior look, as she listed several *Coronation Street* cast members.

'I tend not to watch it,' said Robyn, 'there's always so much rubbish on.'

She caught the end of Maureen's eye roll. A movement diverted her. Carl had taken a seat directly in her eye-line. He leaned in with his group, heads down, deep in conspiracy. Georgia shouted something and Carl threw himself back laughing, almost falling off his chair. Robyn smiled, just watching. As he steadied the chair, he winked at her. She looked away. *Concentrate. Please concentrate.*

'Don't pay any attention to him,' said Fenella. 'He's trying to put us off. He's a smart boy, but he won't have a clue who the second President of the USA was.'

'Do you?' Gillian asked.

'Nope.' Fenella glanced up, smiling.

'John Adams,' said Robyn.

'Wonderful. You see. We have the answers right here.' Fenella scribbled into the box on the answer sheet.

Gillian screwed up her lips. 'Is Carl going to ask Kirsten out, do you think?'

Fenella looked up and frowned. 'I've no idea. Why?' She skimmed past Gillian's head towards Carl, searching for the answer.

'Kirsten's infatuated.'

Fenella sucked the end of the pen. 'Oh dear. Well, I don't interfere. I let my boys lead their own lives. I'm here if they need me, but I don't like to meddle. Carl's never been one for relationships, something always goes wrong. Sometimes I think he's his own worst enemy, but it's not for me to say.'

Gillian sighed and folded her arms on the table.

'I'm quite glad Carl's single. I've got Magnus to worry about, which is quite enough.'

'Why?' asked Gillian. 'What's up with him? I thought he was dating the McNabb girl.'

'Exactly.' Fenella glanced around to check no one was listening. 'I shouldn't really say anything, she's always charming, but I have an odd feeling about her, I don't know, probably just me being an overprotective mother. I know what I'm like.'

Robyn's eyes strayed to Julie, had she changed? Robyn nursed an urge to tell Fenella everything that had happened at school – Fenella's motherly instincts were right – she wanted to protect her child. Maureen hadn't done that. Robyn observed her mother. Her chest filled with pain. Maureen had never protected her from her father's wrath; Robyn had faced it alone. She'd faced everything alone – school, college, interviews, work. Maybe Maureen had done her a kindness, now she was independent and successful. And alone. And sad. Robyn touched the scar before her gaze returned to Carl and Kirsten. A flicker of urgency burned in Kirsten's face. She was desperate to draw his attention. Robyn pulled her brows together. Why was he resigned to be alone? Did he like to play the field? Was there any scope for that on a remote island where everyone knew everyone?

With the final answers folded and posted into Per's box, he tallied the scores as people mingled. Gillian and Maureen headed towards the kitchen. Robyn wondered if she could escape, even to the loo. She hated mingling. Where would she go? To Carl or Julie? Not likely. But before she could escape, Carl plonked himself down on a seat between her and his mum.

'Do you think Dad will give us extra points, mates' rates and all that?'

'I won't,' said Per from the front.

'Too right he won't.' Magnus flicked Carl on the head as he walked by. 'But, as I'm the eldest, if he's giving extra points, they should go to me.'

'You're the brainy one,' said Carl, 'you don't need extra help.'

Except in your choice of girlfriend.

Magnus laughed and moved on with Julie. Robyn kept her head down.

'We won't need extra points,' said Fenella, 'we have the brains of Britain in our team. Don't we?' She beamed at Robyn.

'Hardly,' Robyn replied.

Carl stole a smile at her. 'Well, I was the island dunce.'

'Oh, Carl. You can't have been that bad,' said Fenella.

'You think? Apparently, the tiger in *The Jungle Book* is not Genghis Khan.'

'Oh, Carl, really. Here, I should get your dad a drink.'

'No bribery,' said Carl as she left the table. 'Well.' He turned to Robyn. 'Did you enjoy that?

'Sure.' She clung to the stem of her glass.

'Between you and me. It doesn't matter who wins.' He swung the chair backwards and balanced with his elbow on the table. She took a sharp breath. His next words landed like a warm breeze on her neck. 'It's been a good laugh, what a turnout. I know it'll be a drop in the ocean, but it'll bring a few pounds to the pot.'

'True.' Robyn wanted to recoil but at the same time, she couldn't move. Tapping her pen, she looked up.

A shadow loomed over their table. Kirsten, hands on her narrow hips, frowned at Carl. He bumped his seat firmly back onto the ground. 'Are you going to sing?' she asked.

'Tonight? We're not singing as well, are we? The guitar's at the cabin. We haven't set up the mic.'

'Shame,' said Kirsten. 'It's very romantic.'

'He's just a poser.' Georgia appeared behind Kirsten, placing her hand on her shoulder. 'No singing tonight please.'

She smiled at Robyn before turning her eyes on Carl and casting him a know-it-all look. What did it mean? Carl frowned and looked away. Georgia tossed her tousled bob and dragged Kirsten towards the buffet. Were the two of them fighting it out over Carl? And he didn't want either. Or did he want both?

Robyn took a large sip of gin. Perhaps Carl had told everyone about their teenage misadventures? Which version? No doubt his story was hilarious. Was that what all the little looks meant? Maybe Julie McNabb had stirred it all up again. Why care? Another sip of gin. *I own a business. This stuff is beneath me. Just let it go.*

Per called for order, interrupting Robyn's thoughts. Everyone reclaimed their original seats as he announced the winners.

'It's us!' Fenella jumped to her feet with glee as their name came top. Robyn couldn't restrain her smile. Julie was watching. So was Carl. She could sense it. A cold shiver ran down her back. Why were they staring?

With dinner laid out at the buffet table, Robyn helped Maureen with the fetching and carrying. It was better than serving. She spent a long time lingering in the kitchen and loading dishes into the industrial-strength dishwasher, hoping it still worked. Gillian and Fenella turned up to help. They'd just started when the swing doors opened again and Julie sidled in.

'Hey, Fen,' she said, 'have you heard about the new management position for the Community Woodland group?'

'I saw something about it,' said Fenella.

'It's been re-advertised,' said Gillian, 'it's not a job to be taken lightly. Not after the argy-bargy the last manager caused.'

'I think I might go for it.' Julie picked lazily on a nail.

Fenella frowned and looked up from the dishwasher. 'Do you have the right qualifications?'

'Sure, it's hardly rocket science. And Robyn,' said Julie with a truly fake smile, 'it's a shame we didn't have time to catch up. It took me an age even to recognise you.' Robyn stared, unable to find any words. 'We should have a catch-up. Are you with anyone? Boyfriends? Husbands?'

'No.'

Julie grinned like the Cheshire cat. 'Thought not.'

'Julie, can you pass that pile of plates,' said Fenella.

'Sure, Fen. Robyn always preferred her own company, didn't you? Though I seem to remember you had your eye on someone. Who was it? He might even have asked you out. If only I could remember who that was.' Her fake tone and smug grin made Robyn's blood boil.

The heat in Robyn's neck was unbearable. A sickening throwback. Julie hadn't changed in twelve years.

'Best to leave the past in the past,' said Fenella. 'Tell you what, Julie, let's go and ask Per if he knows about that job.' Fenella took her arm and led her back into the dining room, leaving Robyn and Gillian.

'Never liked her,' muttered Gillian. 'A shameless gossip. Thankfully Beth has a very thick skin because that girl said some nasty things about her. Wouldn't trust her as far as I could throw her. And as for Magnus Hansen, he needs his head examined. No idea what he sees in her. Don't tell Fenella I said that, please.'

The door swung open. 'They're doing a sing-song out here,' Fenella called in. 'Come and listen.'

Gillian's neck turned a little blotchy. 'I hope she didn't hear that. I'm sure Magnus is lovely. It's his taste that's terrible.'

Robyn returned to the room as Carl, Magnus, and their father sang a rather jokey song *a cappella*. The words resonated clear and bold. Julie beamed at Magnus, but when she turned to Robyn, she gave her a pronounced wink. Robyn heard a ringing in her ears.

When the song finished, Julie took hold of both Magnus and Carl. What was she saying? Robyn didn't dare approach. It was easier to disappear. People were leaving, she could do the same. She headed for the side door and the steps leading to her room. Before she'd reached it, warm hands touched her shoulders. She spun to see Carl smiling at her.

'Hey.'

'Oh, no.' Robyn pulled free, her body stiffened. Carl and Julie might want to indulge in the same immaturity they had done at school, but she wouldn't. What had Julie dared him to do this time? Fifty quid if he slept with her? Absolutely no danger. 'Whatever you were cooking up with Julie, just don't. I'm not playing your games.'

'Julie? Listen, Robyn, it was never a game, that's what I've been trying to tell you.'

'Don't lie, I know it was. Julie told me years ago. She took great pleasure in it.'

'I don't deny it. She dared me to do it.'

Robyn reached for the door handle. Carl edged round and held it.

'Let me finish. I wanted to ask you anyway. I just didn't have the nerve. Somehow, their dare gave me the confidence. I never told them anything. They knew I'd asked you, but they didn't know how I felt. Only you knew that. I wish I'd had the guts to do it without any pretext. I liked you. It was never about the dare. Never.' He brushed his rough hand over hers, trailing his fingertip off the end.

Robyn shivered, staring until her eyes hurt, her head hurt. Everything hurt. Rooted to the spot, she tried to take it in. A chain reaction of thoughts had started, every possible scenario shot off like fireworks. She rubbed her head. It might explode.

'Ok. Thanks.' Her insides cringed at the only words she could muster. But until she'd analysed every possible outcome, she shouldn't speak another word.

Carl smiled, his gaze fixed on hers. He was so close; she sensed the heat.

'I mean it, Robyn. You were always special to me.' Bending forward, he placed a kiss on her cheek. Robyn's eyelids dropped slowly. 'Please, forgive me,' he said.

With an effort, she dragged herself from him. 'Yes.' She slipped through the door.

Flopping onto the bed, she shivered. Would she ever stop shaking? Was it true? Could she trust him, or was he a pawn in Julie's pocket once again?

She wanted to believe him. She wanted it so badly her body ached from the inside out.

Chapter Eleven

Carl

Carl finished packing the pendulum clock and wrapped it ready for shipping. With all his tasks complete, he fancied some time on his boat. It might help clear the avalanche of crazy feelings crowding every inch of his brain.

The cabin walls quivered. Carl glanced up and pulled a face. After reading there might be gusts up to 70 miles per hour, he'd hoped they'd bypass Mull. With a shake of his head, he lamented his crazy optimism; Mull never missed the wind or the rain. The roof cowered under its crushing force. Strolling to the window, Carl looked out. His ancient boat rocked up and down, still afloat. No point risking a trip. She was an ongoing, time-consuming and expensive fixer-upper not equipped to deal with severe weather.

Across the lawn, the hotel's grey stone walls blurred as a squall blew in. Carl shuddered. Lending a hand at the hotel was the next job. He'd resolved everything with Robyn. Told her the truth, laid himself bare. What exactly had he expected to happen after? His foot tapped on the floor. Robyn's reaction hadn't given any encouragement or otherwise. Well, he didn't want that anyway. It wasn't like he had plans to get back together with her. No way. She was attractive, hell yes. He'd be blind not to see it. But he wasn't travelling that path again. Robyn had made good.

Having him sneak back onto the scene would only crush what she'd built.

Drawing in a deep sigh, he bounced on his toes. The hollow in his stomach tensed with uncertainty. An unfinished chord strummed. He and Robyn weren't through. Not yet. Because of the hotel. They had to work together. Now, they'd sorted the past, they could move on as friends, workmates, indifferent acquaintances.

After making the decision to go to the hotel, Carl struggled up the path against the wind, barely able to stand. A sharp gust whipped his hat from his head. 'Oi!' He grabbed his hair. Any chance of catching the hat was gone. It was halfway out to sea before he saw it tossed up high.

The back door into the family kitchen banged open and slammed against the wall as he pushed it. Maureen looked around from her cooking. Her hand jumped to her chest.

'Sorry.' Carl forced the door shut. 'What a storm. I lost my hat.' He tried to tame his wild curls. The dogs greeted him with waggy tails; Florrie jumped to his knee and gave him a scratch.

'They're going crazy,' said Maureen. 'High winds always send folks mad. Dogs too.'

'So, how's the building coming along?' He squinted at the ceiling. The lack of thuds, drills and hammering was ominous.

Maureen's chin dipped, and she rubbed her elbow. 'Maybe avoid upstairs for a bit. Robyn's not pleased about the way they've done something – again. I'm keeping well out of it.'

'Can I have a look?'

'Well, if Robyn's in her room, you better knock. I walked in yesterday and she was on a video call with that man of hers. She wasn't happy. Goodness knows what they were talking about. I think he was begging her to come home.'

'Right. I'll knock.' Carl gave a bitter smile. His ribs grew tight, constricting his breath. Someone, somewhere, wanted Robyn. Her partner wanted her home. For twelve years Carl had thought about her return; how she'd run to him with open arms, the past forgotten. But too much had happened in between. If she was happy, that was good. No complications – just the way they needed.

As he got to the landing, he stopped. It was just like the end of the High School corridor. Twelve years ago, he knew Robyn's timetable by heart. Savoured every class they shared or hung about at doors with lame excuses so he could pass her coming out of rooms. Anything to get a glimpse of that face. The things his friends said about her being *weird* or *anti-social* didn't bother him, they intrigued him. When they'd got together she was more than he'd ever imagined. Should he have fought harder? Tried to stay in touch? Her anger had left him in no doubt she didn't want to see him any more. They'd been at a crossroads, both leaving the island for further education. Letting go was the easy course.

For a few weeks, he'd broken into her personal space, found the real Robyn and pulled her out. A deep desire burned low. An overpowering need to save her. He shook his head, glad none of his female friends knew what was going on in his mind. They wouldn't understand what he meant. It wasn't a ploy to undermine her or belittle her. The opposite. He could empower her, showcase her worth. He could do that without crossing any lines.

He opened the door and held back. At the entrance to one of the guest rooms, Robyn leaned casually, wearing dark jeans and an off-white sweater. Her long hair swept into a ponytail hung softly down her back. She had the air of an off-duty film star on location at a ski ranch.

'Hey.' Carl stepped up behind her, forgetting the thick carpet had deadened his approach. She turned with a start and stood up straight. 'Sorry. I didn't mean to surprise you. I came up to see how things are going.'

Robyn absently toyed with her pendant and gazed at Carl. Blinking, she stood aside and he checked out the room. Planks, dust covers, and packaging littered the floor. A wide-open door revealed a bathroom stripped bare. Foreman Bill scratched his head and looked down at a man's rear. A pair of Bart Simpson boxer shorts protruded from the toilet. Carl heard some choice swear words. Robyn raised her eyes and moved into the corridor.

'Honestly.' She shook her head. 'We need a plumber. These guys are out of their depth.'

Carl looked back into the bathroom; Bart Simpson-pants let out more expletives and jumped away as water spouted out. 'Shut it off,' he yelled at Bill.

With a sigh, Robyn closed the door. Carl put his hands behind his back and let his eyes roam over Robyn's face.

'I should get back to work,' she said. 'You can give them a hand if you want. We all know, you can fix everything.'

'No need to be facetious.' Carl folded his arms. Maybe she hadn't forgiven him. Her sharp eyes pierced his, burrowing deep.

'I was being serious. I believe you can fix everything, otherwise, why choose such an unusual job. What made you give up your career?'

Carl ran his fingers through his hair. 'The company went bust.' That was the short-short version. He'd rather not discuss his own part in the matter.

'And you gave up? I mean, there are so many jobs in IT. Why did you come back here?'

'This island is part of me. It's in my blood, my make-up. I wanted to be free.' He sighed and watched her puzzled face. 'I like fishing, cycling, sailing. There isn't as much scope for it in the city.'

'Is the boat at the jetty yours?' asked Robyn.

Carl nodded. 'Yeah. My biggest project so far.'

'I always wanted a boat.' Robyn's gaze roamed far away.

'Your dad had one,' said Carl, 'he took us sea fishing on it.'

'No, he took you.' She pressed her lips together and looked away. 'Only the lads were allowed. I was meant to stay home and help Mum cook.'

Carl shook his head at his feet before looking back. 'I'm sorry, Robyn. If I'd known he was that bad, I would have—'

'What? Sorted him out? Would that have ended well?'

Carl frowned. 'No. I explained all that. I just meant...' His voice trailed off. 'I wish I could have stopped him hurting you.'

Robyn tilted her head and moved her eyes slowly down his face. He drew in his breath and held it.

'It wouldn't have changed anything. He'd have found another way to punish me. I don't understand why they all forgave you and blamed me for Liam's accident.'

'Have they forgiven me? They don't jibe me as they do to you. They control me instead.'

Robyn opened her mouth and closed it again. 'I don't follow.'

'I shouldn't say. Maureen's kind to me. I think she feels sorry for me. She knows I couldn't stop Liam from falling, but she also knows I led him into trouble. All the kindness comes with a price. I'm stuck. I can't get away. I'm trapped here, doing whatever she wants me to. Extra shifts, helping with these renovations. Whatever needs done.'

'Then leave. I did. I couldn't stand living with my father. You could do the same.'

Carl looked away, staring at a patch of torn anaglypta wallpaper. 'I can't. I'm tied up here. If Maureen loses the hotel, I lose the cabin.'

'And is that a big deal?'

Fixing her in his stare, Carl didn't answer immediately. For someone with her cash, it must seem pathetic. 'I don't have anywhere else to go. I won't scrounge off others. I need to find my own path. If I'm going to get my business up and running, I need a place to do it, otherwise, I fail before I've even started. I refuse to walk away without even trying.'

'Just like I did.'

'You're back now.' His eyes returned to her. 'And I'm glad. I often thought about you. Us.'

Robyn slowly closed her eyes and sighed. 'I did too. But it was so long ago. So much has changed. We can't get those days back.' Carl didn't reply. She was right. 'I should get back to work.' Robyn took a step back and swallowed.

'Robyn, I hope you're happy.'

With a weak smile, she shrugged and retreated. A heaviness in his chest smouldered as she disappeared through the door marked private at the end of the corridor. No. They could never go back.

Chapter Twelve

Robyn

Robyn tugged at the dressing table by the window, it was good as a desk and had a great view but it needed to move. Her hand dropped to her scar. Lifting heavy items was banned for several months. Maybe she should draw the curtains and turn on the light. Because she had to stop looking. Why did it matter if she knew where Carl was or wasn't? An excuse to avoid him – no – it had never been that. She'd spent the best part of her time, analysing and over-analysing their recent interactions until her brain was so addled she couldn't make head or tail of anything. With a big conference call planned for the afternoon, she had to get her head in gear. Hopefully, Bill wouldn't knock down any walls in the duration.

She'd completely misjudged Carl's part in Liam's accident and in his motivations for asking her out. He was an innocent, tormenting himself with ideas that he could have saved Liam. *Well, I didn't misjudge my brother, he was an idiot. Why did he do it at all?* A nauseous sensation pricked Robyn's throat. Why had it happened? She steeled herself on the desk, trying hard to keep her eyes focused on the room and not let them stray beyond. If Liam hadn't fallen, what might have happened with Carl? Would they have stayed together? She wrapped her arms around herself and gripped tight. Could she have made such a success in life with him in tow? The solitude had given her the time and the drive.

It didn't explain why the sight of him and the knowledge of his proximity struck such a powerful chord in her chest. Rubbing her forehead, she tried to pummel in some sense. Perhaps it was a form of PTSD – after Liam's accident – maybe she had to cling to the one thing that had ever made her happy. Carl's being so nearby made it seem real. She covered her face with her hands and let out a silent scream. *I'm doing it again – analysing.*

I need coffee. The family rooms weren't equipped with kettles and trays like the guest rooms. Running her fingers out the ends of her hair, she took a deep breath and headed downstairs.

Voices in the kitchen. She stopped, recognising Maureen's sharp timbre. The door was open a crack. Robyn moved closer.

'If I'm honest, I wish she'd go home,' said Maureen. Robyn froze. 'I know she's trying to help, but she's been away for too long. She wants to fit her city-shaped peg neatly into an island-shaped hole. And it's not working. I had Bill down here complaining yesterday. She's rude, she questions everything they do. She even stands and watches them to make sure they do things properly. Bill was raging. She sent Carl in to help them. Carl is very good at turning his hand to odd jobs, but Bill's been in the trade for thirty years. It was insulting. Now, he wants to give up, and it's all thanks to her.'

Robyn couldn't move. Heat fired up her cheeks. She wasn't sure if she was angry, sad, or shocked. Who was Maureen talking to?

'Oh dear,' said a low woman's voice.

Robyn peered through the crack and saw Gillian McGregor standing across the table. A rush of heat to her head joined the flutter of uncertainty. She drew in a breath and held it. Why was Maureen saying these things? Robyn balled her fists, blood rushed in her ears.

'My Beth is the same age and—'

'No comparison,' said Maureen.

What? Robyn frowned through the crack. *I run a business; I've made a lot of money.* None of them really knew just how successful she was. Her whole life had been channelled into it.

'Well, your lass always was a bit awkward, but she's trying,' continued Gillian. 'I think you have to applaud that. I enjoyed her company at the quiz night.'

Robyn's eyes widened. *She did?*

Maureen sighed and sat down. 'I don't know where I went wrong. I thought I saw a change in her. But no. Same old, same old. It's making my life miserable.' She put her head in her hands, flattening the short spiky hair onto her scalp.

Robyn stood back, clenching her fists, forcing herself to breathe evenly. Part of her wanted to crash in the door and tell her mother exactly where she'd gone wrong. *You let my father verbally and emotionally abuse me for years.* She drew in a clear, purposeful breath and counted to five. No way was she getting to ten in this mood. Breathe. Control. She was bigger than this.

'Maureen, she had a tough time too.' Gillian spoke again. Robyn pinned her ear to the gap. 'It can't have been easy growing up here. You know Davie always left her out. You told me yourself. She may have caused havoc around here, but she was lonely and confused. It wasn't her fault. She was a child.'

'She was almost an adult; she should never have provoked him the way she did. It caused so much grief. You wouldn't believe it.'

'Davie was an adult. He should've known better. If Malcolm, God rest his soul, had ever spoken to one of our girls like that, I would have left him. You made the decision to stand by your husband. You have to accept the effect that's had on your daughter.'

Robyn released her fists and furrowed her brow. Gillian's words resonated sense. This woman knew what she was talking about. But what hope of any of it getting through to Maureen? After being friends for such a long time, none of her wisdom seemed to have lodged.

With a fake smile, Robyn opened the door.

'Robyn!' Maureen jumped back in her seat.

'Good morning,' said Gillian, fixing a smile on her face.

'Morning.' Robyn marched to the utility area, grabbing her jacket and gloves.

'Are you, eh…' Maureen picked up the empty cups from the table.

'I'm going out,' said Robyn. 'I heard every word you said. If you want me gone that badly, I'll happily oblige. Who would have guessed I could have offended someone so thoroughly by doing nothing but trying to help.' She zipped the side of her long boot. 'Chewie, Florrie, come on. Walk time.'

'Robyn, I—'

Slamming the back door, Robyn walked down to the seashore. Florrie yapped at the waves as they roared up against the rocks and shingle, some of them reaching as far as the grass. Chewie lumbered along serenely, sniffing occasionally at an interesting piece of seaweed and cocking his back leg.

Robyn's hair whipped up around her head and she pulled up her hood; long strands straggled across her face. She gave up the constant struggle to tuck them in, it was a complete waste of time. Icy cold rain hung in the air, bitter and clinging. She ran her finger across the corner of her eye and pressed her lips together. A swell of pain jabbed her chest. Tears mingled with the rain on her cheeks. Why this weakness? Ever since the operation, raw emotion bubbled close to the surface. The painful ache in her body was a void nothing could fill. Agony and loss. Everything she loved turned to stone. Her best intentions went wrong, her good deeds were misread. Maureen wanted her gone. Hope evaporated. She'd tried to rebuild bridges, but it was too late. Maureen couldn't change.

Robyn stopped walking and turned towards the sea, facing into the wind. The twisted knot in her chest told her this was the end. She had to pack up and leave. This time forever. She couldn't come back. As Florrie and Chewie converged on a seaweed-covered boulder with frantic pawing and crazy tails, she raised her hand to her mouth to stop a further wave of emotion. How could she bear the parting of the two new best friends? Return Florrie to city life after all this freedom? One day it had to happen. Why wait?

'Are you ok?' A weight landed on her shoulder and she heard Carl's voice.

She swivelled round. He squinted through the rain, his hood drawn tight over his face. Robyn might buckle under the weight of his grip. 'Fine.' Her voice held no conviction. 'How are you?'

'Soaked and freezing.' He threw up his arms with a laugh. She couldn't help but smile. Florrie bounded over, her tiny legs going nineteen to the dozen. Carl's eyes travelled over Robyn's cheek. His brows drew together. 'Are you sure you're ok?'

She glanced at the sky, willing the solitary tear welling in her eye to fall back. A row of trees beyond the hotel bent double, leaning low as the wind battered them. She shuddered. Cold emptiness pricked her soul.

'Hey.' Carl raised his hand, suspending it in mid-air. With a fluid movement, he gently stroked his thumb across her cheek. 'What's wrong?'

Robyn turned her head, staring at the rough sea.

'Come here.' Carl pulled her in tight. His touch sent warmth flooding through icy veins. Robyn closed her eyes and squeezed her lips flat, not breathing. The heat of him pressed against her. Tears flowed. His crushing hold steadied her pulse. She allowed herself to relax. Weightless and calm. His bristly cheek brushed the side of her forehead. She kept still, resting against his wet jacket. As he rubbed his hand gently up and down her back, drowsiness crept in. 'I know how difficult this is,' he said.

'Do you?' Her voice was little more than a hoarse whisper.

His breath skimmed her earlobe. 'I've been in tough places too. I know what it's like to feel rough.' His hold tightened. The arms limp at her sides sprang up and embraced him. Through the layers of fleece, she gripped a tight body. The desire to get even closer fired inside. Years of aching for him. 'I hate what happened to you. I never realised Davie treated you so badly. No one deserves that.'

'It isn't just that. It's my mum.'

'I know.'

'When I was younger, she stood by as Dad told me how stupid I was. Mum still thinks I'm bad news. She hates me.'

Carl stroked her back. 'She can't bear it that you've done so well. You're a successful woman. She's not.'

Robyn straightened up, hating the sudden cold. 'I've lost my family because of how I acted when I was a child, when I didn't know any better, when I was shy and awkward. After I left, I trained myself to be someone else.

No one knew me. I could be whatever I wanted. I knew coming back wouldn't be easy. I tried to help. I shouldn't have bothered. I'm not like this anywhere else. This island brings out the worst in me.'

'Robyn.' Carl shook his head with a sigh. The wind knocked off his hood, tossing his curls wide. 'Stay. I'd like you and Maureen to reconcile.'

'She doesn't want to. She's stubborn. She won't accept me now because it'll mean admitting she was wrong and she'll never do that.'

Dragging his hair onto the top of his head, Carl scrunched up his face. 'I don't think it's that simple. She doesn't believe she *was* wrong. Her memories are skewed by loyalty to Davie. She's different from you. For her, it was easier to go along with things and keep the peace. But you—'

'Don't tell me. I stirred things up, provoked him.' Robyn held out her arms and walked backwards, her hair swirled in the wind.

'No. You were brave. Maureen's a coward. If she had guts, she'd sell the place to Calum Matheson and move on. Instead, she clings to old ways. You're the one with nerve. I wish I could be as strong as you.'

'You want to be strong like me?' Robyn gathered up her hair and shoved it into her hood. 'It's easy. Just shut down every emotion and put people to the side. If you want to leave this place, go. Forget about how it might affect others. Cut all your ties.'

'I can't.'

'Because you let sentiment win. I love this island so much, but it's never loved me.'

Carl tilted his head and gave a sad smile. 'Has shutting down really helped you? Are you happy?'

'What?'

'When you're in Manchester, in your normal life, are you happy?'

'That's irrelevant.'

Carl brushed his hand down his face and looked out to sea. 'Is it? I thought coming back would make me happy. I'm not sure it has. I don't know how to make it up to the people I've wronged.'

'Then don't. Live your life. Leave my mother to her misery. Go out on your own, it's safer.'

'It comes back to the same thing. I don't have your strength. Or your money.' He observed his feet. 'I almost killed your brother through my own misguided stupidity. I've never been successful in business. The hotel's almost bankrupt. Even that's partly my fault because so much money was spent on Liam's rehab and tutoring.'

'Is that what my mum said?' Robyn folded her arms. 'The hotel didn't go bankrupt from that. That's like a drop in the ocean. Years of misplaced spending, poor marketing and complacency caused the problems here.'

Carl shuffled his feet in the sand and sighed. 'I wish things could have been different.' He looked her in the eye. 'A lot of things.'

Turning away, Robyn covered her mouth, her head spun and her chest bubbled in turmoil. It was too late. That ship had sailed long ago. What they'd had was a dream, a teenage fantasy. She always misread people. Maureen, Liam, Carl, Pete. She'd interpreted Pete's interest as love. How wrong had she been? Their date nights were well-planned and followed strict timetables. No romance, no spark. They talked shop and conversations rolled on from day to night like one long meeting. Their one spontaneous night had ended in disaster. If Pete ever found out... Robyn bit her bottom lip.

Was she mistaking Carl's signals too? Did he want more from her? What crazy path of upheavals and changes would that send her down? Her life wasn't here. Carl was a man who valued his solitude. Maybe what he wanted was something transient. Something he could forget as soon as she left. She didn't want that. Did she? Maybe that was all she needed.

'I should get back.' She checked the time. 'I have a conference call later.' Carl tugged at his zip-pull, his eyes boring deep into hers. She gazed back, trying not to blink. Hugs weren't her thing, but the warmth and safety of his arms had crammed her with contentment. She craved more. Back in Manchester, she wouldn't want or need it. 'Come on,' she called the dogs.

'Robyn.' Carl stared and took a deep breath. 'If you want to talk. About anything.'

'Such as?'

'Anything.' He ran his fingers through his wild hair. 'What you're doing for your mum is hard. You've got a big heart. If you need to vent, I'm here.'

Was there anything left to tell? Pushing her hands into her pocket, she rubbed her scar through the fabric. Not that.

'Before you go,' said Carl, 'can I give you something?'

'What?' Robyn frowned.

'This.' Carl walked forward, leaned over, put his hand under her chin and tilted it towards him. His lips brushed hers, softly, gently, just long enough to feel his breath, the warmth of his skin. Robyn closed her eyes, forgetting the wind rush and the bite of the rain. A deep sense of calm welled in the void. Carl pulled back and ran his finger across his chin. 'You take care.'

Running back toward the hotel, the shingle impeded her. Wind howled, rain crashed, blasting her in all directions. Nothing compared to the typhoon of thoughts spinning around her head. Holding her hood firmly in place, she made it to the hotel door. Before she opened it, she looked back at the beach. A tiny figure strode along the shore, wild hair tangling around.

Soaking, bedraggled and confused, Robyn slumped into a seat in the kitchen. Maureen was nowhere in sight, which suited just fine. Chewie's head landed on her lap, and she stroked his wet fur.

'Oh, my word,' she said, 'this is such a mess. I need to put some distance between me and Carl. I can't afford to get too close.'

Chapter Thirteen

Carl

Carl stooped to pick up another branch from the lawn. The storm the day before had left a messy trail. He collected as much wood as he could carry; it was always useful. A movement near the jetty caught his eye; he squinted towards his boat. Something didn't look right. The boat rested at an odd angle.

Making his way across the wooden slats on the jetty, Carl squinted into the hull and pulled his hair onto his scalp. Slopping about in the bottom of his beloved boat was months of work… and cash. How could he afford to repair it? Lobbing a stick into the sea, he sighed. Just add it to the list of things he couldn't have. Walking away, he kicked a stone and palmed his throbbing head. No way out of the rut.

The Glen Lodge drew closer, casting its austere presence on the landscape. What a place it should be; packed with holidaymakers escaping to the wild. Instead, it lay cold and empty. The dark green shutters at the guestroom windows remained tightly shut. As he moved towards the rear, Carl's eyes leapt to the family windows above the kitchen. Was Robyn there? She'd crept into his head every hour since their meeting on the beach. When she left. What would he do? He cracked a thick branch across his knee. Yesterday, she'd turned his world upside down. Seeing her so upset had crushed him. How could he fix her? He couldn't. Leaving was what she wanted. That was all she needed. Being here was the root of the pain.

A sharp call echoed across the lawn. An apron-clad Maureen waved to him. Shoving his hands in his pockets, he approached. 'Carl, I don't know if you remembered, but it's Rabbie Burn's night. I haven't arranged anything big this year, just a few friends. Please come over.'

'Eh, ok.'

'Is your boat ok?' Maureen rubbed her arms against the cold. 'I saw you down there.'

'Full of water.'

'Oh dear. I wish we'd kept Davie's old boat; you could have had it. No one else ever used it, which was why we sold it.'

'Yeah, well, never mind.' Carl ran his fingers through his hair. The love and attention he'd poured into that boat. Months of work sabotaged by the forces of nature.

Maureen placed her hands on her hips. 'Have you seen Robyn?'

'No.' Carl roughed up the hair at his forehead. 'Not today.'

Maureen rubbed her hands on her apron. 'Me neither. She was in a right state yesterday. I think she was annoyed, she overheard me saying something and misunderstood the context. She wouldn't let me explain. And she had a conference call, or something like that, I don't even know what it means. I think there are problems with her business. She was very edgy. I'm not sure why she doesn't go back and sort things out.'

Carl tugged the front of his jacket. 'She wants to. But she also wants to help you. She's trying really hard. That's why she's upset.'

Maureen raised her hand to her chest. 'She has her own agenda. I don't know why she's really here. Something's going on with her business or she'd have left weeks ago. I think it's in trouble and she doesn't want to admit it.'

'No. It's nothing to do with that. She wants to make things up with you.'

Maureen held her forehead. 'For what? I don't hold a grudge.' Carl disguised his cough by ducking from a sharp gust of wind. 'Everything she does either undermines me or upsets her. She'd be better going back to Manchester and letting us all get on with things ourselves.'

'I'm glad she's here. She's doing an amazing job.'

'Oh Carl, Carl, Carl,' sighed Maureen. 'I remember she had this effect on you before, flashing her pretty face at you.'

'Pardon? What are you talking about? She's had no effect on me. I'm just stating facts. And she's got a lot more going for her than a pretty face.' Carl glowered, balling his fists. 'She runs a big business.'

Maureen rubbed her hands together. 'Don't I know it. Just don't let her hurt you again. You know she's involved with someone, don't you?'

'Yes. Well aware. I'm not getting involved with anyone. I'm fine on my own.' His cheeks and hands burned hot despite the cold. He jogged back to the cabin, but he wanted to sprint, and dispel the restless energy bouncing about inside him. He grabbed his waterproofs and pulled them on. He knew he had no business pursuing Robyn. That wasn't his intention. He'd kissed her to comfort her, but also to satisfy his own desire. It hadn't. Now he wanted more, but he also knew she had a partner. He knocked his head. What an idiot. He'd used her moment of despair to come on to her.

He jumped into the boat, up to his ankles in water. Robyn's face loomed strong in his mind. *It's just pheromones – or whatever. It'll pass. It'll pass. It'll pass.* He said the words over and over as he bailed water, trying to find the breach.

Keeping away from Robyn was the best way to stem the craving. He'd agreed to go over that evening for the Burn's Supper and couldn't see a way out of it. Would she be there? Should he apologise for overstepping? After an hour of fruitless attempts to find the problem with the boat, he returned to the cabin and collapsed into his chair, trying to think up some excuse for not going.

After showering, he knuckled down to repair a bizarre little tin toy soldier he'd been sent. Its ugly mug stared. Why anyone wanted it fixed, he couldn't quite fathom. A knock on the door. Carl peered up from ugly soldier.

Georgia's head popped round. 'Look at this.' She stepped inside and pulled a piece of driftwood from a box. Three upside-down wine glasses were suspended from it.

Carl raised his eyebrows at her beaming face. 'What is it?'

'Can't you tell? It's a chandelier! I made it. I don't suppose you can work out how to get a light bulb to work in it? I should probably have considered that first.'

There were days when a challenge like that would have appealed. Today, however, Georgia's crackpot ideas drew nothing but a long sigh. 'I'm sure I can figure it out. Leave it with me. I'll have a think.'

'Are you ok?'

'Fine. My boat's breached. I guess it's made me a bit down.'

'Aw, that's a shame.' Georgia flopped into a seat. Carl tapped his foot and glanced towards the window. 'You seem distracted.'

He pulled a one-shoulder shrug. 'It was a good boat.'

Georgia sat back and tented her hands over her middle. 'I think you might have another problem.'

'Nope.' He turned back to the tin soldier and picked up his tweezers.

'How's Robyn?'

'What?'

Leaning forward, Georgia rested her elbows on the chair arm. 'I know you still like her.'

'I don't know what you're talking about.'

With a pronounced blink, Georgia rested back and folded her arms. 'Yeah, right. I saw it at the quiz night. You couldn't stop staring.'

'You're way off.' He looked away from her know-it-all face, keeping his expression calm. She was a nosey parker. And she was right. Her eyes drilled into him; he could feel it. Laying down the tin man, he glanced back. 'Ok. I like her. *Like.*' He stressed the word. 'She has a good heart. I feel sorry for her. I'd like to help, but I don't know how. If she and Maureen could just see eye to eye.'

'Maureen's a stubborn old mare,' said Georgia. 'I think Robyn is crazy even attempting to help. I don't know why she doesn't go home. What is she trying to avoid?'

'Nothing. She just wants to build bridges.' Carl rolled his eyes and looked back at the ugly soldier.

Georgia left at four, after hours of speculation. Carl had switched off. It was getting dark and low mist crept in from the sea. He spent the remaining two hours finishing the ugly soldier before heading to the hotel.

The McGregors' Land Rover was parked outside. Carl pinched the bridge of his nose. Would they notice if he didn't turn up? He could hardly bear an evening with Kirsten; trying to dodge her puppy dog eyes and hints at dates. One step inside and he saw her, sitting opposite her mother and Beth. She patted the seat beside her. What could he do?

With a fixed smile, he scraped back the chair and sat next to her. Gillian watched him with a beady eye. He flicked his gaze to her, smile still intact, feeling like a rabbit below a hungry buzzard. For once, the kitchen looked vaguely tidy. Fingering his fork atop the tartan tablecloth, Carl could see Maureen had made an effort. There were purple candles and little sprigs of snowdrops on the table and the dresser. Carl screwed up his nose. The floral scent from the candles mixed with the mellow spicy aroma of the haggis and the slightly noxious smell of turnip created an unusual blend.

'I'll call Robyn.' Maureen left the kitchen and an awkward silence followed. Carl couldn't find any words to fill the gap. His fixed smile was getting painful. Robyn was coming. He tapped his foot under the table and fidgeted with his fork.

'Maureen's not happy,' muttered Gillian.

'Her daughter is causing all sorts of problems,' said Kirsten.

Beth nodded and sipped her drink. 'She had a reputation for being a troublemaker. Didn't she cause her brother's accident? She pushed him off a roof.'

'No,' said Carl. 'Liam fell. Robyn wasn't even there. She didn't cause trouble. *We* caused it for *her*.'

'Maybe you're right.' Beth placed her glass on the coaster. 'Was she bullied? Some kids in our year were awful, like Julie McNabb.'

'Yes, she was. And I think we should all respect just how difficult it's been for her to come back here at all.' Carl picked up the wine bottle and poured himself a large glass. It was ridiculous that his hand shook. He needed to get a grip and not just on the bottle.

'Fair point,' said Beth.

'Why bother?' said Kirsten. 'Maureen said she was leaving.'

'Is she?' Carl gulped his drink.

Gillian nodded, her eyes darted to the door as she whispered, 'I've told Maureen for years some of her choices would come back to bite her. For Robyn's own sake, I hope she goes. Though this place will come crumbling down around Maureen's ears.'

With a frown, Carl considered, maybe Robyn would be happier far from this mess. The door opened, creaking like something from a horror film. Maureen's hard stare cast a cloud of doom over them. Robyn followed, dwarfing her mother in her high heels. Her gaze cast downwards, she took the empty seat beside Beth, opposite Carl.

'Right.' Maureen smoothed her red shirt. 'Now, we're not doing this officially but would anyone like to read some Burn's poetry? How about you, Carl? You're good at things like that.'

'Am I?' His gaze fixed on Robyn. So much for letting her go. He couldn't tear his eyes from her. Before he could refuse, a book poked him on the shoulder. He took the tartan bound volume from Maureen and ran his fingers down the contents.

He enjoyed things like this – normally. But his heart wasn't in it. Maureen sat back, hands clasped on the table, waiting. Carl blinked. Kirsten's smile was like an interrogation lamp in his face.

'Ok, here we go. "Tae a Haggis" is an apt one.' The showman in him took over, and the words carried him away. Maureen beamed brighter than he'd seen for months as she stood up to get the starters. The others clapped. Carl's eyes fell on Robyn. She hadn't moved her head. Her solemn stare fixed on the candle flame. Where had she gone to escape? A special place – maybe with a special person? Was she wandering in the woods of twelve years ago? Or was she in Manchester with someone else?

'Perhaps you'd like to try "Tam-o'-shanter" next,' said Gillian, 'I enjoy that one.'

'I don't know.' A clatter behind Carl made him look round. 'That's a really long and tricky one.' Maureen stood still at the worktop. 'Are you ok?'

She nodded. He heard a sniff. 'Fine. It's just Davie used to always…' Maureen picked up some plates.

'Well, I'm sure he wouldn't mind,' said Gillian.

Robyn side-eyed the door.

'Maybe not.' Laying the plates on the table, Maureen's lip quivered.

After Carl topped up his wine, he passed the bottle to Beth. She poured, then offered it to Robyn.

'So, are you going home soon?' Beth asked. Robyn frowned as she accepted Beth's top-up. 'Sorry, that came out wrong.' Beth placed the bottle back in the middle. 'I blame it on too much time with animals. I end up sticking my big muddy farmer's boots in everywhere. I wondered how long you were here for. It must be hard leaving your job. I can't leave the farm for five minutes, but something goes wrong.'

Robyn took a sip of wine. 'I have a very efficient deputy.'

'I didn't think you planned to leave until you finished the work,' said Carl.

'I haven't decided.' Robyn raised her gaze to him and bit her lip. Sadness pooled in her cool blue eyes.

'But you're doing a great job,' said Carl.

'Apparently not.' She took a small mouthful of smoked salmon.

Maureen frowned.

'I liked the millionaire idea.' Kirsten beamed at Carl.

'That was Georgia's idea, not mine.' Carl wrinkled his nose. Robyn raised an eyebrow questioningly. 'She thought we should advertise for rich investors.'

'I think she was specifically hoping for a young, very single, extremely handsome male type of investor,' said Beth.

Gillian rolled her eyes. Carl smirked at Beth's accuracy – pinpoint.

'Well, it wouldn't have worked anyway,' said Maureen. 'Who'd have invested in this place? It's a shame. We could have done with a millionaire to bail us out.'

'How do you know you didn't get one?' Robyn put down her fork and took a slow sip of wine not making eye contact with anyone.

Kirsten looked across the table at Robyn. 'What do you mean?'

'Has someone made an anonymous donation?' said Maureen.

'Maybe a millionaire bailed you out already, but you've never taken the trouble to find out,' said Robyn.

'I don't follow,' said Maureen.

'You have no idea what I'm worth. You can sit here and discuss your pie in the sky ideas all night. But even if a fantasy millionaire turned up, you'd have to break some eggs. If you think you can turn this place around quicker without me, then fine. Do it. And maybe the next time you open the door, your fairy prince with the money bags will be standing outside ready to wave his magic wand.' She scraped her chair back from the table and shook her head. 'I'm done. I can't take any more.'

Silence ensued. Carl didn't make eye contact with anyone.

'Wow. She's a millionaire.' Beth lifted her glass. 'That's amazing.'

'Of course she isn't.' Maureen put her head into her hands. 'I am so sorry.'

Gillian narrowed her eyes. 'You don't need to apologise to us.'

'Yes, we all know what she's like.' Kirsten frowned at Robyn's empty space.

'That isn't what I meant,' said Gillian. 'We're not the ones that need an apology.'

'Well, she's rude,' said Kirsten, 'that much we can all see.'

'Can we?' Carl glared at her. 'Is it rude to be upset when you've tried to help and all you get are insults and nasty remarks?'

'Well, I...'

'No one's denying her help,' said Maureen. 'It's her methods. She doesn't see how her actions affect others.'

'Do any of us?' Gillian's voice was quiet like she was speaking more to herself. When she looked at Maureen her steely eyes flashed. 'It's time to cut her some slack for things that happened long ago. Look at what she's become, not what she was.'

'Or what you think she was.' Carl ran his finger round the top of his glass before facing Maureen. 'She was nothing like as bad as me. I almost killed Liam. Yet, you let me sit here, you give me a rent-free cabin. Why treat me so well? Why not her?'

Maureen lowered her eyes. 'What you did was an accident.'

'That I should have prevented. I provoked Liam into it. What has Robyn ever done that warrants this? Argued with her father? Left and became a success without you?'

'Yes, Carl. All of that.' Maureen stood up. 'You don't know what she was like. You may think you do, but you never had to live with her or Davie. If you're angry with me for helping you, then sorry. I thought I was doing you a favour. I know how upset you were about Liam. I wanted to help. But don't feel obliged to stay on my account.'

'I didn't say that.'

'You're right, Carl,' said Beth. 'She's had a raw deal. God, life is complicated.' She grabbed a drink and knocked it back. 'That's why I like farming. The animals aren't anything like as twisted as this.'

'Sit down, Maureen,' said Gillian. 'Let's eat up. Come on.'

With a hardened jaw, Maureen sat down. Carl ate his haggis quietly, stabbing at it with his fork, giving monosyllabic answers to Kirsten. He was in no mood for small talk. Robyn was upstairs, alone, her anger flying around. And it was their fault. He wanted to talk to her.

As Maureen cleared away the plates, Carl excused himself. He jumped the stairs two at a time and headed through the door into a short hallway. It had a matching door at the other end that led into the hotel corridor. If he knocked on every door, one of the four would be right, unless Robyn had gone down the guest stairs and left by the main exit. Maybe she'd gone home, back to the man and the place where she was happy.

Before he could attempt any of the doors, the one at the end opened. Dark shrouded the hall, Robyn's elegant shape was framed in the doorway.

'Hi.' Carl coughed.

'What are you doing?'

'I eh, came up to see if you were ok.'

She raised her fingers to her head. 'Why wouldn't I be? That was quite mild for this place.'

Carl approached. Where to put his hands? Great clumsy things. These fingers fixed tiny objects, painted intricate details, and strummed precision notes on the guitar, but right now, they felt about as deft as a pair of outsized Marigolds. 'I'm sorry.'

'Why? Like I said, it's normal. I just couldn't sit through another several hours of it.'

'I wish I could fix it.'

'Well, you can't. Not unless you can fix everything that goes on inside my mum's warped brain.'

'No, I can't do that.'

'You know, when I'm back in my own life, I run a business. I have over thirty employees. I'm respected. I earn… a lot. But here.' She drew closer. 'Here, I'm stupid, socially awkward, or whatever they're saying about me.' Her face shone ghostly white in the pale light emitting from her room. 'There's just no shaking the child-Robyn. Everyone thinks I'm some backwards kid.'

'Not everyone. Just Maureen. I certainly don't.' He put his hand on her arm, trying to reassure her.

She batted him off and turned away. 'You do. You feel sorry for me.'

'No.' He shook his head. 'Well, maybe. It hurts me to see you like this. I'd like to help you shine. I wish I could make Maureen see.'

'You can't.'

'I've seen a different side to you. The real you.' Clenching his sweaty hands, Carl let his gaze wander across her ashen face.

'I'm not that girl any more. Too much has changed.'

'I know. And I haven't helped.' He held his forehead. 'What happened yesterday. I shouldn't have.'

'Why?' Her voice was a little higher than usual.

He looked away. 'I took advantage. I just meant to… I don't know.' He raked his hair, staring into the darkness at the corridor end.

'I'm glad you did. It helped me more than anything else has since I arrived.'

'I want you to stay. Please,' Carl whispered.

'Why?'

'Because… I… you're the one who can fix this place, not me.'

'Not with my mum behaving the way she is.' Letting out a sigh, Robyn slid her fingers around the back of her neck.

'You can do it. Look at where you are in business. You didn't do that by giving up.'

'This is completely different.'

'It isn't. It involves the same principles. Keep trying and take some risks.'

'Such as?' Boring into him, her glassy blue orbs were like searchlights. What was she looking for?

'I er… Come down. We could…'

Robyn raised her hand and placed the tip of her index finger on his neck. An electric spark forced him into the wall. *What's she doing?* So little air. Carl's heart thumped a tattoo in his eardrum. 'I'd rather stay here,' whispered Robyn.

'Why? Do you…' He grabbed her hand as it lingered on his neck. In the faint light, he saw her eyes move to his lips. The charge building inside him was about to go into overdrive. He closed his fingers tightly over hers. '…Want to?'

He released her and stared. Suddenly she grabbed his neck, pulling him forward. Their lips met with a crash. His hands slid round her waist, drawing her close. He let out a groan as she slipped her fingers into his waistband. Pushing her backwards, they collided with the wall. The burning inside shut down his rational brain. Fumbling for the door, he nudged it fully open with his knuckles. They edged into her room, still kissing. Robyn's fingers entwined in his hair.

'Oh boy.' Carl gasped. The romantic glow from the bedside lamp increased the surge of endorphins. He nudged her backwards.

Crash! Everything went dark. Robyn stumbled.

'Holy shit.' Carl held her firmly around the waist. 'What was that?'

Robyn broke free, breathing fast. She slapped her hand to her forehead. 'Damn it,' she muttered. 'I knocked the bedside table and the lamp. Careful, it's smashed.'

'I can fix that. Let's just…' He edged towards her in the darkness.

'Hello!' A shout from the corridor. 'Is everything ok up here?' said Beth's voice.

Carl froze, a cold sweat crept over him. The corridor light went on. Robyn pushed him behind the door.

'Yes.' Her voice was hoarse; she cleared it with a little cough. 'I knocked over the light.' Bending over she picked up the base.

Footsteps. 'Is it broken?' Maureen's voice. Carl swallowed and tipped his head back against the wall, realising with a jolt of panic Maureen was on the opposite side. He held his breath – or tried to – but he was in such a feverish state; he needed more air, not less.

'Yes,' said Robyn. 'But I'll replace it.'

'Pity, I loved that lamp. Is Carl here?' asked Maureen.

'What? Why would he be?'

Carl kept his head back. Only his eyes moved. The edge of Robyn's cheek flushed.

'We had a bit of a falling out. He went out, and he didn't come back,' said Maureen, 'I thought maybe he came up here.'

'I eh, don't know.'

'Do you want a hand with the table and the light?' said Beth.

'What? Eh, no. I can sort it. Really, it's fine.'

'If you're sure.'

'I wonder where Carl went,' said Maureen. 'I hope he isn't mad with me.'

Robyn kept the door open until Maureen and Beth had gone downstairs. She peeked out, then rounded on Carl. 'Get back downstairs quickly. Go through the hotel corridor. Say you were at the bathroom or something, hurry.'

'Robyn. I—'

'Just do it. I don't know what we were thinking. I've had far too much wine, so have you. Now go.'

Feeling punch-drunk, he arrived back in the kitchen. Gillian and her daughters were getting their coats on. Beth raised an eyebrow and gave Carl a searching look.

'It's snowing quite heavily,' said Gillian, 'we better get on our way.'

Maureen glared as she came in from outside. 'Oh, there you are, Carl. Where have you been? I thought you must be back at the cabin.'

'Oh. I eh, I went to the bathroom. And looked around at the building work.' He wrapped his scarf tightly around his neck, wanting to pull it tight enough to choke himself.

Chapter Fourteen

Robyn

Robyn woke with a panic akin to an exam day. Had she missed something? Forgotten to do something important? Left it too late? She spotted the glass-and-brass lamp in pieces beside the broken cabinet and threw back her head. *Shit. We crossed the invisible line. Both of us! Thank goodness, we were saved by the lamp.* Its retro chic was gone forever. Closing her eyes, she sighed and ran her fingers across her lips, caressing the barely tangible reminder of what might have been. So vivid, yet so far.

It had taken so long to get to sleep with the *Generation Game*-style conveyor belt of analysis streaking by that she was exhausted. Drawing back the curtain with a yawn, she blinked. So bright. She pressed her hand to her pounding forehead. A picture-perfect scene rolled out. Crisp and clean snow covered the grounds almost to the sea, the trees and the cabin. Its door opened, and warm light spilt out, setting Carl in sharp relief. He clapped his hands and stretched. Robyn drew back on the off-chance he'd look up. What must he think of her now? So much for not wanting to give into transient feelings. She'd fallen straight into the pit.

Fastening his cycle helmet, Carl pulled a colourful bike out from the lean-to shed and sped off towards the trees, the mist of his breath carried in his wake.

Robyn slumped into the chair at her dressing table and held her face in her hands. The things that had happened in the past couple of days drummed in her head. She rubbed her temple. Being so close to him in that corridor had set every sense in her body buzzing. Controlling herself had become about as easy as manoeuvring a unicycle on an ice-rink.

Memories had spurted out, and all the old feelings. How badly she'd wanted him. A shiver ran through her. She still wanted him, but she mustn't make it any more difficult to go when the time came.

Why had she let him get under her skin? Normally she could regard attractive men with serene equilibrium. Pete was a good-looking man, and she'd dated him for almost three years without allowing feelings to complicate things. She groped around on the dressing table for her hairbrush. Whatever they'd had never produced anything remotely like what she'd felt in a few alcohol-inflamed moments last night. Her hand strayed to her stomach. Something had been produced, not from love, but a silly mistake. Now it was gone. No more mistakes.

Brushing her hair with strong rhythmical strokes, Robyn considered how best to tackle her mum. 'She'll be mad,' Robyn told her reflection. 'I walked out on her meal. Just another fault in my long list of felonies.'

The bristly stair carpet poked through her socks on the way down. Her thoughts returned to Carl. Rubbing her forehead, she tried to shake him out. She'd let him in. Only a crack. But it was enough. The craving deep inside smarted for more. She'd walked away before. Could she do it again? Detach and move on. Deal with the Pete-shaped problem lurking in her office. If she kept schtum about what had happened, she and Pete could muddle along. But why should he be allowed to get on with his life, as though nothing had happened? It was his baby too; he had a right to know. Whether or not he wanted to.

Maureen didn't look round as Robyn entered the kitchen. 'I have to go to Tobermory today.' She fixed her eyes on the table.

'Do you want me to come with you?' Robyn put her hand on the fridge door. 'We could discuss how the plans are going.'

'No, I don't. I'd like you to explain your behaviour last night.'

Robyn examined the jumbled assortment of magnets on the fridge, forcing her expression calm. 'No.'

'No? That's it? No reason why you stormed off from the table and smashed some hotel furniture in your rage?'

Robyn swallowed a laugh, not out of humour. What was funny? 'That was an accident, but there's no point in me explaining. Unless I was to say, sorry, Mum, I'm a completely unhinged and awful person. That's the only thing you want to hear.'

'Of course, I don't. You sat there and claimed you'd made millions, then in the next breath you got up and stormed off like a child.'

Robyn raised an eyebrow and placed her hands on her hips. 'Because I'm sick of the way you speak to me. All I'm doing is trying to help.'

'You should go back to Manchester. Get on with your life and leave us to muddle along here as we always do.' Maureen threw some wrapped packages into a box, picked it up and ran to her car. Drips of melting snow spattered around the door as she left.

Setting the kettle to boil, Robyn leaned on the worktop and let out a sigh. If Maureen wanted her gone that much… fine. She could leave at the end of the week. Things had got too hot to handle. Not just with her mum.

A knock at the door. Chewie looked up and barked half-heartedly.

'Come in,' Robyn called. Who bothered knocking round here?

A ruddy-cheeked Georgia peered around the frame and scanned around the room.

'My mum's out,' said Robyn.

'I know. I passed her in the drive. Is Carl here?'

'No.' Robyn fiddled with her pendant. 'Isn't he at the cabin?'

'I must have missed him.' Georgia clapped her gloved hands together and stamped her feet on the doormat.

'I think I saw him going for a ride.' Robyn rubbed her forehead; why was she giving away her creepy stalker tendencies?

'Hmm.' Georgia looked around. 'Would you like to go for a walk with me? I'd love to get some photos out there before the snow melts. I'd appreciate your company.'

'I, eh.' Robyn searched for an excuse, but Florrie and Chewie jumped up at the 'W' word and wagged their tails at Georgia.

'I'll get my stuff.' Georgia bounded outside, leaving the door wide open.

Robyn got her boots and coat and followed. The dogs sniffed everything, knocking snow off bushes, sneezing and snuffling as it tickled their noses. Chewie did some crazy leaps, looking a lot younger than his nine years.

'I doubt I'll make any money from the photos, but they'll look nice on my blog.' Georgia unzipped a large padded camera bag. Robyn threw her hands into the pockets of her grey wool coat and fell into step. 'It's cut-throat trying to break into the market. You'd never think it in a small place like this. But artists are two-a-penny and you have to cut a niche. I'm not sure if I've done it or not.

This is my first winter and I'm sinking. Basically, no tourists and very few sales. I'm doing all sorts on the side just to keep up with my rent. I've even taken on some shifts at the shop, which is not me at all. I hate being cooped up behind the till for hours on end, but the bills keep coming. I have to up my game come the summer if I'm going to survive living here.'

Robyn craned over diminutive Georgia, lowering her shoulders in a vain attempt to fit in. 'Cutting a niche might be difficult with both photography and art. You need careful branding.'

Georgia frowned and poked out her lip. 'You think? I mostly photograph landscapes, but I'd like to do wildlife as well. I might try more of that this year. I love all kinds of art. I used to fancy doing interior design, but that never took off. Gosh, that's all over the place, isn't it?'

'It is a bit, but it's not impossible to market. Nothing is, if you know how. Your work just doesn't fit neatly into a box, which also isn't necessarily a bad thing. It's really about the brand you're trying to forge. What you want people to see.'

Georgia's eyes widened and her red lips fell open. 'I am so clueless about business. I'm not sure I even know what you're talking about. I just like painting pictures and taking photos.'

'Well, if you want some interior design work, there's plenty here, but I've decided to leave at the end of the week, so you'll have to sort it with my mum.'

'You're leaving?'

'I have to. Business.'

'You're so like my sister,' said Georgia. 'Not in looks. But your business skills. I wish I'd learned more about running a business before I started doing this. That's part of my problem. I'm a tad impulsive.' She pulled an 'eek' grin. 'But I don't miss the grind. Life can be hard here, but there's always the sea, a woodland or a hill to escape to.'

'How sentimental,' said Robyn, but the vision tugged her; a house by the sea, a family, some more dogs, maybe a boat.

'I know. I'm a crazy romantic. I dream of meeting princes and shining knights. And I look for kelpies in every loch and unicorns in every forest.' With a giggle, Georgia knelt to capture some snaps and flicked through the results.

'Hello.' A hand landed on Robyn's shoulder; she nearly collapsed. Turning around her eyes met Carl's. 'What's going on here?'

'Nothing.' Robyn's gaze trailed over Carl's mud-spattered legs. She nibbled the inside of her lip. Looking away wasn't an option. He had her pinned.

Georgia tapped him on the arm. 'Where have you been? I was looking for you.'

'Cycling.' Carl gave his filthy gear the once over. 'I left the bike at the cabin and ran down to catch you. Why don't you both come back for a drink?'

'Sure,' said Georgia, 'I've got something to show you.'

'Another chandelier?'

'Better than that.'

'I can't wait.' His gaze returned to Robyn, he flattened his lips and blinked.

'I'll head back,' she said, unable to look at Carl. Her cheeks reddened at the crazy ideas spinning around her brain. She'd like to wrap herself around him and never let go. Even the mud wasn't a deterrent.

'Come with us,' said Georgia. 'See what you think of my creation.'

'I need to get out of these clothes,' said Carl.

Robyn's heart skipped about twenty beats. If he was going to do that, she had to keep far, far away. But her disobedient feet followed.

A zany pink van covered with floral decals sat outside the cabin, displaying Georgia's creative tendencies for all to see. What imagination and bravery. Carl flicked Robyn a smile as he held the door. Passing him, she lowered her eyes. The scent of cold air on his warm body was divine. A tremor ran through her. Whatever they'd started the night before was begging to be finished.

Georgia flopped into a seat and began skimming through her pictures, chatting nonstop. Robyn took the other seat and fidgeted with her cuff, listening to the sound of the water running in the shower. Her rebellious eyes wanted to drill a hole through the rustic wooden wall and watch. The gushing stopped with a clunk. Steam filled the alcove behind the kitchen area, by the front door, staining the panelled walls. Carl emerged wearing nothing but a towel. Robyn averted her eyes as he passed through the kitchen area and the bi-fold doors on the other side. If she looked, she might have to jump up and grab him. He'd barely set foot in the bedroom when he nipped out again and grabbed a white t-shirt from the radiator. Robyn trained her eyes forward. *Don't move.* Chewie, having no such scruples, lifted his head off the floor and stared.

'Right, some drinks.' Carl reappeared two minutes later, wearing the white t-shirt with Nordic patterned lounge pants that hung too low to be legal on that tight waist. He took a few steps into the kitchen area. 'Hot chocolate?' Nothing he served could be as hot as him. A few moments later, a mug landed in front of Robyn. Carl thrust himself onto the beanbag on the floor and ruffled up his damp hair.

'Is this you channelling your Norwegian roots?' asked Georgia. 'You look like a model in my *How to Hygge* book.'

'I'm ready for my close-up now.' He jokingly coiffed his hair, rested his hands behind his head and casually elevated one knee, exposing a lithe ankle, his long feet poked out. *Oh!* Robyn pulled her head back, expecting to squirm, usually she hated feet, but his were pink and healthy, with every nail neatly trimmed. She suppressed an urge to lean forward and massage her thumbs over them. 'How do you want me?' He raised his eyebrow. He may joke, but the pose had a volcanic effect on her insides. She bit her lip. Her imagination answered his question with a hundred completely inappropriate and highly censorable scenarios. Even Florrie peeped up from her nap and lifted her left eye.

With a wry grin, Georgia lifted the camera and clicked. 'You utter poser,' she said laughing. Robyn grabbed her hot chocolate and gripped it; the china burned.

'So,' Carl stretched out his legs, 'what did you want? Apart from an excuse to take photos of me?'

'Haha,' said Georgia. 'It's in the car. I'll nip and get it.'

'But your drink will get cold.' Robyn blinked. What an utterly stupid thing to say, but being alone with Carl set her heart plummeting into a tunnel of panic. Unfinished business sat before them like the last chocolate in a box. Who would grab it first, or were they both too polite, leaving it for the other to make a move? Carl rested his head back and smiled at the wall.

'I'll only be a second.' Georgia ducked out the door.

Robyn shivered, feeling completely naked. *Oh heck.* She smacked her forehead. Not good.

Carl glanced at her. She could read his mind.

'Listen.' Her eyes darted to the door. 'Last night. It was—'

'Too much wine?'

'Exactly.' She'd only had one glass. Hopefully he hadn't noticed.

His gaze lingered on her face. 'I'm sorry if—'

'It's fine, I…' Robyn frowned. Words fluttered about but she couldn't grab the right ones. Her cheeks burned redder and redder. She tugged at the neckline of her grey sweater, flapping it at her throat. Where was the businesslike Robyn when she needed her?

The door opened. Carl rubbed his fingers and observed his bare feet. Georgia glanced between the two of them. 'It's getting windy out there.' She laid a lumpy piece of wood on the table and sat back, grinning. 'What do you think?'

Carl leaned forward and raised his eyebrows. Robyn noticed some pebbles placed round the wooden object in a neat circle. 'Am I supposed to know what it is?' Carl turned it round and squinted.

'A clock,' said Georgia. 'Can you put a mechanism in it so it works?'

'I guess.' Carl sighed.

'It's cool,' said Robyn. 'In a wacky sort of way. No offence.'

'None taken.' Georgia smirked and drank her hot chocolate. 'That pretty much sums me up. I'll leave it here. No urgency, and I'll pay you. No refusal.' She pointed at Carl as he opened his mouth. 'I should go. It looks like more snow's coming and I hate driving in it. The van isn't the most dynamic vehicle in bad weather, or in any weather, come to think on it.'

'Ok,' said Carl, 'I'll see what I can do.'

'Thanks.' Georgia swigged her hot chocolate. 'And Robyn, if I don't see you again, it was nice to chat.'

Carl sat up straight. 'You're leaving? I thought?'

'At the end of the week.' Robyn gulped her chocolate. 'I have work.'

'Well, good luck.' Georgia shook Robyn's hand. Her smile was kind and genuine. After looking at her for a few seconds, she pulled her in and hugged her. Robyn stood poker straight. 'Sorry, can't help myself,' said Georgia, giving both dogs – and Carl – a pat on the head before she left.

'I should go too.' Robyn fiddled with her sleeve.

'Why? Stay and talk to me.'

'No,' said Robyn far too quickly.

'Fair enough.' The side of Carl's hair closest to the fire had dried into fluffy curls; he dragged his fingers through them, muddling them together with the damp side.

'Listen.' Robyn bit her lip. 'I have to leave, but while I'm here, I'd like to get those bathrooms finished. I checked this morning and, well, they look awful.'

Carl raised his eyebrow. 'Ok. Business it is.'

'Yes. Let's stick to that. Whatever I say to the builders will be wrong. So, would you… Could you speak to them tomorrow? I think they'll take it better from you.'

Carl leaned back into the same pose he'd done for the camera. He was too smoking hot to be allowed. 'Yeah, of course. No problem.' Florrie dragged herself closer to him and he lazily dropped his hand over the side of the beanbag to tickle her. Robyn's brain tried to keep her eyes busy, but they wouldn't obey. They fixed on Carl and wouldn't move. He looked back. His smile was still warm, but tinged with something else – sadness? *I've hurt him; led him on.*

'Thank you.' Robyn drowned the words in the dregs of hot chocolate powder at the bottom of the mug. 'Now, I really must go.' She had to get the distance back before the hammering in her heart changed her mind. 'Come on, you two.'

Carl stood up and walked to the door as Robyn hustled the dogs into action. Chewie groaned, heaving himself to his feet. Carl placed his hand on the door, holding it shut. 'Why are you leaving? I thought we agreed to work together, to take some risks.'

'I'm not sure we were on the same page.'

'Look, I overstepped last night. I'm sorry, I know you have a partner. I lost control—'

'I don't blame you. I started it. I just needed an escape. But it was silly.'

Carl's gaze drifted across her face. Flattening her lips, Robyn looked away. For a second, she imagined the eighteen-year-old boy with the cheeky glint in his eyes. How he'd grown. Could she wrap him around her like a cosy blanket and never put him down?

'I just want to see you smile.'

Robyn's brows lifted. She put two fingers to her lips; her other hand rested on the void. 'I can't.' She pushed open the door. Carl released it. Bitter cold stabbed her.

'Robyn.' The chill vanished, replaced by warmth. The heat of Carl's arms wrapped round her. Closing her eyes, she slid her hands around his back. 'I never meant to hurt you,' he said. 'Ever. I've made so many mistakes. I really hoped you'd stay and sort out things with your family.'

'It's too late, Carl.' Robyn looked up.

'Because of last night?'

'No. Because of my mum. If you want the truth of what I feel in here.' She pulled back and planted her fist into her chest. 'I wanted you last night. I still do.' Her balled fist uncurled onto his torso and slid upwards. His breathing snagged as she raised her lips to his. They melted together. He slipped his hands inside her coat, hoisting her closer. Blood rushed to her head and surged through every vein. The kiss deepened. Her lips parted. Carl groaned, pushing her gently against the doorframe. He pinned her fast. Robyn moaned and lifted her neck to breathe. Carl's arm braced rigid against the wall.

'Oh, boy.' He flexed his neck, breathing rapidly.

Robyn swallowed. 'This is a mistake, isn't it?'

'It doesn't have to be.' He leaned in again. Robyn lodged her fingers in his thick hair. The world stopped spinning, transferring its revolutions into her head. No one else but the two of them.

When he pulled back, she blinked.

Carl took a deep breath. 'You're smiling.'

She touched her lips. 'I am.' Her brows raised. 'Thank you.' She drew her hand down his chest. A car door slammed. They glanced towards the hotel.

'Maureen,' muttered Carl. He stepped inside the door. 'I hope she didn't see that.'

'She isn't looking. I need to get back. I—'

Carl pulled her inside. 'Just one more.' Lacing his arms round her waist, he placed a soft kiss on her lips. Throwing caution to the wind, Robyn curved into him, clinging to his toned abs. His breathing intensified. Hot lava filled the void with tremors of pleasure. Robyn moaned as her nails dug into his back.

*

Giddy and shaky, Robyn opened the back door and edged into the kitchen. She could hardly breathe. The feel and smell of Carl lingered. Crushy girl feelings of never wanting to wash again tingled on her skin.

Maureen wasn't in sight. With a quiver of relief, Robyn settled the dogs and sank into a high-backed armchair in the deserted guest lounge. From the expansive window, she looked out trying to think of anything other than what had just happened. During the summer as a youngster, she'd seen this room packed with guests. The austere bottle green décor and the emptiness was unsettling

With Carl and all the rogue thoughts swirling around her brain, it was impossible to concentrate on anything. Closing her eyes, she wondered if she might fall asleep.

'Is everything ok?' Robyn opened her eyes to see Maureen at the door, arms folded, chewing the corner of her lip.

'Yes.' Robyn sat up.

'Hmm.' Maureen narrowed her eyes.

Cursing the blood-rush to her cheeks, Robyn tried to keep a level head. Her insides cringed. Had Maureen seen?

'How's Carl?' Maureen walked to the window.

'I, eh, don't know.'

Maureen rested her hands on her hips. Robyn flattened her lips and breathed deeply. Where was this going? Her body felt rigid and thoughts scrambled through her head. Maureen turned and pressed her palm to her forehead. 'Well, you won't believe what happened to me. I met Calum Matheson in Tobermory – the cheeky sod that wants to buy this place.'

Robyn furrowed her brow. 'Right.'

'Yes. I was chatting to Fenella and up he comes bold as brass. Honestly, those Mathesons are always muscling in. Do you know what he said?'

'Can't imagine.'

'There's an open viewing on an old cottage in Carsaig on Thursday afternoon. Apparently it would be a good place for me.' Maureen touched her chest and widened her eyes. 'He was actually suggesting I sell up here, buy the old ruin and live there. It has *potential*, so he insists. Honestly, if he's that interested, he should do it himself. Fancy having the nerve to suggest that.'

151

'Fancy indeed. Though it sounds quite idyllic. Carsaig is beautiful.'

'Why would I want to live away down there? It's far too remote. He's a shady trader if you ask me. His dad, Ron, has been a boat skipper all his life, but I've seen him sailing round in a boat that belongs in Monte Carlo. They're all at it, the whole family.'

Robyn sighed and held out her hands. 'Some people are good at making money.'

'Oh, yes. Like you.'

'Like me. And on Friday, I'll go back to Manchester and make some more.'

'Go back? You've only just started?'

Robyn furrowed her brow. 'No, I started over a month ago. I think that's long enough.'

'Oh, for heaven's sake.' Maureen gripped her chest. 'It doesn't seem fair starting something as big as this and not seeing it through.'

Looking out the window, Robyn bit the inside of her lip, trying to hold in the scream desperately trying to escape. She was beyond confused.

Chapter Fifteen

Carl

Foreman Bill smirked as Carl handed round packs of homemade tablet – his mum's legendary baking. Carl smoothed the front of his sweater and laughed. 'I thought you might appreciate it.' Maybe a little sweetener would speed them up.

Bill opened his packet and scoffed half the bar before he said, 'Maureen's lass has no right coming in and telling us our job.'

Carl looked into the bathroom they were working on and raised his eyebrow. Nothing was remotely finished. 'She's very organised though.'

'Full of airs, you'd never know she was born here. Thinks herself superior and all that.' Bill shoved his half-empty tablet packet into his back pocket.

'I'll give you a hand here.' Carl hoisted off his sweater and cast it onto a pile of boxes. 'It's tough with just the two of you. Where are all the others?'

'Ach, we've had bad luck. The flu, Kev's wife just had a bairn, and Ross is off to a funeral somewhere – the borders, I think.'

'Well, tell me what to do and I'll muck in. I haven't done plastering for a while.' Not since he'd helped his dad when he was about fourteen. He remembered why it wasn't something he was particularly drawn to when he almost choked on the dust. Some hours later, Carl's eyes glinted as he scanned over a perfectly smooth wall. 'Not bad.' He knocked his tools together and dumped them in the bucket.

As he checked his phone, his tummy rumbled. Nearly three. Where had the day gone? No wonder these jobs took so long, on paper it seemed like they should be quick, but this couldn't move faster, not without several more people.

'What are you doing here?'

Carl turned to see Robyn standing in the doorway. He rubbed the back of his hand over his hair, hoping he didn't look like he'd opened a bag of flour over his head. A burning sensation deep down rerouted his rational brain. Had she asked him something? Everything he desired stood before him. But he'd acted like a testosterone-fuelled idiot the day before. She hadn't been exactly blameless, but she'd admitted she only wanted him as an escape. Well, he'd had his fun. Now to business.

'Oh, I'm helping. But I should have put on my mucky clothes.' He eyed his dusty jeans. 'I forgot this was so messy.'

Robyn stepped back from the cloud and frowned. 'Very hands-on.' Drawing her lips together, they curled upwards.

Carl blinked and looked away. 'Yeah, well.'

'Where's Bill?'

'In the next bathroom.' Leaning out the door past Robyn, Carl checked neither Bill nor his assistant was in earshot. Keeping his voice low, he said, 'They're struggling a bit. It's a big job for two of them. Everyone else is off for whatever reason. And between you and me, they're a bit sloppy.'

Robyn stood up tall and folded her arms. 'I already told you that. Plus, I said right from the start, we should get contractors from the mainland.'

Carl nodded, ignoring the frantic pound in his chest that began every time she came close. 'They'll manage. They just need a bit of support.'

'So, how about I contact some people to come and do just that?'

'I don't want to offend them. My dad knows lots of people on the island: handymen, joiners, plumbers—'

'But they're all busy on jobs already. I tried everyone at the start. We can't afford to wait. This is the season when all the hotel owners want repairs done. We were lucky even to get these guys.'

Carl screwed up his lips thoughtfully, Robyn glanced at them. He leaned forward a fraction, her neck tilted. Just another inch. A curl of hair slipped across Carl's face, knocking dust into his mouth. He coughed and stepped back. 'Well, if you put it like that, I guess we need help.'

'Great. I'll go make some phone calls.' Robyn looked at him as though she might say something else, then backed away a few steps.

Carl gave a little cough. 'Robyn.'

'Please, Carl. Things are hard enough. I appreciate you being here for me. But—'

'You're leaving, I know. And I'm, well, I don't want anything from you. I just want things to be ok. You deserve to be happy.' His hand shaking slightly, he brushed his finger down her cheek, leaving a chalky trail.

Robyn pressed her hand on top of his. 'I need to get my head together. Mum's attitude is, well, confusing, to say the least. She wanted me gone, but when I suggested it, she accused me of running away. I'm already doing that. I ran away from things I needed to face up to in Manchester. I have to go back and do it.'

With a nod, his hand trailed away. 'Ok. But I'll always be here. As a friend. If you need anything.' He took the incline of her head as a thank you; she turned away quickly.

Carl watched her retreat through the door marked 'private'. His fingers formed a steeple. What was she running from in Manchester? The man? He shook himself both mentally and to knock off more dust. He didn't need to know. Not his business. He just had to knuckle down and accept things. They'd shared a brief moment, lost themselves. Part of her had been healed. Though in some bizarre symbiotic way, Carl felt part of him had been ripped from his soul to staunch her wound.

*

As bills snapped around like sharks trying to grab him and pull him under, Carl accepted some IT work thrown his way by a former colleague. He hated it, but it was a good earner. He could remotely fix several problems as well as offering some consultancy. It reminded him of days in the office, stuck in a suit. He shut himself away for a couple of days to focus. His dwindling coffee supply sent a constant stab of panic to his chest.

Fenella dropped in on Wednesday after her teaching was done for the day. Carl's heart sank when he saw Aunt Jean doddering out the car behind his mum, leaning heavily on her walking stick.

'Ludicrous place to live,' said Aunt Jean. 'It's like a kennel. But then your hair reminds me of one of those English dogs; the paint ones, you know.'

'An old English Sheepdog.' Fenella rolled her eyes and shut the door. 'Jean's bored in the house. She fancied an outing. I've brought some freezer food for you.'

'Thanks, Mum.'

'Can't you cook yet?' asked Aunt Jean.

'I can, yes.'

'Go, sit down, Jean,' said Fenella.

'Not enough room for me to get inside, never mind cross the room. How will I get to the seats?'

Carl let her figure it out while he helped unpack the bag of freezer supplies.

'It was like anarchy at school today,' said Fenella. 'I'm so glad I cut my hours. It's wonderful when Wednesday becomes your Friday.' She squinted at Carl. 'Is everything all right? You look a bit pale.'

'Yeah, well.' He opened his arms and hugged her, towering above, feeling like he might crush her.

Fenella looked up. 'Oh, Son. What's wrong?'

'Nothing. I'm good.' He ruffled her hair and released her. 'Just… You know, the boat.'

Fenella folded her arms. 'I know you love the boat, Carl, and if anyone can fix it, it's you. But why not buy a house?'

'I can't afford it.'

'You might be surprised. Don't waste what you have on boats and bikes. Invest.' Fenella stroked his arm and drew her lips flat with pity.

Carl shook his head. He'd followed this doctrine as a teenager and landed a job he didn't want. Sensible but dull. On one hand, he had Georgia telling him to follow dreams, on the other, his mum telling him to keep his feet on the ground. In the middle, the Sherratts pulled his destiny on a string.

'I have an idea. I'll come for you tomorrow at twelve. Don't tell Magnus and Julie, I don't want them muscling in on this,' said Fenella.

'On what?'

'You'll see.'

'Can I come too,' said Aunt Jean.

'No!' said Fenella and Carl together.

Chapter Sixteen

Robyn

Robyn walked into the kitchen on Thursday morning and stopped dead. Not just the surprise at how clear the dresser looked, but Julie McNabb! Of all the people, she hadn't expected to see, Julie was top of her list. A rush of furious heat spread up Robyn's neck.

Julie had her back to the door as she said, 'I could do anything. I'm sure I'd be just as up to it as her.'

Robyn coughed and let the door slam. 'Up to what?'

Maureen dropped her tea towel.

'Oh, hi.' Julie turned, looking rather pink.

'Talking about me?'

'What?' Julie laughed. 'No.'

Her tone made Robyn want to hit her. 'Why are you here?'

'Julie saw the advert for new staff, she fancies the front of house position,' said Maureen.

Robyn sat and crossed her legs, rocking back in the chair. The opportunity for revenge was almost too delicious. 'Well, you can apply through the proper channels. I'll see you at the interview.' Robyn tapped the table and looked up slowly.

'*You'll* see me? I'll sort this with Maureen. It doesn't concern you.'

Robyn raised her eyebrows. 'It concerns me a great deal. If you have your CV, I'll look right now and let you know if you're suitable.'

'Robyn, maybe we should—' began Maureen.

'We'll follow the procedures. I don't agree with nepotism. So, do you have the CV?'

'Oh, never mind,' said Julie. 'If you're involved there's no chance of anyone on the island getting the job. You've alienated everyone by contacting these mainland workers. And honestly, who wants to work with you anyway?'

'Excuse me,' said Maureen, 'please don't talk like that in my house.'

'Sorry, but it's true. Once she's gone, you can get your hotel back and make everyone happy. No one on the island will set foot in it while she's here.' Julie stormed from the room.

'Robyn, I'm not sure that was a good move. Julie has good credentials.' Maureen frowned, sorting through a wad of envelopes.

'I don't care. I hate her.'

'You can't live in the past.'

'Me? I'm not in the past. It's me getting this place to look like it belongs in this century.'

Standing still, Maureen stared at Robyn. 'But you're leaving tomorrow. So what's the point?'

'I've extended my stay. One more week. When the mainland workers arrive on Monday, I can set them to task. I can also do the interviews.'

One more week wouldn't hurt, especially if it meant Robyn could oversee the hiring. Maureen's amazing knack for handing out charity to everyone she knew would ensure jobs for all her friends even if they were totally incompetent. Of course, she didn't extend this generosity to Robyn.

A secondary motive for not leaving immediately lingered on the fringes of Robyn's imagination. A swarm of butterflies erupted even at the thought. Vague possibilities or unfeasible ideas about Carl and the future rose and fell, messing with her head. Was there a future? In a parallel universe, perhaps? Even as she got in the car that afternoon, she wasn't sure exactly what was driving her. An unseen force guided her south on the long Glen More road. Stunning scenery whipped past. Snow-capped hills, waterfalls, gushing streams and wide-open spaces flooded her vision.

'Amazing,' she whispered, rounding a bend and looking downhill over a huge expanse of forestry leading to the sea. So free. This was life on Mull. Not the hotel. Not Maureen. Peace, serenity, freedom. She sighed. A pang grew in her lower midriff. Had things gone differently, she could have retreated here. If Pete didn't want any more children, she wouldn't have burdened him. She and the baby could have roamed free. But it hadn't happened.

At a sign for Carsaig, she took a left turn up a steep road. After a narrow and twisty drive, a stunning sea view panned out. A wide bay curled beneath rocky cliffs. Scattered houses nestled around the shore. A few miles along the road, a For Sale placard caught her eye. She indicated and pulled down a track towards the sea. At the end was the cutest cottage imaginable. Close to the sea with a wild garden backing onto the beach. 'We don't need to go in,' she told Florrie. It seemed important to justify herself. 'We could just go for a walk.'

She imagined carrying a little tot down to the water's edge and her eyes misted over. *It won't happen now.* Stopping on the grassy verge behind two other cars, she pulled on the handbrake and stroked Florrie. 'It's just you and me. Let's go and see. Just for fun.'

As she walked up the stony path lined with snowdrops, a prick of terror and a flutter of excitement battled in her chest. This cottage had figured in so many of her dreams. Although she'd never been to it before, she knew it was the place. Even in the dead of winter, it was perfect. A peaceful haven. A place to enjoy crackling fires, thick blankets and hot chocolate every night.

A man at the door shook her hand and gave her a property schedule. 'It's an open viewing, so look around, take your time.'

Wide-eyed, Robyn soaked it all in. Dated interiors were nothing. Her hand covered her nose as she peered into the small kitchen. The smell. She recoiled. The previous resident obviously hadn't liked cleaning. As she moved into the living area, she realised why. That view of the garden and the sea. Stunning.

'Wow,' she mumbled. Another viewer gave her a look. She skimmed the schedule. Pretending to examine a blank wall, she waited until the other viewers left. 'I don't need this place,' she told Florrie. 'But I love it. It's what I always imagined. But only if…' She pinned her lips shut and stared forward, hearing footfalls. More viewers approached from the corridor.

'Robyn?' A low voice spoke. The footsteps stopped dead.

Spinning around, she jerked back her head; her mouth fell open. 'Carl!' They stared at each other. No words came. Chewing the inside of her lip, she could hardly breathe. What magic had drawn him here? Was it really him? She felt like pinching him to check he was real.

Behind him, Fenella stepped into the room, her eyes up high, checking the ceiling. 'It's not in the best of nick,' she said. 'I suppose that's why it's so cheap.' Dropping her gaze, her eyes landed on Robyn. 'My goodness, Robyn. I didn't know you were interested. I didn't expect to meet you here.'

'I, eh. It was just a whim. My mum.' With a struggle, she turned her full attention to Fenella.

'Oh yes,' said Fenella. 'Maureen was with me when we met Calum in Tobermory. He was quite insistent this place would suit her. Is she here?'

'No, but I thought I should check it out.'

'Personally, I don't see Maureen here at all. But Carl, it's your kind of place.'

'It certainly is.' Stuffing his hands into his back pockets, he looked out the sliding patio door. 'My dream house.'

'Mine too.' Robyn said the words so quietly no one heard. She glanced at Fenella.

Drawing her eyebrows together, Fenella spoke with a soft tone. 'It is beautiful. Maureen won't want to live here though. Will she?'

'It doesn't matter anyway,' said Carl. 'I can't afford it.' He pulled open the door and stepped outside. Wind whooshed by, abruptly eclipsed as he slammed the door.

Robyn blinked and glanced around, tucking her hair behind her ear. Fenella trod forward, watching Carl walking round the seashore garden. 'He's not himself.' She checked her watch. 'And Magnus might turn up as well, I hoped he hadn't found out about this place. I'm not sure it's what he wants at all, but Julie is so demanding. Well, I shouldn't say anything, I try not to interfere. Maybe I shouldn't have brought Carl. Was that silly? My poor boy. I don't know how to help him. He used to have a good job, but the company went bust. I think he blames himself.'

'Why?'

'A deal he was negotiating failed. The company went under.'

'Oh no.'

'It all hit him hard. Then his girlfriend left him.' Fenella drew in a deep breath. 'I'm not sure how serious he was about her. Carl never gets too serious about anyone. Anyway, she ran off with his housemate. He came back to heal, maybe to hide. Maybe just to get away.' She watched him from the window. 'I thought he might get together with a nice island girl and settle. But he's adamant, he doesn't want to. Pity. But it's his choice, I respect it. I don't agree with it, but, well.' Letting out a long sigh, she glanced at Robyn.

Robyn looked out the window. If things had been different, would they have been here together? Holding hands, laughing, trying to work out how big an extension they'd need for three kids and six dogs. She touched the void. Here they were as individuals, up against each other. If Carl wanted it, she'd walk away and let him have it. That was pretty much what she had to do anyway. She really didn't need this place, no matter how much it tugged on her heartstrings.

'I'd like to look outside.' Robyn gripped the door handle. 'Are you coming too?'

'You go. I'll stay and give Carl some privacy. It's bad enough me bringing him. I can't buy the house for him, I don't have the means.' Fenella fingered her earlobe. 'I hope I haven't upset him.'

'I'm sure he appreciates it.' Robyn stepped into the bitter wind, her hair whipping around her face. Florrie shivered. Picking her up, Robyn held her close. Fenella was a kind mum, but she was probably right. Carl wouldn't thank her for this. It must be tormenting to find the dream house and be unable to afford it. Almost as gut-wrenching as finding it, but having no need for it.

Robyn caught up with Carl. He side-eyed her. 'Why are you really here?' he asked.

With a wistful smile, Robyn looked away. 'Curiosity. I heard Mum talking about it. It sounded like somewhere I would like.'

'You and me, both.'

She glanced up at him. He looked back. A force tugged her closer. 'This is the place, isn't it?'

His eyes moved on, following the sea line. 'We dreamed it. But it's not real.'

'Isn't it?'

He moved his head a fraction. 'No. What we had is lost. You have a career. Your life isn't here.'

'And what about you?' Robyn took a step back and clung to Florrie.

'What about me? I live as best I can from day to day. Many regrets, no expectations and each day as it comes.'

Robyn drew her lips together. 'What if things were different?' A tremor ran up her arm, shaking her nervous system. Could they be? She'd run the business remotely for over a month – it was possible.

Tilting his head, Carl's gaze drew inward. 'How can they be? I can't afford this place, and even if I could. Why? What are you suggesting?'

Cold panic spread into Robyn's chest. How to reply? 'I'm not sure. I just wondered if—'

'It was a beautiful dream, but it's never going to be real. I have nothing to give. Nothing you'd want.' Shoving his hands into his pockets, his chest heaved with a sigh and he walked away. Following his movements, Robyn stood quite still, watching. A leaden weight sunk into her tummy and her shoulders sagged. The sea of broken dreams crashed onto the shore, beating its slow rhythmical refrain.

*

On the return journey, Robyn drove quietly. Waves of sadness bubbled inside her. The void Carl had filled for a couple of days was empty again. However long she prolonged her stay, it wasn't going to change. She'd tried, but it was hopeless. Even if she'd followed Carl, and begged him, what good would it do? What did she want from him? He'd said he had nothing to give. But he did. Something that warmed her heart and filled it with peace. Something that made her life feel worthwhile. Inside, she craved it. For a few short weeks, a new life had bloomed inside her. She wanted to feel that again, but not with Pete. With someone who loved her. Someone who would love their child. Could that ever be Carl? He'd always made it quite clear that life wasn't for him. Sadness and pain collided inside her like a boat on turbulent seas.

The road rounded a hill at Pennygown Cemetery where her dad was buried. Making an emergency stop, Robyn swung the car around and drove up the track towards the gate. Sitting still, she stared ahead, seeing nothing. With a heavy chest, she got out and walked up the hill. Pushing open the creaky iron gate, she battled against the wind to the grave. Beyond the cemetery wall, waves rolled up, breaking softly on the shore. Clouds gusted in, obscuring the view of mainland hills across the sea.

As Robyn stood in front of the cold marble headstone, her hair twisted and flowed out behind her. She pulled her long grey coat tight. 'Dad.' A lump rose in her throat. Lifting her brows, she flattened her lips, trying to hold back the tears. 'I don't know why I never lived up to your expectations. For a long time, I blamed myself. What did I do wrong? I was a child. I needed care and guidance. I'm sorry you couldn't give it to me.' She crouched down, touching the stubby grass. Tears clouded her vision. She didn't stem the flow as they slid down her cheeks and off the end of her chin, watering the hallowed ground. 'If you could have seen me as I am now you might have been proud. I know you can't hear me, but I need to feel wretched. I wish I'd come sooner, but I couldn't. I was afraid. I was in pain. I was in hospital.'

For a long time, she sat, struggling with the wind. 'I wish things could have been different. So many things.'

*

A video call with Pete later sent Robyn's fluff-filled brain careering down the work path. The panic in his voice got her attention. Losing a big contract was about the only thing to get Pete in a flap. Not something he wanted on his plate. He wanted to pass it on before it got too hot. She ended the call and sat on the bed. *Great, just what I need.* This wasn't how she'd planned to spend the weekend; back at her bedroom desk, watching Carl's every move. How must he feel? Robyn couldn't rid herself of the pained look in his eyes. If anyone belonged in the house at Carsaig, it was him. *And me.*

The whole weekend was sacrificed to keeping the contract. She toasted Pete on Sunday night with a strong gin. *Where you fail, I succeed,* she told the geometric wallpaper.

After an alcohol induced deep sleep, she woke to the sight of builders' vans rolling up on Monday morning with a team of workers from the mainland. Bill sulked as Robyn passed round copies of the job folder, explaining the work. The mood in the family kitchen was equally grim. As Robyn entered, she jerked back her head, frowning at an almighty clatter. Maureen knelt amidst a sea of junk next to an open cupboard, muttering to herself.

'Are you all right?'

Maureen flung a cooking pot on the floor. 'No. Of course not. It's a disaster. What will people think of me? Having all those workers here? I've always tried to stay local.'

Robyn pinched the bridge of her nose. 'We've been through this. The work needs to be done.'

'Yes, thank you. I am aware. But don't you see what this has done to me?'

'What?'

Maureen's head sunk into her hands, and she started to sob.

'I don't understand. This is what we agreed.'

'It's not that.' Maureen stood up, grabbed a tissue from the box on the table, and dabbed her eyes.

'What then?' Frowning Robyn looked around, the room had been gutted, it barely resembled the mess she'd seen when she arrived.

Maureen continued to sob. 'It's the idea of reopening.' Maureen blew her nose. 'Without Davie.'

Robyn sighed louder than she meant to.

'And that is why I find it difficult to talk to you.' Maureen's voice pierced with a sharp edge. 'I know you and your father didn't get on. But he was my husband. For years, we ran this place together. It wasn't always easy, but I always had someone. Now, with all the repairs and changes, it's like thirty years have been erased. It doesn't look like my hotel any more.'

'But...' Robyn rubbed her forehead. 'It had to change.'

'I know. It looks good. But it's wiped me and Davie off the slate. This is a new place. I feel like a stranger about to open a hotel I know nothing about. If things go wrong, who do I turn to? Before, there was always Davie.'

'You have me.'

'But you won't always be here. And no matter what you say, if you go back to Manchester, the concerns of this place won't interest you.'

'Carl will help you.'

'Carl?' Maureen put her hands on her hips. 'Funny you should mention him.'

'Is it?' Robyn swallowed and twisted her pendant.

'Fenella phoned me. She said she'd met you at a house viewing. And you were there on my behalf.'

Robyn looked at the floor, her cheeks flushed.

'She's all upset because she'd pegged the house for Carl. Now she thinks you'll swoop in and buy it for me. But I don't want it.'

'I know you don't.'

'Which makes me wonder what you were doing there.'

Robyn sat down and rested her head on her fingertips. 'I just wanted to see it.'

'Why? Are you planning on buying a house here? I had no idea you wanted to stay.'

'No. I don't. It was just curiosity.'

'Well, I don't know what Carl's financial circumstances are, but I don't think he makes a lot. Maybe with savings and family money, they might be able to do something to get the house. But you need to back off. Fenella's very worried.'

'I'm not going to buy it. I told you, I don't want it.' A sorrowful weight pounded in her chest. Robyn rubbed it, staring at the table. All they had left were the interviews, then the path was clear. She could leave any time she wanted. And there was no time better than the present. What could possibly keep her any longer?

Chapter Seventeen

Carl

'Hiya, Bill.' Carl popped his head around a guest bedroom door. The extra workforce drafted in from the mainland had powered through the rooms. The smell of fresh paint wafted along corridors. Light flooded in; the old shutters had finally been pulled back.

'Hi.' Bill looked up and waved.

'What progress. I hope you guys are ticking along together.'

'Aye, we're all getting on great. Things are moving a lot quicker and that's pleased Lady Muck.'

Carl attempted to smile along. 'She's pulled off the impossible.'

'Aye, or *we* have.'

'Well done.' Carl patted him on the shoulder.

Neither Maureen nor Robyn had been in the kitchen when Carl had come through. Maureen had maybe forgotten she'd called Carl to help. It happened so often. What was he to do this time? He scuffed his feet on the way down.

For twenty minutes last Thursday, his mum had talked him into the possibility of moving out and on. But doing that needed cash. Even using all his savings, he couldn't amass enough. There was every possibility his brother would swoop in and buy it as his island pad. What fun that would be, visiting Magnus and Julie in *my* dream house. Carl ran his fingers through his hair. Even if he could afford it, it wouldn't be a dream house. Not on his own. The dream didn't belong to him alone. It was Robyn's too.

As Carl made his way into the private corridor, a man's voice from inside Robyn's room made him stop. Had she left the TV on?

'Robyn, where are you?' The voice echoed.

Who was in there? Carl couldn't help himself stepping up to the door. He peered around but couldn't see anyone. 'Hello?'

'Is Robyn there?' retorted a grumpy voice.

Carl looked towards the window. Propped on the dressing table was Robyn's iPad, a man's face frowned from it.

'Hi.' Carl walked over, squinting at the screen. 'I don't know where she is.'

'Right,' said the man. 'This is so inconvenient. She popped off for something, but I bet she's forgotten. She seemed distracted.'

'I could go and look for her. Who should I say it is?'

The man frowned. 'I'm Pete, she'll know who I am.' His eyes shifted about. 'What is she doing? She said she had something important to tell me, then she disappeared. I have another meeting in five minutes.'

'You're Pete.' This was the man. Maureen had said his name was Pete. Something about him induced a nauseous sensation in Carl's stomach. Pete looked slick, businesslike and handsome – exactly the type that would suit Robyn. If they stood side by side in a photo, they'd look picture-perfect. 'You're her partner?'

Pete raised his eyebrows. 'Is that what she calls me? Well, listen, I need to end this call. If you see her, tell her to call me. I can't wait any more. And tell her to hurry and get back. I need her here. I miss her.'

Carl's eyebrows knitted together as Pete vanished. He backed out of the room and closed the door. So that was Pete and he missed Robyn. Yeah, well who wouldn't. What important things did they have to discuss? Business? Or something more? A possible reunion. Pete hadn't seemed averse to the word partner. Carl rubbed his forehead. *None of my concern.*

Friday loomed like an ugly black cloud. Carl swallowed. After Robyn had gone, what would he do? Lapse into his old life, muddling along? Yes. Exactly that. He leapt down the back stairs and into the kitchen. It was still empty. Should he look for Robyn and give her the message? It was only fair. The soft new carpet in the corridor led to the side door of the dining room. Carl's hand rested on the handle. Robyn had stood here at Maureen's party. He'd sung to her. 'You're Beautiful'. Because she was. Inside and out. People misconstrued her diligence and meticulousness as coldness. If only he could scoop her up and save her. He let out a cold laugh. Him, save someone? He couldn't even save himself.

He pushed the door slightly. The new bar side blocked his view, his eyes travelled over the rows of glasses hanging above, the pristine wood and bright new floor. Behind the bar area, a swing door opened into a shiny kitchen fitted with all mod-cons. Someone spoke.

'I can't move that.' Robyn's voice sounded high and anxious.

'Why not? Give it a push.'

'No, I can't. Why don't we ask Carl?'

Carl frowned. He could walk in and help with whatever it was, but before he moved forward. Maureen said, 'Now that you mention him, I want to ask you something.'

'What?'

'I saw you with him the other day when I came back from Tobermory. I didn't say anything. Well, you're both adults. But the more I think about it, the more I wonder. What were you doing?'

Carl held back and drew in his breath. Maureen had seen. He screwed up his face and cringed.

'Nothing.'

'Oh, Robyn.' Maureen sighed. 'I'm not blind or stupid. So, why lie? Your lies have never got you anywhere.'

'Pardon? I do not lie. And I'm not accountable to you. It's none of your business. Carl's about the only person who's shown any kindness to me.'

'Kindness? And have you shown kindness to him?'

'Yes. Why do you say that?'

'Is it kindness to tease him? Use him? Just like you did twelve years ago, then you dumped him.'

Carl drew back, listening.

'I left him because I thought he'd caused Liam's accident. Plus I heard some other lies about him. I was wrong. I see now. I should have tried to find out the truth. We were all in shock. Carl didn't deny his part because he couldn't think straight. It was a mess. I didn't know how to sort it out.'

'So, you left. Like you always do.'

'Yes. Just like that. As I always do.'

Silence. What were they doing? Carl peered in. He couldn't see around the corner.

'He still blames himself,' said Robyn. 'That's why he helps you so much. He's caught in your web and he can't get out. He doesn't want to cause you any more pain.'

'My web? What does that mean? Oh dear.' A scuffle of chairs. 'I never meant it to be like that. I know he beats himself up about it. I tried to help him because I know he still hurts.'

Carl tugged at his sleeve, running his nail across the scrape on the back of his arm.

'It wasn't his fault. If anyone's to blame, it was Davie.' Maureen let out an audible sigh.

'Dad? How?'

Drawing his brows together, Carl slipped forward. What did Davie have to do with it?

'Davie hated Carl seeing you,' said Maureen. 'It made him furious. Carl was like his protégé. You were his nemesis. When he found out, he went through the roof. Liam took great pleasure in telling him. Especially after you'd shopped him for spying through keyholes. But Davie was annoyed with Liam too. You might think he favoured Liam over you, but it irritated him that Liam was always the one at the bottom of the tree while the other boys were at the top. He'd be the last one in the water, the seasick one, the one who came home crying because he never won the races. Davie told him he needed to man up. He said Carl had gone off with you because he was fed-up with Liam whining, and it was time Liam proved himself. Davie was full of it. He told Liam all sorts of rubbish about what he'd supposedly done by his age: jumped off the end of the old pier, ridden his bike down a sheer cliff face and scaled the old folly to name a few. Liam was incensed to do something dangerous.'

'Oh no way,' said Robyn. 'Didn't you try to stop him?'

'I thought Davie was talking nonsense and it would wash over Liam. When you came running for help, I couldn't believe he'd done it. Whatever Carl said, it wouldn't have made a difference. Liam was ready to do something stupid.'

Digging his short nails into his arms, Carl dragged them across his skin. A rush of fury and confusion clouded his brain. He stepped into view, his jaw set.

Maureen looked up from the table. Her eyes widened, and her mouth fell open. 'Why didn't you tell me any of that before?' Carl glared, tapping his foot.

Robyn jumped and spun around. Her hand clung to the bar top. 'Carl. Were you—'

'Listening. Yes, I was.' He glared at Maureen. She lowered her head.

'What difference would it have made? Davie was crushed enough; I couldn't make it worse for him by letting him think he was to blame.'

'But he was,' said Robyn. 'So, instead of letting him deal with his own guilt, you put it all onto Carl? And Dad obviously didn't want that, so he twisted it onto me. What a ridiculously tangled mess. And all to protect a man who didn't deserve it. Do you know what we've suffered because of this?'

'And yet you've still made a success of yourself,' said Maureen.

'That is not the point!' Carl's voice shook the room. His fists bashed the table. 'Davie put the idea into Liam's head. He knew how gullible Liam was. How could he goad his son into doing something like that?'

'And you, Mum.' Robyn trained her gaze on Maureen. 'Why did you let him?'

'How could I stop him? Davie had suffered in the army. It made life difficult at times.' Maureen rubbed her forehead. 'Carl, when you came back last year, I saw the accident still affected you. I couldn't change things, but I tried to make it up to you.'

Carl shook his head and rubbed his face. Hot rage surged up his neck. 'I can't believe you didn't tell me. Do you know what I've put myself through thinking about it? And all the time, Davie? He told his own son to try a stunt like that. It's pathetic. This family is… I wish I'd…' Throwing up his hands, he growled under his breath.

'Never met any of us?' Robyn's ice-blue eyes sparkled with tears. She put her hand to her lips.

'Davie wasn't well,' said Maureen.

'That was years later,' snapped Carl. 'It doesn't excuse what he did to Robyn. Even as a dying man, he never apologised.'

'I don't mean that.' Maureen looked at her hands. 'He was mentally unstable.'

'I think we've all worked that out.' Carl pinned his hair to the top of his head and glared.

'He wouldn't admit to anything or be seen by doctors, but he was sick. He needed help but he wouldn't let me do anything. This mess. It was all him.'

'No, Maureen, it wasn't.' Carl faced her, the burning fury threatening to boil over. 'Some of it was you. You might be in denial. You might cover it with your concern and charity, but you're almost as much to blame as him. You've stood by and done nothing for years. You let him tear Robyn apart. Ruined her childhood. If she wasn't as strong as she is, it could have ruined her whole life. That's what it's done to Liam. His father goaded him into almost killing himself. He spent his last years at school and his university days wheelchair-bound. And what about me? All those years blaming myself, feeling like I owed you. If you'd told me the truth, it would have helped. I could have had a completely different life.'

Maureen buried her head in her hands and sobbed.

'It's too late. Too late for that.' Carl walked past her, through the main door and into the corridor. Sitting on the bottom step, newly carpeted in smart grey, he lowered his head and tangled his fingers in his hair. The imprint of bitter memories thumped inside. He wasn't to blame. Liam had already made up his mind to do something stupid. Even if he hadn't seen Carl with Robyn, Liam would have done it anyway.

The door clicked. Carl peered up. Robyn stepped out, her face twisted with pain.

Closing his eyes, Carl pushed his palms over his eyelids, producing total darkness. Footsteps crossed the hall. He winced as Robyn brushed the scratch on his arm and he breathed in her perfume.

'Carl, you're bleeding.' Her voice was hoarse.

'What?' He tugged his sleeve. Robyn put her hand over his and held it.

'You didn't do that to yourself, did you?' She pursed her lips. Carl let out a sigh and rubbed his fingers over the broken skin.

'I… I can't help it. It happens in my sleep sometimes.'

'Carl, I'm sorry. I can't believe what my family have put you through.'

'Both of us,' said Carl. Robyn leaned on his shoulder. Sliding back, he eased his arm around her. 'It's ok.' His fingertips slowly caressed her arm. Soft hair brushed his neck. He tilted his cheek and stroked it over her head, breathing in the floral scent of her conditioner.

Lifting her gaze, she gave a weak smile. He leaned in and kissed her. Slowly at first, savouring the taste of her lip balm. His stomach clenched. With a groan, he moved closer, holding her firm, needing her. She gasped, breaking away to draw breath.

'Carl—' she whispered.

'Yeah, I know. I know.' He released her, ran his hand down her cheek and immersed himself in her cool blue eyes. Her long lashes glistened.

'No, you don't know. Please, let me finish. What if I stayed here?' She swallowed. 'Would you? Could we?'

Carl's eyes burned hot. No. It would be disastrous for Robyn. Whatever she believed she wanted from him now, he couldn't sustain it.

'I can't. You're leaving soon and none of this will matter. You said it yourself, this is something you only want just now. Once you're away, you'll quickly forget. I'm no good for anyone. I should go.' With a sigh, he stood up. 'Don't leave without saying goodbye.' As he reached the stained-glass front door, he stopped. 'I forgot the reason I came down here was to tell you. Pete was on your iPad. I had a message to give you.' He rubbed his forehead. 'I'm sorry, I can't even remember what it was.'

He closed the door behind him and stared out to sea. Oh, for the wind to carry him away. Far away.

Chapter Eighteen

Robyn

Robyn ended the video call. Her hand shook as she pressed the button. The look on Pete's face. The shock. The horror. It said it all. She fingered the scar – or where the scar had been. So small now, almost gone. Soon there would be nothing. No external memory. 'You were saved,' she whispered. 'From a father who couldn't love you.'

Next time she saw Pete it would be in the flesh. Could she ever look him in the eye again?

She was packed, ready to leave. The ferry booked for the following day. Slumping onto the bed, she covered her face. There was nothing to keep her here. After putting her foot in it so thoroughly with Carl the day before, she realised it was too late. The tiny fragment of the dream she clung to had washed away.

With a shudder, she pulled her knees to her chest. Why couldn't she have kept her silly thoughts to herself? As the cold February sunlight split the sky, it lit up her stupidity. Why had she muddied the water? They'd been ticking along just fine, playing out the dream's end. But what had she expected? How could it ever be real? Instead, she could add another few weeks to the Carl Hansen memory box.

Maureen had been quiet. Robyn couldn't find it within herself to care. It was too late. Every feeling she had was turned over to a deep-seated grief. Trying to put it down to the pain of leaving, she switched on Robot-Robyn; it had seen her through many long years so far, and very successfully.

The bridges she'd hoped to build hadn't even got off the ground. Maureen didn't want to cross the cavernous breach. Let her wallow. *I'm so over it.* Robyn whistled for the dogs and headed for the beach. The hollow ache in her chest yearned for Carl. Just one more hug to keep her going. His cabin was dark, his pickup gone. Where was he? Maybe he'd left. She hadn't seen him since the chat, since he'd learned such horrible truths. He'd stood up for her through it all. Hearing him defend her was like being wrapped in a blanket by his fireplace and held tight. A safe place, a happy place. Somewhere she wanted to stay. But it was reserved for dreams.

The wind whipped around, tossing her hair in all directions. Carl's battered little boat tossed up and down in the bay. Closing her eyes, she transported herself to the dream cottage. Carl sailed up in a brand-new boat. She waved to him, ready to run to his arms as soon as his feet hit dry land. Her eyes opened. The fantasy evaporated. A solitary tear ran down her cheek. He'd said not to leave without saying goodbye, but where was he?

As she walked back towards the house, the wind picked up. Opening day festivities were planned for March the fifteenth, only a few weeks away. Robyn wouldn't be there. She pulled up her hood as rain tore down. Running the rest of the way, she dived indoors.

Drying off in her room, she checked the forecast. High winds, rain, sleet, and possible snow flurries. Flicking to the ferries, she slumped back on her bed. All sailings the following day were cancelled. One more day to hang about. And still no Carl.

Everything in the hotel was taking shape but Robyn watched as if through a fogged-up window. Things that happened hereon after would be in another world. She'd be in Manchester, and Mull would be nothing but a memory. Life would go on ticking by, but she wouldn't be part of it.

A delivery truck rolled up. The driver stood outside almost blown horizontal. Robyn watched him unloading boxes. He stopped to talk to someone. She leaned forward, trying to see who it was. Perhaps one of the McGregors. It looked like their Land Rover parked nearby.

Squaring her shoulders, she set off downstairs. The boxes were stacked in the new foyer. Ripping one open to reveal packets of new sheets, Robyn smiled. At least her time wouldn't be wasted, she could dress the bedrooms. The boxes didn't feel too heavy, but should she lift them? She'd been advised not to after the operation. Had three months past? How quickly it had gone by. Taking hold of the top box, she carted it up the stairs. On her way back, she heard voices and stopped.

A door snapped shut and Maureen spoke. 'No. I can't ask Carl.'

'Why not?'

Robyn leaned over the banister and saw Gillian McGregor frowning at Maureen, her hands on her hips.

'We argued.'

'What about?'

'All sorts of things. But mostly me. I've upset him… and Robyn.'

Peering through the gap in the stair rods, Robyn saw Gillian frown. 'Well, I'm not in the least surprised. I've told you before, it would come back to bite. It's time you noticed what that girl has to offer and stop walking in the shadow of a man with a crooked side. I know Davie did a lot for the community, as do you. But instead of worrying about everyone else, consider your own family. Mend the bridges before it's too late. Look around, look what Robyn's done here. And as for Carl, let him go. He can find his own path without you.'

'Maybe, but it won't be with Kirsten if that's what you think.'

'I don't think anything of the sort. He can do what he likes with his life. It isn't for me to decide. Or you. I'll help Kirsten get over it if need be. That's what mothers do, Maureen. They comfort their children in times of need.'

Maureen threw up her hands. 'Stop lecturing me.'

'Fine.' Gillian drew in a sigh and opened the dining-room door. 'Where's Beth gone? She could carry them.'

'I think she's outside,' muttered Maureen.

'She'll be soaked,' said Gillian. 'Let's go and make some tea. Warm everyone up.' They headed for the kitchen. Robyn waited for their footsteps to die away. Sitting on a step, she bowed her head and raked her hair. Nothing could change Maureen. Hearing Gillian's words loosened the ache in her chest a little, but they'd fallen on Maureen's deaf ears.

Heavy footfalls clumped up the front stairs. Robyn stood up, half-expecting Carl. She tucked her hair behind her ears. A barrage of rain and wind gusted in as the door flew open.

Beth McGregor grabbed the handle and kicked a pair of mud-caked wellies onto the stone step under the porch. Closing the door, she looked around the foyer.

Robyn hopped down the stairs. 'Hi.'

'Oh, hello.' Beth rubbed her fingertips together. 'Is there anything else needing done? I've shifted the planters round the front.' She brushed a strand of wet hair from her face and smiled.

Robyn lifted her eyebrows, frowning. 'You must be Superwoman. You did that in this weather? I couldn't even lift those things off the ground.'

Beth gave a little shrug as though it was nothing. Robyn rubbed her eyebrow and stared. Beth was tall but not exactly a bodybuilder; she must have hidden muscle power. She looked like she'd raided her granddad's wardrobe and found the muckiest clothes possible.

'Well, if you don't mind more weightlifting,' said Robyn, 'these boxes need to go up, and there are some dressing tables to go back in place now the walls have been painted.'

'Sure.' Beth took off her massive wax jacket, opened the door, and threw it outside. In her normal clothes, she was surprisingly thin. She pulled up her sleeves, looking ready to take on some burly men at arm-wrestling – and win. Picking up three boxes, she peered over the top. 'Where are these going?'

'Eh, just to the top, please. I'll sort them once they're up.'

Not able to match Beth, Robyn trailed behind with one. As she reached the top, Beth bounded back for more. It didn't take her long to get them all up.

'Ok, the tables.' She dumped the last set of boxes. 'Where are they?'

'This way.' Robyn led her to the first bedroom.

'Just as well this is happening now. In a couple of weeks, I won't be able to help anyone. The lambing will kick-off and that'll be me until April.' Beth picked up the table by herself as though it was a fluffy cushion and deposited it by the window.

'Do you do it all yourself?' Robyn frowned. Islanders all knew lambing was a laborious process even if they were clueless about farms, *like me.*

'We have a farmhand, but I mostly do it. Mum does the B&B side of things, Kirsten works for a tour company. The owners are retiring this summer and she's going to take it on herself. It's a big step.'

'She'll have her own business and you run a farm. That's great.'

'It was a necessity for me. My dad died, and there was no one else to do it.' Beth stood up and massaged her back.

Robyn's brows creased. She took a step closer. 'I bet it's hard work.'

'It is. Tourists come to Mull thinking it's an idyllic beauty spot, but it's a tough place to live at times.'

'So true. And what about your sister? Does the tour business do well?'

'It does in the season. That's the problem. Everything runs well in the season. Winters can be harsh. Kirsten's had a lot of downtime recently. It's not good for her. She broods. She's got a thing for Carl. You probably noticed on Burn's night. I wish she'd snap out of it and leave him alone; it's an embarrassment.' Beth let out a sigh. 'She won't accept Carl's happy on his own. I know how he feels, I'm the same.'

Robyn looked out the window; its frames gleamed, newly painted. Sometimes solitude seemed the answer, but now when it faced her so bluntly, she didn't want it. Not any more.

'Maybe that's why I'm thirty and still living with my mother,' said Beth. 'I don't get out much. I guess I'll die an old spinster who can drive a tractor, birth a lamb and never has clean clothes.'

Robyn smiled and frowned. Beth was pretty if you could see past the mud. Robyn wanted to say something to help, but what? 'Do you remember me from school?'

'I do, yes.' Beth blinked and flattened her lips. 'I didn't take time to get to know you. I was a bit of a tomboy. You'd never have guessed.' She gestured at her outfit.

'I remember you hanging out with the boys; you were a bit intimidating, and I was never any good at making friends.'

'Me neither. Not really. Boys were easier; they didn't talk, not about anything important anyway. I couldn't keep up with all the gossip. It's not my thing.'

'I tried to escape it, but I couldn't. I was usually the brunt of it. Thanks mostly to Julie McNabb.'

'Her! Don't get me started. But pity her, if we happen to meet alone in a dark alley one night.' Beth winked.

Robyn's eyebrows drew together, and she let out a laugh. 'I wish I'd spoken to you at school, I think we might have got on well. Though I wouldn't be much help in the dark alley.'

'Don't worry, I've got that covered.' Beth flexed her forearm and Robyn smiled.

'Listen, seriously, I'm sorry I can't help you lift this stuff. I… I had an operation a few months back. It's probably fine now, I'm just paranoid.'

'No worries,' said Beth. 'I don't mind doing it.'

Robyn led her to the next airy bedroom, very chic in its crisp new linen. She pointed out the table.

'What happened? Was it an appendix?' asked Beth.

Robyn swallowed, she hadn't told anyone other than Pete. But it would be ok. 'An ectopic pregnancy.'

Beth dropped the table into place and looked around. 'Wow. I'm sorry. That must have been terrifying. They can kill you. I'm not an expert in humans, I only know from sheep.' She cringed and covered her cheeks. 'Sorry, totally insensitive.'

'No, it's not. I was lucky, I guess. They found it early. I knew something was wrong. I got it checked out.'

'Just as well you did. And what about the father? Is he—'

'We separated at Christmas. He already has three kids and doesn't want any more. I only told him this morning, I wasn't sure if I should, but I felt he had to know.'

'Yeah, definitely. The guys always get off lightly. I guess having kids in the future will be hard because you would have lost…' Beth hovered her hand over her lower midriff.

Squeezing her hands together, Robyn nodded. 'It might not happen and it could go wrong again. I'm not even sure where things go from here. I'm almost thirty-one, no partner, and if I'm honest, I don't know where to start. I'm not one for pubs, clubs or online dates. It's all a bit terrifying.'

'I hear you. Sometimes, I'm glad I have my farm to keep me busy and stop me thinking about things like that. But you're a smart woman, I'm sure you'll find someone.' Beth fixed the table into place. 'Shame you're leaving so soon, we could have gone for a drink when the lambing was over.'

'That would've been nice, but I really can't stay.'

'Yeah, I get that,' said Beth. 'No worries.'

She moved the rest of the furniture before leaving to find Kirsten and her mother. Robyn felt lighter. She'd found a friend and shared her secret. Even if it was only for a fleeting moment, it relieved the tight pain in her chest.

*

Howling winds kept Robyn awake that night. She got up, crossed to the window, pulled back the heavy jacquard curtains, and looked into the gloom. The cabin looked dismal beneath the vague shadows of swaying trees, but it was still standing. Was Carl even there? No lights were on.

Had he come home? Robyn hadn't noticed his pickup. It was too dark to see now. Was he ok?

The following morning, Friday, she was dismayed to see no pickup. Carl hadn't come home. Or had he left early? Robyn bit her lip. What to do? She didn't have his number. She'd never needed it. He'd always been just there.

Eight o'clock. Nine. Ten. Eleven. Twelve. Still not back. One o'clock. The panic was so strong; she wanted to jump in her car and go look for him. The trees in the wood crashed around in the wind. Rain slapped the windows. The phone rang, making her jump.

'Hello.' Robyn's eyes widened when she realised who was speaking. 'My bid was successful?' Tapping her finger on the dressing table, she waited. Her heart thumped like a bass drum in her chest. Here was an opportunity, but should she take the risk?

Chapter Nineteen

Carl

Carl trudged along the edge of a cliff, looking out to sea. Behind was the tiny village of Carsaig. A few scattered houses dotted around a wide, curving, picture-perfect bay. In the distance was the dream house. 'It's not for me. Since when have I ever got something that good?' Wind hurled round. Health and safety be damned. He was sure-footed and the need to be somewhere wild hammered in his head like a nail-gun. Raking his hair off his face, he threw his arms wide. The wind pummelled his jacket, it shuddered at his sides. He jumped down the track. A stream of rocks dislodged under his foot and crumbled over the edge. *Whoa.* Pulling back, he steadied himself, then crept forward and looked down. What a drop. A gust caught him; he wobbled. Grabbing the rock face, he gasped for air against the mighty swirls of wind. A sharp edge jutted out. Crouching down, he sheltered in its wake.

Should he go on? The narrow path funnelled beyond to an almost impassable ridge. Crazy in any weather. Waves roared below, crashing onto rocks with angry blasts. Carl rubbed his forehead with his soaking glove. Why this madness? What was he trying to prove? *I'm doing exactly what Liam did, only no one's here to see me, or save my skin.*

Dropping onto all fours, he peered over the ledge. Was it worth the risk? If he fell, who would care? He closed his eyes. Images passed inside his eyelids – his parents, brothers, friends. Robyn.

Even out here, there was no escape from her. Carl wanted to go back and say goodbye. The ferries would be off, and she'd be stranded, but it only prolonged the agony. Robyn was leaving. What reason did she have to stay? *Not for me, that's for sure.* She'd tried to tell him something. He'd had to stop her. The words were too heavily influenced by the island's spell – the pull of Mull. Once you were here, you never wanted to leave. But Robyn had to. What they'd shared was something to get her through the dark days. It wouldn't last forever. When she was back in Manchester, she wouldn't need it any more. He had to keep his distance to protect her.

Clambering back up the ledge, he ran along the path, into the village and the pickup. He'd already cleared out the cabin, shoved everything in the back and left in the dead of night. A day and a half he'd spent driving about. Last night he'd huddled in the backseat, hoping not to be blown out to sea as the car shuddered and shook.

If he turned up at his parents' door looking like this, Fenella might faint. If she found out about Maureen, she might commit murder. Carl didn't want to risk either. Only one option remained. An hour later, he banged on Georgia's door. Rain lashed his face, and he jigged his foot.

Georgia prised open the door. Her eyes widened, sizing him up. 'What's happened to you?'

Shaking his hair, he stepped in. 'Nothing's happened. I eh.' He looked around. 'Could I borrow your shower? The one at the cabin's broken.'

Georgia lifted an eyebrow and thumbed her ear. 'Right. Yes, you can. It's upstairs. Grab a towel from the cupboard on the landing.'

Ignoring her suspicious look, he ran up and turned the water on hot. The tiny bathroom filled with steam. Sloshing water across his face, he scraped his fingers through his hair, tossing back his head. Warmth flooded his numb limbs.

Cold air on the landing shocked after the heat of the bathroom, but it was a relief to be in clean clothes. A cloud of steam billowed out. He shut the door and shivered.

'I'm in here if you're looking for me.' Georgia's voice came from behind a door next to the bathroom.

Carl poked his head into a small room, presumably meant to be a bedroom. His mouth opened. He'd never been up here. Georgia had fitted it out like a tiny studio. Carl could barely see the floor or walls. A table and chairs, shelves, boxes, easels, canvases, and paints covered every available space. He blinked. So much stuff in one tiny room. Georgia bent over the table, drawing something with a thin black pen.

'So this is the studio.' Carl eased in and sat opposite. 'Makes me a bit jealous.'

'Seriously? You like this?' Georgia continued to draw. 'I feel like such a fraud. People think I'm an artist, so I must have a beautiful studio in a summerhouse, with a gallery nearby. Not this mess.'

Carl ruffled his damp hair. 'I'd love this.'

Georgia replaced the pen lid, sat it to the side and rested her chin on her hand. 'So, what's going on?'

With a half shrug, Carl grunted, 'Nothing.'

Throwing her head to the side, Georgia stared. 'Seriously, Carl? You expect me to believe that?'

'Yeah.' His gaze darted around the room. Anywhere other than those question-all eyes.

'So, the shower in the cabin broke, and at…' She woke her phone. 'Fifteen-forty-three, you decide to come here for a wash.'

'Yup.'

'Even though, you live about 400 metres from a hotel where every other room is a bathroom?'

Carl closed his eyes with a sharp sigh. 'Pretty much.'

'Just spit it out,' said Georgia. 'Better out than in.'

Turning in the seat, Carl stretched out his legs, leaned back, and took a deep breath. 'I fell out with Maureen. We argued. I packed my stuff and left.'

'You left? Ok.' Georgia looked around and screwed up her face. 'And you want to stay here?'

'No. I'm done scrounging. I need to do something else.'

'Such as?'

'I don't know, maybe go back to IT, get a proper job and start over.'

'Why?'

'Because I'm pathetic. Look at me? I'm thirty years old and what do I have to show for myself?'

Georgia frowned. 'Carl, you've helped hundreds of people by fixing so many precious things. I know it's the world's worst paid job, but don't knock it. I've read some of the messages on your webpage. Why not see if you can do more IT stuff on the side? Don't just give up.'

'It's not a case of giving up.' Carl stood up and raked his hair. 'It's like my whole mess of a life has caught up with me. I can't take it in. I found out Davie put Liam up to the dangerous climb in the first place. I still wish I could have stopped him, but if I'd known, I wouldn't have felt entirely responsible. It's like my life's been on hold. If only I'd known what Davie was really like. I'd have—'

'What? You were a child yourself.'

'I wouldn't have stayed in the cabin, that's for sure. Then I might have seen sense sooner. Instead of wasting my time on that toxic family.'

Georgia tilted her head to the side. 'Yep, they've got a lot of issues. Maureen does anyway. She scares me. What about Robyn? Has she gone?'

'No.' Carl picked his way to the window through stacked boxes and canvases. 'I guess not, ferries won't be on.'

'Poor Robyn.'

'She suffered, you know, from Davie's poison. More than me.' Carl shook his head. 'She deserves better. If she could just be happy. With someone.' He leaned on the windowsill and breathed, trying to quell the sick feeling. Someone who loved her. Someone who wanted her more than anything. But he couldn't inflict that on her. *She deserves so much more than a waster like me.*

'And does she have someone?'

Carl flipped his hair. 'She has a man in Manchester. They're separated. But she'll go back to him.'

'Did she say so?'

'No. When I saw him. I just had a feeling.'

'When did you see him? Is he on the island?'

'He was on a video call. He looked smart and suave. Very well suited to her.'

Georgia tented her fingers and pressed her lips together. Carl peered out the window onto the tiny triangle of garden between two other houses.

'I liked her,' said Georgia. 'But she always looked sad.'

'I know. I wish she could be happy. That's all I want. She told me to make a clean break. I don't know how, but I need to. She's good at shutting down and keeping out the problems so she can get on with life. I'm not.'

'I don't think that's all.' Georgia frowned and folded her arms. 'Spit it out, Carl.'

'There's nothing else.' He faced her and leaned back on the windowsill.

'Really? You didn't try and rekindle an old flame?'

His eyes darted heavenward. 'No.' He swallowed. 'It just happened. She and I… We have a bond. I feel it anyway. I think she did too. But it's only because she's here. She appreciates a shoulder to cry on. I was there for her when she needed it.'

'Let's go downstairs.' Georgia pushed her pen back into a case and zipped it. 'You need a coffee.' Carl followed her down. She pointed him into the petite living room, and he slumped onto a squashy grey sofa. What comfort after two nights sleeping in the pickup. The kettle boiled through a wall somewhere behind his head. A clink of china. Georgia padded in and placed a steaming mug on the glass coffee table.

She flopped into an armchair and held her cup on the side. 'I'm not an expert, definitely not. Me and relationships, well, let's not talk about that. But I get the feeling you're going to regret this forever if you don't tell her.'

'Tell her what?'

'How you feel.'

'And how do I feel?'

Georgia smiled and sipped her tea. 'Only you know that. She's obviously important to you. Tell her.'

'What's the point? She's leaving anyway.' Carl burned his tongue on the scalding coffee. He pulled his head back.

'Is that what you said to your last girlfriend?'

Lowering his eyes, he rubbed his hand across his brow. 'Yes.' He'd let her walk away with his flatmate, someone he'd considered a friend. 'No point in forcing her to stay. She was happier with him.'

'Was she? Or did you just have an eye on the exit? Sometimes Carl, you don't seem to know what's good for you.'

'She was better off without me.'

'And Robyn's the same?'

'Yes. She runs a business. She's successful. She's smart. She's got everything going for her. What would she want with someone like me?'

Georgia's thick, dark lashes blinked, and she smiled gently. 'Love.'

'What?' Carl furrowed his brows.

'That's what she needs. Can you give it to her?'

'But I… I have nothing. Everything I own is in the back of my bashed up old pickup. I'm not good enough.'

'You have a heart. Try, Carl. If she says no and leaves, at least you'll know. You don't want to spend another twelve years or more wondering how things might have been.'

Chapter Twenty

Robyn

Robyn slammed the boot shut and glanced towards the cabin. Still no pickup. Where was Carl? Ferries were back on a limited timetable. She had a place on the one-thirty sailing. Frowning, she checked her phone. It was early yet. Would Carl come home in time? He'd told her not to leave without saying goodbye, then disappeared. Did he know she was still here? Maybe he thought she'd gone the day before. Carl knew the island so well; he'd have known the ferries were off. Why not come back? Robyn's heart was in tatters, it might bleed out inside her chest. If she could just hug him one last time.

Her daring didn't stretch to asking Maureen if she'd seen Carl. Even speaking to her was difficult. Silence spiralled every time Robyn was near her, and Maureen had gone quiet, which wasn't much better than the constant nitpicking.

Robyn flapped out her car mats; she could do with giving them a proper clean. The car's normally pristine interior was covered in stones.

'Robyn!' Maureen stood at the top of the main stairs holding her phone. 'There's a disaster. You need to come quick.'

Adrenaline burst into Robyn's veins. She darted up the stairs with wide eyes. Her pulse rate rocketed; she could hardly breathe. Carl. Something awful had happened. Maureen's revelation had cut him deep. Had he done something dreadful? Robyn had seen the marks on his arms. What else might he do? 'What is it?' she gasped, clutching her pendant.

'I just had a phone call.'

Robyn trembled, her insides stone cold. 'And?'

'The woman we employed for the front of house, she can't do the job any more, she's changed her mind, it's a disaster.'

Pressing her palm to her chest, Robyn let out a gritty sigh. That was it? Forcing her breathing to remain calm, she said, 'I thought someone had died.'

'Don't be ridiculous. I knew this would all end in tears.'

'Pardon?' Robyn glared.

'Oh, whatever. I'll sort everything, as usual.'

'Well, as I'm leaving, why not phone Julie McNabb? She's desperate for a job.'

'Julie? Why would you give her the job? I thought you hated her?'

'I don't particularly like her. I won't be here though, so it doesn't matter. She might be the one to save the place. That might make you happy. As you probably like her more than me. Do you have her number?'

'Why would you think I like her more than you?'

'Because you like everyone more than me. There's no point pretending. I came back to build bridges. I've done everything you needed here and more, but you're still cross with me; you snap at me, you put me down. I can't change who I am, and the person I am is never going to be good enough for you. Now, do you have her number?'

Deep grooves furrowed across Maureen's ashen forehead. 'That's quite hurtful. What you just said.' Maureen searched through her phone.

'Good. Now you know how I feel.'

Stiff-jawed, Maureen turned her phone for Robyn to read the number. Robyn punched it in and waited, biting her lip until Julie answered.

'It's Robyn Sherratt. I have a job here for you if you want it.'

Maureen stared at the carpet as Robyn spoke. After she ended the call, Robyn shoved her phone into her jeans pocket and pulled out her car keys. 'She's delighted to do it.' Gripping her keys hard, Robyn supressed an urge to throw up. 'I'm going for a drive. I might not be back before I go to the ferry.' Staring at Maureen, she took a deep breath, leaned forward and kissed her on the forehead. 'Goodbye, Mum.'

She was out the door before she heard Maureen at the top of the stairs. 'Robyn. Thank you. Drive safely.'

Lifting an unsuspecting Florrie, she swept her into the car and gave Chewie a big hug. No prolonged goodbyes. Holding her lips tight together, Robyn pulled off, not looking back.

The storm had blown off enough for ferries to run, but the roads were dicey. She drove north towards Tobermory. 'I'd like to look around, I didn't have a chance yet.' But even browsing the shops couldn't calm her mind. As she peered in windows and bought a few bits and bobs all she could think of was Carl. Where was he? Should she have waited for him at the hotel? It had been two days.

Giving Florrie a pat, Robyn hopped into the driver's seat and put down some bags. The heavenly smell of handmade soap filled her lungs, momentarily relieving the ache in her chest. 'Right, a quick walk.' She drove to the Aros Park and let Florrie run about while she breathed clean air. Soon she'd be back in the city with noise, people, and anonymity. Alone.

Covering her lips, she walked behind Florrie. 'Time to face up. I *am* alone. Quite alone.' She could cling to the memory of Carl's hugs and kisses, as she'd done for twelve years, but it didn't change the cold hard facts. 'And look what I accomplished in those twelve years.' The words burst through exasperated tears. 'I'm meant to be alone. That's who I am. How I work. What a success I've made.' But to what end? She dried her tears with her fingertips.

Back at the car, she put Florrie into the passenger seat and shut the door. Checking the time, she glanced up with a desperate sigh. *I can't go back to the hotel.* But what if Carl was there? Was there any chance? For the last goodbye. Her trainers crunched on the stones. She put her hand on the door. Goodbyes were the worst.

'Robyn! Hello-oo!' A sing-song voice resonated around the car park. A wood pigeon flapped out of a tree with a disgruntled coo. Wrapped up in a padded green coat, tartan scarf and wellies, Fenella Hansen waved across the car park. Opening the boot of a silver Land Cruiser, she hustled two spaniels and a retriever inside.

Robyn returned the wave. What now? Drive away? Or did Fenella want to talk? Hovering with her hand on the door, Robyn swept a stray hair from her face. Fenella slammed the tailgate, pulled her jacket tight and hurried over.

'I thought you'd left.' She threw her arms around Robyn and hugged her. Standing bolt upright, Robyn returned it stiffly. 'I'm so glad I caught up with you. I meant to call in, but I've been so busy. Honestly, people think teaching is an easy job, but I've been rushed off my feet. And my Aunt Jean lives with us. She's more demanding than a toddler.'

'I, eh, I'm going now. The one-thirty boat.'

Fenella checked her watch. 'You've got a few hours yet. Would you let me buy you a coffee? I'd love to have a chat before you go.'

Biting her lip, Robyn glanced around. 'Ok, thanks.'

'We can nip over to The Pottery. I'll meet you there.'

Robyn was parked and out as Fenella pulled up. Her dogs jumped about to get to the window, watching Fenella as she dashed across the car park. The wind whisked her feathery hair, and she lowered her head, clutching her bag as she battled forward. 'I hope the dogs behave. Sometimes, they leap around and set off the alarm.' Fenella stroked down her hair as they claimed the warmth inside. 'It's getting windy again.'

They headed upstairs to a smart mezzanine restaurant with a view over a misty Tobermory. After hanging her coat over a chair at a window table, Robyn watched the trees around the bay swaying to and fro.

'I thought it was meant to get better today, but it looks like more stormy weather is coming,' said Fenella. She put her hands on the rustic wooden table and beamed. 'I had a message from Julie this morning. She said you'd offered her a job. She's over the moon. It was so kind of you.'

'Oh, well. She, em.' Robyn picked up the little wooden block, which displayed their table number, and spun it in her hand.

'It's ok.' Fenella pulled a face. 'I know what she's like. Honestly, sometimes I wish I was a meddlesome mother. If I was, I'd tell Magnus to kick her out, but I have to accept his choice. Personally, I think the relationship only works because he's away so often. But, oh my goodness, you've made her so happy. Thank you. It makes my life much easier when she's in a good mood.'

Robyn tried to smile. Just seeing Fenella's joyful features had a powerful effect on her insides. She looked so like her son.

'Are you quite alright?' Fenella put her hand across the table and rested it on top of Robyn's. 'I hope I haven't spoken out of turn.'

'You haven't. Not at all.'

'Let's get a drink, and how about a cake? That'll cheer you up. I guess it's hard to leave, but you must miss your work. Carl told me what a success you are. I think it's marvellous. You'll be glad to get back into the routine.'

'Actually, I don't want to go back. I feel like I should, but I'm dreading it.' The words came out before she'd considered how true they were.

'Only because you've been away for so long. It's like that for me every August after the school's been off for six weeks. I hate the thought of going back, then ping, one day in class and it feels like I've never been away.' Fenella waved to the server. She chatted to her for some time and Robyn stared out the window, wondering. Was it just that? The fact she'd been away for months? Or a deeper niggle. A spatter of rain hit the glass. Robyn shivered.

'She's my neighbour's daughter, lovely girl,' said Fenella as the server headed off with their order. 'What was I saying? About your work. I'm sure it'll be fine. You've been doing lots from here anyway, haven't you?'

'It's not the work.' She swallowed. 'It's Pete.'

'Who's he?'

'The deputy manager. I was in a relationship with him. It was all very well-organised. Pete has three children and he doesn't want any more. I didn't want any either.' She took a deep breath. 'But I fell pregnant. It wasn't planned. I didn't even realise, not fully. But things weren't right.'

'Oh dear. You had a miscarriage?'

'An ectopic pregnancy.'

'Oh no.' Fenella jumped out her seat and plonked herself beside Robyn, throwing her arms around her. Speechless, Robyn took shaky breaths as Fenella hugged her. 'So devastating. You poor girl.' Fenella rubbed her back. 'Tragic. And so unfair. Life can be terribly cruel sometimes.'

'I was so alone. I only told Pete a couple of days ago. He was angry and not in the least upset. He didn't care what I'd been feeling for the past few months. I know he wouldn't have wanted me to keep the baby. And although I didn't think I wanted children, I know now that I do, and it might never happen.' Robyn's eyes misted over. The rib of Fenella's jumper pressed into her cheek as she rested on her shoulder. Robyn held her breath.

'Oh, Robyn. I'm so sorry. Life has no guarantees, but I think it'll happen for you. I really do. I had a miscarriage early on, I never believed I would have children. Then suddenly I had three. At the time, it's the most dreadful feeling. I'll never forget it.' She stroked Robyn's hair.

'It's just all got so complicated.'

'Yes. I understand.'

Robyn believed her. The warmth of her hold relaxed her nerves.

'And what does Maureen say about it all?'

Robyn pulled back and wiped her eyes with her fingertips. 'She doesn't know. We don't really get on. I tried. But I never get it right.'

'I always wondered.' Fenella shook her head to the side. 'I count myself as a friend of Maureen. I've known her for a long time, but she's an odd woman. I thought things were strained between the two of you.' Fenella reached up and stroked Robyn's hair out of her eye. 'Well, she's missed out. You're bright as a button, and I don't understand how anyone could shut you out. I had three boys; I always wanted a girl too. I'd have loved a daughter like you.'

Tears crowded Robyn's eyes and she covered her face. Fenella patted her back. Something might burst any second. *Why am I crying, and in public too?* Robyn dabbed her eyes with a napkin as the server arrived with the food. Fenella thanked her with a gentle nod.

'Why not try a bit of cake? I know you've probably lost your appetite, but it might do you good. Listen to me, preaching cake as being good for you.'

Robyn glanced at her. 'Thank you,' she whispered.

'No, don't thank me. More and more I've wondered about Maureen. After the accident, she changed. Not unexpectedly. It was a shock. But I saw a different side of her. I was glad my boys were old enough to not want to go over there every weekend. I wish Carl had never moved into the cabin last year. I'd rather he'd just stayed with us, but he values his independence. My aunt, Jean, winds him up. She's batty, but harmless. Nothing compared to all the horrible memories tied up at the hotel. I don't think it's good for him, but I try not to interfere.'

'He's fallen out with my mum. They argued. She told him some things she should have told him years ago. My father goaded Liam into his accident days before it happened. Carl always thought Liam did it because he'd seen Carl and me together, and Carl had called him immature. But it wasn't that. That was just a catalyst. Liam was going to do something crazy no matter what. And if he had done it when Carl wasn't there to get help, it could have been a hundred times worse.' Robyn pressed her fingertips to her forehead. 'Carl got really angry with my mum. I've never seen him like that.'

'Maureen kept that quiet all these years. When was this? Carl didn't say a word.'

'Wednesday. Have you seen him since then?'

'No, I haven't seen him since we went to view the cottage. Oh dear.' Fenella touched her cheek. 'He was upset about that too. He loved it. I know he wanted it, but I hadn't quite grasped how little savings he had left. I think he's a bit cross with me. He usually sends me nice texts, but I haven't had any for a while.'

'I think something might have happened to him. He hasn't been at the cabin since. I thought he must be with you.'

Frowning, Fenella stabbed her cake. 'Hmm, no. I'll message him. Oh, now what's this?'

Damn the tears, they wouldn't stop. Robyn rubbed them away.

'Oh, you're in such a bad way. You're not worried about Carl, are you?'

Robyn nodded, pressing her lips together.

'Well, don't. He'll be fine. Sometimes, he just doesn't know what's good for him. He hits the self-destruct button and off he goes. For someone so good at fixing things, he's blind when it comes to himself. Tell you what, give me your phone number, and as soon as I get a reply, I'll forward it to you. You never know, he might even reply before we leave.'

He didn't. Parting with Fenella hurt. How to leave the warmth of her motherly hugs?

'You must come back for a visit, and don't leave it so long this time. Call me whenever you need to, or just for a chat. You have my number. I really would love to hear from you.' She stroked Robyn's cheek and gave her one last hug.

As Robyn got back in the car, Florrie greeted her. Robyn breathed slowly. 'Fenella is so kind, but I just wish I knew where Carl was.'

Chapter Twenty-One

Carl

Carl rubbed his back and stretched. Sleeping on Georgia's sofa or the back of the pickup weren't long-term options. A ten-year-old would struggle to lie straight, never mind a six-foot man. Two nights… or was it three. Lack of proper sleep had addled Carl's brain and his back was feeling it too. Days and nights blended into a spiral of hopelessness.

He'd returned to the hotel earlier, hoping to catch Robyn. Parking the pickup in the trees near the main gate, he'd run through the woods past the old folly, now completely fallen in, surrounded by metal fences to keep out would-be adventurers – and idiots. As soon as the hotel was in sight, he'd craned his neck and peered through the trees. Robyn's BMW was gone. Throwing himself onto the ground, he'd sat on the stone-cold earth and waited. Trees swayed and creaked all around. The wind roared. Maybe the ferries would be cancelled again. At twelve-thirty, he'd given up. She'd probably gone on the early boat. He'd missed her… and his chance.

After coming back to Georgia's and sitting through an hour of chatter, Carl had perfected his listening face, but barely a word filtered in.

'If you rented an office, you could set up a workshop, and combine your fixing with some IT. I think there was some office space up for grabs in Tobermory.' Georgia stopped to draw breath.

Her concern was great. Her help appreciated. But he had nothing. 'This is all great in theory.' He rubbed his forehead. 'But I have no source of income. Fixing things barely gets me enough to scrape by on. I guess I can pick up seasonal work in a month or two, but right now, there's no way I can afford to rent an office. And without the cabin, I'm homeless.'

'But not alone.' Georgia smiled. What eternal optimism. 'I know you can't stay here indefinitely. Not that I'm throwing you out.' She drummed her fingers on the chair arm. 'I get how hard it is. I don't make a lot either, and doing shifts in the shop, and the like, does not fill me with joy. But you also have your parents, your brothers, and so many people who care about you. Don't forget that.'

'I haven't forgotten. But I can't move back with my parents. They haven't the space, not with Aunt Jean.'

'Hey, it's ok. I understand. Nothing would drag me back to living with my parents. Much as I love them, small doses are enough.'

'And as for Magnus, can you see me living with him and Julie? Or just Julie when he's away working.'

'Hmm, ok, when you put it like that, no. But he's quite well off, couldn't he sub you?'

'No!' Carl frowned and rested his head back. No way was he asking for a loan or a handout. 'I won't beg. I just need to get online and look for a job.' He padded his pockets. His phone battery would be dead. 'I have to accept things are never going to be the same again.' A cold, sharp pain struck his chest. The idea of donning a suit and returning to an office made him sick. Plugging in his phone, he set it to charge on the windowsill. Horizontal rain flashed by.

'What about Robyn? You could still get her number. Maureen would have it.'

Shaking his head, Carl sighed. 'I'm not going back. I don't want to see Maureen. I can't face her yet.'

A loud knock. Georgia jumped up. 'Who's that? If they knock that hard, they'll smash my window.'

Carl listened as she bustled into the hall and opened the door. She sounded surprised. Then a familiar voice. Mum? Carl sat up and rubbed his cheeks, jeez, he needed to shave. Georgia returned, followed by Fenella.

'There you are, Carl. Honestly, what a scare you gave me.'

'What are you talking about?' He rubbed his chin and frowned.

'Where have you been?'

'How do you mean? Did Maureen say something?'

'No. But when I see her, I will have quite a few things to say to her.' Fenella braced herself on the armchair and glared.

'Mum? What have you heard?'

'Everything I need to.'

'What?'

Fenella pulled off her gloves. 'Robyn told me all about it. Honestly, what a stubborn, unforgiving, thoughtless woman. I am furious with her.'

'Robyn?' said Carl.

'No, Maureen! I'm so angry.'

'But you saw Robyn?' said Georgia. 'Is she still here?'

'She's just left. Well…' Fenella checked the clock. 'She's heading for the one-thirty boat.'

'What?' Carl jumped up and swivelled to see the time. One o'clock. He could still get there. 'I have to go.'

'Carl. Where are you go—'

'I need to catch her.' He grabbed his keys and ran from the house, skidding on the wet path as he made his way to the pickup door, but unless he fell and broke all his limbs, nothing would stop him.

He knew the road between Salen and the ferry port at Craignure like the back of his hand, in fact, much better, because who the hell knew what the back of their hand looked like?

The windscreen wipers worked overtime, screeching back and forward. Icy rain slapped the pickup. Concentrating hard, Carl didn't allow himself time to think. He didn't know what he would say, how he felt or anything. He just wanted to catch her.

He entered the village and cursed the need to obey the thirty miles an hour sign but did it. He didn't want to be responsible for another accident. The terminal emerged through the gloom. His heart stopped. The ferry's black hull loomed in the bay, but the car lanes were empty. He was too late. The cars were on board.

He screeched to a stop and jumped out. A man in a high-vis jacket squinted through the sleet and waved his hands. 'Sorry, we've called off the sailing. It's too risky. No more sailings today, I'm afraid.'

Carl's shoulders sunk and he pressed the bottom of his palm into his forehead. Where now? Where would she go? The hotel? His eyes darted about, hoping to see Robyn's car, anything.

Making a wide U-turn in the pickup, he belted back towards the Glen Lodge. Narrowing his eyes, tension jabbed his shoulders, he leaned forward, pushing the wheel. Seeing Robyn was all he wanted. But Maureen would be there. How could he face her?

The rain turned more to sleet; he slowed as it intensified into a thick flurry. A set of tyre tracks had grooved a path in the slush-covered driveway. Carl's brows raised as he reached the parking area. His mum's car. *Oh no.* Carl shook his head as he got out. What was Mum up to? Glancing around, his heart sank. No Robyn – unless she'd hidden her car. Approaching the door to the family kitchen, he heard raised voices. Should he knock? He'd never knocked on that door before. The hotel had been like a second home for almost a year. Pushing open the door, he pulled off his beanie hat.

Maureen stared across the kitchen, her jaw set. Fenella's eyes flashed, she blinked as they settled on Carl. 'Did you find her?'

Carl twisted his hat in his hands and shook his head. 'Ferries are cancelled for the rest of the day. She wasn't there.'

'I'm sure she'll be fine,' said Maureen. 'She goes off for drives all the time. The day she arrived, she drove around the island before coming here and didn't appear until the middle of the night.'

'And why does that not surprise me?' said Fenella. 'She didn't know what to expect coming back here. It certainly wasn't a warm welcome. To put it quite frankly, I'm disgusted. Your attitude has left me utterly bewildered. How any mother could treat their child the way you have is beyond me. The faults and wrongs you've accused her of are nothing. She was shy! She found it difficult to relate to people. So what? Does that warrant years of hatred?'

'Stop.' Maureen crossed her arms over her chest. Her face flushed. 'Stop. Just stop. I know what I've done, but there's nothing I can do now. I was on edge all my life; always wondering what would happen next. Davie was so volatile, and Robyn didn't help. And I know, don't tell me, she was a child. I've failed. I didn't have the energy to deal with her too.'

'Well, get your finger out, before it's too late,' said Fenella. 'Let her know you appreciate what she's done here. Because if you don't, you're a cold-hearted woman, and I, for one, will never set foot here again.'

Maureen turned away and braced herself on the worktop.

'Come on, Carl,' said Fenella. She grabbed his hand and pulled him out.

'Mum.' He broke free as they got outside. 'I'm not five!' Taking a cleansing breath, he stared at Fenella then pulled her towards him and embraced her. 'Oh, Mum. I'm sorry.'

Patting his back, Fenella looked up and frowned. 'I hope Maureen takes heed. I'm furious with her.'

'I noticed.'

'We need to find Robyn. I have her number.'

'What is going on?' said Carl. 'How do you have her number?'

'I met her this morning. She's such a lovely girl. So sad, so lonely. She just needs—'

'Love.' Carl rubbed his forehead and looked away. His old boat swayed about in the wind.

'Well, yes. Carl… do you?'

He nodded, flattening his lips, willing the great swell of emotion to stay firmly inside. 'For twelve years I've tried to hide it, forget it, ignore it, but it's not going away. It's just got a whole lot worse.'

'Oh, Carl.' Fenella put her hand to her mouth. 'I'm very glad to hear it.' The wind twisted her fair hair around her face. 'Has she told you about the baby?'

'What baby?' A million impossible ideas splintered through his head in a split second. He had nothing to do with *that*.

'She lost a baby. It's ripped the carpet from under her feet, thrown her world upside down. That's why she's here.

She couldn't face her ex. A horrible man by the sound of things. Pete, I think she called him. He didn't want a baby, then she lost it anyway. She's bottled it all up.' Fenella shook her head, the corners of her lips turned down. 'She's heartbroken. Poor, poor girl. Let's find her. She needs you. You can fix this.'

'How? You're talking about mending hearts. That's beyond me. I can't.'

'You'll find a way. Now go. Wherever she might be, just go. I'll text her. I'll send you her number too. Just find her, for goodness' sake.'

Fenella pulled out her phone and gestured Carl to go. Where? He started the engine, gave a toot and pulled off. Three hundred square miles of Hebridean land lay between him and finding her. Mull suddenly seemed too big. She could be anywhere. He could miss her going south as she drove north on the other side of the island. He knew some quiet spots off the beaten track; places he'd slept in the pickup after leaving the cabin. Robyn would know places too, but she wouldn't do that. Sleeping in a car was not her style. She would come home. Much later but she'd come. He bit the inside of his cheek and shook his head. Could he be sure? Howling winds battered the pickup. He headed south, passing back through Craignure, checking every car parked outside the shop as he drove on. Nothing. The road beyond led to the small village of Lochdon. A few roads shot off to other villages and hamlets. Beyond, uninhabited countryside spread for miles. Slamming on the brakes, he pulled into a passing place and stopped the engine. The tightness in his ribs paralysed him. How could he possibly find her?

'This is crazy.' He leaned back and tried to breathe normally. Waiting back at the hotel was the best idea.

A ringing sound. His phone. Scrabbling about his pockets, he found it. *Let it be Mum. She's found her.* He frowned at the screen.

Liam calling

Liam? Since when did he ever call? Carl swiped the green dot. 'Hello.'

'Hey, buddy. What's going on?'

'I don't know. What do you mean?'

'I just had Mum on the phone in a right state. She says your mum was shouting at her and she's all upset about Robyn.'

'Yeah? And about time.'

'What do you mean? So, Robyn missed a ferry and isn't back yet. She's always driving off, avoiding people. What's new?'

'Nothing. Nothing's new for you. Or for Maureen. What's new for Robyn is this time someone cares. I want to know where she is, how she is. I want to make sure she's ok and not on her own, dying inside because everyone she's ever cared about has thrown her under the wagon.' Carl swallowed. Deafening silence. Pulling the phone from his ear, he checked it was still connected.

'Carl, this is Robyn we're talking about. The one who abandoned—'

'Do not say she abandoned her family. *You* abandoned *her.* You threw her to the dogs. All of you. Davie ripped the skin from her with his cruel words, Maureen left her hanging for the buzzards, and you swooped in and pecked what was left.'

'I don't appreciate—'

'And I don't appreciate what your family has done to me either. You never bothered to mention your father was the one who goaded you into climbing the folly. You let me think it was me. All I did was call you immature, and you know what? You still are. All those years, I beat myself up about it. You would have done it anyway. All to prove yourself to that feeble excuse of a man.'

'What does it matter now? It happened. And so what? Your feelings were hurt. You didn't need several years of therapy to regain mobility. You can live a normal life, you don't need adapted furniture, accessible living. You think you've had a raw deal?'

'I'm not saying you didn't suffer. I know you did, and I hate myself for it, but if you think I've led a normal life since then you're wrong.'

'Look, Carl, I don't want us to fall out—'

'I have to go. I'm not in the mood for caring. I don't give a shit how you feel or whether or not Maureen is upset. Both you and her have a lot of soul-searching to do. Because if anything has happened to Robyn, I will never forgive either of you. Ever.' He swiped the *end call* button and threw the phone onto the passenger seat. How had it come to this? The pickup shuddered in the wind. Somewhere out there was Robyn. What if she'd finally had enough?

A sharp pain stabbed Carl's chest. 'Please, just let me find her.'

Chapter Twenty-Two

Robyn

Carsaig Bay – even through the dismal squall, it was one of the most beautiful places Robyn could imagine. Carefully she drove the BMW along the bumpy track. At the end was the cottage. The dream home. Deserted and dark. How cosy it could be inside with a fire in the stove, a plush sofa, soft blankets. And Carl. Her eyes closed as she imagined falling asleep in his arms. Safe as the storm pounded.

Florrie jumped onto her knee. Robyn stroked her. The car got colder and colder. She shivered. What now? This was the end of the road. Not just the track. Her journey. Nowhere to go. She couldn't go back to the hotel. 'I never want to see it again,' she muttered. Checking her phone, she wasn't surprised to see *no reception*. Had Fenella found Carl?

After the ferry was cancelled, Robyn had let the road carry her. She'd been sure Carl would be here. Just there, on the beach, or walking along the cliff-side path. Her stomach flipped. If he tried that in this weather. No. She shook her head. The pickup. She would have seen it. The village had only a tiny parking area. If he was there, she would know.

'I wish we could go inside,' she whispered in Florrie's ear. Florrie nuzzled her and curled back into her coat. 'No one lives there. But no. We better not.' Throwing back her head, she sighed. Darkness crept down. Great grey rainclouds rolled in, covering the dramatic cliffs with an ominous, grim ceiling.

Florrie got restless. Robyn bit on her lower lip and fingered the door handle. 'Come on then.' Icy wind bit her face, sleet nipped at her cheeks. She faced it head on, but she couldn't see the way forward. The queen of business, and mistress of her office was lost out here in the wild. A million miles from success, money, order. She'd built a comfortable life; she couldn't knock it. Many people didn't have half as much. But the void inside ached. Sharp shots of pain flicked upwards, burning her chest. Clasping her hands across her front, she looked up. Sleet stung her forehead. Darting about, Florrie sniffed some boulders.

Waves crashed in. Robyn kicked the shingle as she walked. Where did she go from here? Squinting around, she rubbed the water from her face and frowned. 'Florrie?' Where was she? Stepping forward, Robyn called again. Her eyes roamed around the darkening shoreline.

'Oh my god! No!' Her hands slapped her cheeks. Adrenaline pushed her quivering legs forward; her boots bolted across the rocky beach. Florrie's tiny body dipped up and down. Huge breakers rolled closer. Robyn trembled, her breath rasped. 'I'm coming! I'm coming!' Stumbling over a boulder, she reached the water's edge. The pulse thrashing in her ears eclipsed the waves, the wind. Everything. *Please, just get me to her.* Water flooded into her boots and hampered her progress, her grey wool coat dragged. She pushed forward.

'Florrie, swim, please. Come on, come to me.' Robyn clenched her fists, wading further. The weight of her boots tugged as she forced her legs to move. The chill. The clag. *Breathe. Move!* Her lungs constricted. She couldn't get there. A colossal breaker rolled over. Florrie vanished. Robyn stumbled. Pressing her nails into her cheeks, she let out an anguished shriek.

Gasping and shaking, she staggered forward. A sudden shout. She spun around. A man charged across the beach, ripping off his jacket, and tossing it aside.

'Robyn! What are you doing?' Strong hands grabbed her arms. Her eyes widened and her heart thumped. Carl! Where had he come from? He pulled her back. 'Get out the water, come on.'

'Help me.' Her finger shook. She tried to point. 'Florrie. She's gone. I can't see her.'

'What?' Bending down, Carl pulled off his shoes, slung them onto the shore and ran into the sea. It was almost up to his middle, but he pushed his way out. Frozen rigid, Robyn held her face. Dread shot through her system, choking her. If he turned around holding a limp body, she'd throw herself in. She couldn't bear it. She shouldn't have let her get so near the edge. Why hadn't she watched more closely? Everything had slowed. The waves seemed to be rolling up with leisurely deliberation. All sound ceased, except for the rushing in her ears.

Robyn's heart stopped. Carl was cradling something in his arms. Florrie. Was she…? Robyn couldn't bear to look.

'She's ok.' Carl's shout switched everything back on. Suddenly the waves crashed, and the wind moaned. Carl waded back to the beach, grabbed his coat and wrapped Florrie inside. Hardly able to drag her waterlogged boots an inch, Robyn forced herself forward. Staggering towards him, she threw out her arms and took the bundle.

'Oh, Florrie. My little one.' She held the shivering terrier close. 'Do you think she'll be ok?'

Carl nodded and sank to the shingle, pouring water from his shoes. 'Bring her up to the car, I'll put the heaters on, and we'll dry her out. She's probably in shock, but she'll be fine.' His teeth chattered as he pulled his soaking shoes back on.

Robyn clung tight, patting Florrie's dripping head. Her wet nose nuzzled Robyn's fingertips, and Robyn let out a little laugh. 'Oh, baby, you scared me.' Carl stood up and pinched his soaking jeans. Robyn's head shifted into gear. She stared at him. 'Why are you here?'

He swallowed and scanned about. 'I had a feeling you might come here. I thought you were trying to…' He hung his head. 'I thought you'd given up.'

'No. But, thank god, you came.' Robyn's eyes misted over. 'Why were you looking for me?'

'Because…' Carl's shoulders shook with cold. He rubbed his arms, and his gaze roamed over her face. 'Why do you still wear this?' He gently tugged the pendant from beneath Robyn's coat.

Her hand leapt to it and she gave a half shrug. 'Habit. And because. Well, I hoped.'

'I came to tell you that… Well, that I love you.' He raised his hand and ran his thumb down her cheek. 'I just wanted you to know.'

Robyn pressed her lips together, her eyes welled, and she looked up, bottling the air in her chest. 'It was meant to be forever.' Her fingers clung to the pendant.

'I know. I lost my way. But no matter what you choose now, to stay or go. I just want you to know how I feel. I had to tell you.'

A watery smile forced its way onto Robyn's lips. Strong arms pulled her tight. Her eyes shut, unleashing a stream of tears. Florrie snuggled into the warmth between them. Robyn pressed against her and leaned on Carl's shoulder. He stroked her hair, letting out long breaths across her neck.

'I don't know what to say,' Robyn whispered.

'I can't offer you anything. I have nothing – except what's in the back of my truck.'

'You just offered me something no one else ever has. Love. And I want it.' She burrowed into his shoulder. 'I thought I was fine on my own. But I'm not.'

'Me neither.' He rubbed her back with his broad hands. Warm lips touched her cheek, and she smiled. 'My mum told me what you'd been through. The baby. I'm sorry. I really am.'

'I never thought I'd feel like this. I thought I was happy without kids. Until I lost the baby.'

'I've never trusted myself. A guy should be able to provide for kids, protect them.'

'Carl, you're the most caring man I know.'

He breathed a laugh. 'If you and I have a future, maybe I'll be brave enough to try.'

Her gaze met his grey-blue eyes. They shone bright. 'We do. Don't we?'

Carl gently rubbed the end of her nose with his; the cold tickled. Robyn smiled as he leaned in and kissed her. Trying not to squash Florrie, Robyn immersed herself in Carl's lips. Moments drifted by. 'Let's get to the car and warm up.' Carl breathed. 'We've got plenty time to finish this.'

With the aid of the blowers in the pickup, Florrie perked up, her coat fluffy, warm and dry. Robyn sat in the passenger seat, stroking her. Letting out a sigh, she attempted to take stock. The distraction of Carl changing into dry clothes beside her was enough to stop the conveyor belt of analysis kicking into action.

'Right.' He swivelled around, adjusting his dry jeans. 'What are we going to do?'

'Drive off into the sunset?' Robyn flashed him a smile. 'Though it's too dull for that.'

'Good plan. Unfortunately, I'm homeless and I doubt you want to go back to the hotel. I don't fancy spending another night on Georgia's sofa.'

Robyn sighed. 'I don't really care. I'd happily sit here all night. As long as I can stay with you.'

'Likewise.' He leaned over and kissed her. She wanted to leap across the gearbox and grab him, but Florrie had been exposed to enough trauma for one day.

'How about your mum? Could we stay with her? I like her, she was so kind to me.'

'Ok. I guess, but Robyn.' He took her hand and squeezed it. 'I'm penniless. A waster.'

'No, you're The Fixer, and together we'll sort this.'

Letting out a sigh, he pushed back his mop of curls. 'I don't see how.' With a puzzled look, he scanned around. 'Where's your car?'

'I left it at the cottage.'

'*The cottage?*' He smiled. 'It's exactly like the dream we had, isn't it?'

'It is.' Her eyes widened.

'Well, we missed out there. Maybe we should go back to the cabin before we go anywhere else. I think Maureen is actually concerned about your whereabouts.'

'Really?'

'Hmm, let's get your car and we'll find out. You can follow me back.'

'I'll get my case, but I'd rather come with you.'

'And leave your car at the cottage? What if the new owners show up?'

Her lips curled up. 'They already did. And they don't mind.'

Carl frowned and leaned forward, trying to see along to the road end. Perhaps looking for the twinkling glow of lights. 'Someone's in already? Who are they?'

A smile split Robyn's face. She couldn't hold it back. Months, perhaps years of tension lifted from her chest. The release left her light-headed. 'You and me.'

'Pardon?'

'You and me. I bought the cottage. Though I don't have the keys yet. I only heard yesterday my bid was accepted.'

A grin and a frown battled on Carl's features. He shook his head. The grin won. 'Why?'

'I couldn't let it go, especially when I heard Julie McNabb was interested.' Robyn smirked, then touched her cheeks. 'Though I didn't mean any offence to your brother.'

Carl laughed. 'Well, if anyone deserves to miss out, it's her. She's caused enough problems. I call it karma.' He shook his head, still beaming. Robyn mirrored it. 'You have a beautiful smile,' he said. 'I just wish I had more I could give you.'

'You're my missing piece.' She traced her hand down his cheek. 'What more could I want?'

Chapter Twenty-Three

Robyn

When a knock came on the cabin door early the next morning, Robyn looked at Carl. No words were necessary. Robyn knew who it was. Carl's fixed jaw said he did too. The previous day's euphoria hadn't worn off. Snuggling inside one of Carl's woolly jumpers, Robyn basked in the assurance of change. The uncertainty of the future wasn't as terrifying, because she wasn't alone. Pinching her lip, Robyn eyed the door. The hammering increased. Tension spread across her shoulders as Carl stood up.

'Let me,' she said.

'Don't you want to keep a low profile?'

'No. Let's see what she has to say. Shall we take bets on just how furious she'll be? What will I have done wrong this time?'

With a sharp tug, Robyn pulled open the door. An ashen-faced Maureen gaped. Her hands flew to her cheeks.

'Robyn! You're here.' Maureen fixed a disapproving sideways look on her.

'Yes, she is.' Carl stepped up behind, putting his hand on the door across Robyn's shoulder, sheltering her. The warm woody scent was calming. Robyn breathed it in, letting it flood her with comfort. 'And don't you dare say anything about it,' continued Carl.

'I wasn't going to. I just… Where have you been? You've had me worried sick. I haven't slept a wink.'

Robyn crossed her arms. 'You expect me to believe that? Since when? You've never given me a passing thought in over twenty years. Even before that. As soon as Liam was born, you threw me aside. I wasn't a quiet, compliant and biddable child like him.'

Maureen rubbed her thumbs together and chewed her upper lip. Tiny flakes of snow fell, landing in beads on her short spiky hair. 'I'm sorry,' she said quietly, looking away.

'Sorry doesn't cover it,' said Carl. 'I'd like to forgive and forget. We both would. Hell, we know better than anyone what it feels like to be blamed and shamed. But, Maureen, this isn't a quick fix. You can't just say sorry and expect us to crumble and fall into your arms.'

Maureen swallowed and rubbed her chest. 'I realise that. And you're right. I've said some terrible things. Nothing I say can make it up to you. I suppose actions speak louder than words.'

'Yes, they do,' said Robyn. 'But we're going to have lots of opportunities to make up for things.'

'We are?'

'Yes. I'm staying. With Carl.'

Maureen's normally slit-like eyes bulged wide. 'As in… together?'

'Yes. I bought the cottage in Carsaig.'

Perhaps Maureen was trying to reply, but her mouth opened and closed without a sound.

'Robyn's the love of my life,' said Carl. 'We've missed out twelve years of what-might-have-beens. No more time wasting.'

Robyn turned to Carl and smiled. He pulled her in for a hug.

*

Opening day dawned misty and grim, as was not unusual for Mull in mid-March. As Robyn hustled the dogs back into the family kitchen at the hotel, the chill wind bit her cheeks, reminding her that winter wasn't quite through.

A shadow near the corridor door gave her a start. A man's head poked around, his expression sullen, his dark eyebrows drawn together.

'Good morning, Liam,' said Robyn. As she'd spent the previous evening at the cabin, she'd missed his arrival and had allowed Carl to get their 'man to man' chat out of the way without her.

'I guess I have some apologies to make,' said Liam. 'I've been a total git, haven't I?'

'Pretty much.'

'Well, I'm going to try and make it up to you. Both of you. Mum and I did a lot of talking. Blaming others has always been the easy option for us. We need to grow a pair if we're going to fix this mess.'

Time would tell if his words were idle, but Robyn's chest still tingled with the thrill of new adventures. She was willing to accept his words as a good start.

Shortly before twelve, Robyn met Carl in the foyer talking to Maureen. Even now, there was an edge to his voice. Maureen's part in Carl's grief would take a long time to assuage. Robyn's eyes met Maureen's. Maureen blinked and pulled a tiny smile. Tentatively, Robyn returned it.

'Everything's ready,' said Maureen. 'Carl's just fixed up the ribbon.' Maureen straightened her shimmering black satin top and glanced around. Gone was the 1980s carpet and mahogany. A smart new desk and country décor welcomed guests to the foyer. Light shone through the landing window, glinting on the polished floor and handsome staircase.

The front door opened. Julie McNabb swanned in. Robyn flicked a glance at Carl. He pulled a face and stretched out his hand. Robyn clasped it.

'Hello,' said Julie. 'The sun's just come out. It's freezing, but it looks good out front. I ducked the ribbon.' Her eyes skimmed over Robyn and Carl's entwined hands. She smirked.

Carl leaned in and whispered, 'Don't look now, but I think a seagull likes her jacket.' Julie turned round to straighten some files on the shelf. A greenish-yellow streak dripped down the back of her new blazer. Robyn covered her mouth, holding in a smirk. 'Karma.' Carl smiled.

'Looks good, doesn't it?' Maureen stepped onto the stairs and surveyed the foyer.

'It does.' Liam walked behind Robyn and patted Carl on the back. 'We owe you both. This place should be yours.'

'Well, I don't want it,' said Carl. 'Running a hotel is not for me.'

Elsa came down the stairs, carrying baby Harris. 'Hey everyone.' Her eyes darted about nervously. She'd obviously been keeping out the way. Harris cooed, and she passed him to Liam.

Carl slipped his hand round Robyn's waist and steered her away from the others. She leaned into him. 'One day,' he whispered, 'we'll have our own.' Robyn threw her arms around Carl, a buzz of warmth cascading through her.

Cars started to arrive. Robyn tugged Carl outside to wait. Rays of sun dappled across the lawn. 'I should have put on my coat.' Robyn took her place at the bottom of the steps, clutching Carl's hand.

'Hello!' Fenella waved, heading down the path. She steadied an old lady with a walking stick.

'Oh joy,' said Carl. 'Here's Aunt Jean.'

Fenella drew level. 'Now, Jean, let me introduce you to Robyn.'

A bony hand popped out. Robyn shook it.

'Nice firm grip,' said Jean. She glanced up at Robyn. 'I hear you're a business tycoon. Hopefully, you can teach Carl a thing or two. I'm very glad to hear he's moving out of the shed. No place for a respectable man.'

Carl rolled his shoulders into a shrug. 'Who said I was respectable?'

Robyn grinned as they took their places on the flag-stoned area at the bottom of the main steps. Friends from all over had arrived to watch the opening. Georgia beamed at Robyn and Carl, giving them a bright wave as she huddled beside Beth. Robyn raised her hand in return. Her eyes landed on Kirsten, whose face did not reflect a happy occasion. Beth gave her a stoic nudge. Kirsten shrugged it off, pulling up a furry hood.

Letting out a sigh, Robyn rubbed her cheek on Carl's shoulder. She knew what it was like to ache for him.

Maureen stepped up carrying a large pair of scissors. People clapped. She turned on the top step and raised a shaky hand. 'I have some things to say before I cut this. I would like to thank some people. First, my friend, Gillian, for helping me through this difficult time. Second, Carl. Carl was roped into this and gave up so much of his own time to help. Third, and most importantly, my daughter, Robyn. In fact, I'd like Robyn to come up.' Maureen beckoned her. Robyn swallowed. Carl gave her a gentle nudge.

Keeping her eyes down, she climbed the five steps to the top; it felt like a lot more. Turning to face the crowd, she looked around. Carl beamed and winked.

'Without you,' said Maureen, 'none of this would have happened. You've worked tirelessly and in poor conditions. Because, everyone here knows me, I hate change and I can be a cantankerous old devil.'

An outbreak of laughter erupted. Robyn exchanged a glance with Carl. At his side, Fenella folded her arms and nodded. But Robyn's eyes were glued to Carl. He loved her. A warm tingling sensation crept over her. He smiled and she responded in kind. Maureen tapped her shoulder.

'I'd like you to do the honours. You deserve to.' She handed the scissors to Robyn.

Robyn stepped forward, hardly able to take in the magnitude of what had happened in the past few months. 'I declare the Glen Lodge Hotel, open.' She cut the ribbon; it fluttered on either side of the door. Rapturous clapping broke out.

'You're all welcome for a drink. Our first customers,' called Maureen, flinging the door wide.

Robyn backed off as the guests streamed up the stairs.

'Well done, and I'm happy to hear about you and Carl.' Beth patted Robyn's shoulder. 'That drink's back on the cards then.' Kirsten stormed in without speaking to either of them. 'Though it might have to wait until after the lambs.'

'I'd like that.' Robyn regarded Beth. She'd cleaned up well – so feminine, almost elegant. 'Is Kirsten ok?'

'She'll get over it. I tried to tell her for a long time Carl wasn't interested, but she wouldn't listen. Now, she's annoyed with me too. I'll go and see her.'

At the bottom of the stairs, Georgia chatted to Carl, Fenella, Per and Aunt Jean. With a wink, Georgia hopped up the steps. 'I'm so excited you two got together. It's made me feel like a big fuzzy ball of candyfloss.'

Per gave Carl a fatherly clap on the back as they stepped up beside Robyn. Fenella helped Aunt Jean before embracing Robyn. 'You wonderful girl,' Fenella said. 'I'm so happy you're ours.' Robyn felt the wave of emotion rising. 'Let's get in.' Fenella patted her back.

'I hope they have sherry,' said Aunt Jean. 'I like a good sherry.'

Carl grabbed Robyn's hand as she moved to follow. 'Wait a bit.' He watched until everyone had disappeared inside. 'You're amazing. You really are.' He stroked his thumb down her cheek and tilted his head. Robyn took a deep breath, drawing in the sea air and him.

'I couldn't have done any of this without you,' she said.

'We make a good team. Just think about what else we can accomplish if we put our minds to it.'

'And we can start with our own dream cottage.' Robyn wrapped her arms around his neck and pulled him in for a long kiss. One she hoped would never end.

Epilogue

Robyn

With dainty feet, Florrie bounded up the path towards the cottage door. Robyn smiled, breathing in the cool sea air, as she watched the sparkle of the sun poking through the clouds, and twinkling on the water.

Carl inhaled and threw back his head. 'Perfect.' He slid his hands into the back pockets of his jeans and looked around. 'This is our dream come true.'

Robyn put the key in the lock; her hand trembled as she turned it. 'Are you going to carry me in?'

'Ha, no sweat.' Carl swept her up and lifted her over the threshold. She squealed. He was so strong. Florrie yapped and dotted about. Setting Robyn back on her feet, he laughed.

'Imagine all the things we can do here.' Robyn gazed around. 'I think I might even give Bill a call, I can see some building work in the offing. Do you think he'll want to work for me again?'

A shadow clouded Carl's eyes. 'Robyn. I can't help feeling I don't deserve this. You bought it, you worked for it. I've just stepped in and taken what's not rightfully mine.'

Robyn tipped her head to the side. 'If it bothers you that much, I'm sure we can come to some arrangement.'

'Such as?'

'I get breakfast in bed every morning, you do all the cleaning, cooking. You know, that kind of thing.'

Carl frowned and flipped back his hair. 'Yeah, ok. I guess that's fair.'

With a laugh, Robyn poked him in the tummy. 'Don't be silly. If you were a man with money and I was a penniless woman, it wouldn't bother you. It's only hard because the tables are turned. You're a man. You like to provide. But Carl, you have different talents. Look around. This place is in a bad way. It's cute and I love it, but it needs fixing. And there's only one man for that job.'

'And you just said that was Bill.'

Robyn chuckled, peeling off a loose bit of wallpaper. 'Some of this is beyond him. Only you can make it the way we dreamed it. And you can build yourself a studio, or a workshop, or both.'

'You're going to banish me to another cabin?'

'I thought you liked it.' Robyn flashed him a grin and walked to the window. The sea rushed across the boulders, spreading in white foamy puddles. 'But you could always fix it up so it was part of the house, then you'd always be here. And it could double as my office – you on one side, me on the other.'

He nodded and smiled. 'That I can do. It sounds almost perfect, but there's room for improvement.' He stepped up behind her, wrapped his arms round her waist and planted a kiss on the nape of her neck. 'After it's all fixed up, we can add the most important touches.'

She leaned back, absorbing his warmth. 'Which are?'

'Five more dogs… and three kids.'

Robyn smiled; a wave of ambient heat flooded her chest. So much to look forward to. New adventures called.

She clutched Carl's hand; he squeezed it in return. With him at her side, she had the strength to face anything and she couldn't wait to get started.

The End

Share the Love!

If you enjoyed reading this book, then please
share your reviews online.
Leaving reviews is a perfect way to support authors
and helps books reach more readers.
So please review and share!
Let me know what you think.

Margaret

About the author

I'm a writer, mummy, wife and chocolate eater (in any order you care to choose). I live in highland Perthshire in a little house close to the woods where I often see red squirrels, deer and other such tremendously Scottish wildlife... Though not normally haggises or even men in kilts!

It's my absolute pleasure to be able to bring the Scottish Island Escapes series to you and I hope you love reading the stories as much as I enjoy writing them. Writing is an escapist joy for me and I adore disappearing into my imagination and returning with a new story to tell.

If you want to keep up with what's coming next or learn more about any of the books or the series, then be sure to visit my website. I look forward to seeing you there.

www.margaretamatt.com

Acknowledgements

Thanks goes to my adorable husband for supporting my dreams and putting up with my writing talk 24/7. Also to my son, whose interest in my writing always makes me smile. It's precious to know I've passed the bug to him – he's currently writing his own fantasy novel and instruction books on how to build Lego!

Throughout the writing process, I have gleaned help from many sources and met some fabulous people. I'd like to give a special mention to Stéphanie Ronckier, my beta reader extraordinaire. Stéphanie's continued support with my writing is invaluable and I love the fact that I need someone French to correct my grammar! Stéphanie, you rock. To my fellow authors, Evie Alexander and Lyndsey Gallagher – you girls are the best! I love it that you always have my back and are there to help when I need you.

Also, a huge thanks to my editor, Aimee Walker, at Aimee Walker Editorial Services for her excellent work on my novels and for answering all my mad questions. Thank you so much, Aimee!

More Books by Margaret Amatt

Free Hugs &

Old-Fashioned Kisses

Do you ever get one of those days when you just fancy snuggling up? Then this captivating short story is for you!

And what's more, it's free when you sign up to my newsletter.

Meet Livvi, a girl who just needs a hug. And Jakob, a guy who doesn't go about hugging random strangers. But what if he makes an exception, just this once?

Make yourself a hot chocolate, sign up to my newsletter and enjoy!

A short story only available to newsletter subscribers.

Sign up at
www.margaretamatt.com

A Winter Haven

She was the one that got away. Now she's back.

Career-driven Robyn Sherratt returns to her childhood home on the Scottish Isle of Mull, hoping to build bridges with her estranged family. She discovers her mother struggling to run the family hotel. When an old flame turns up, memories come back to bite, nibbling into Robyn's fragile heart.

Carl Hansen, known as The Fixer, abandoned city life for peace and tranquillity. Swapping his office for a log cabin, he mends people's broken treasures. He can fix anything, except himself. When forced to work on hotel renovations with Robyn, the girl he lost twelve years ago, his quiet life is sent spinning.

Carl would like nothing more than to piece together the shattered shards of Robyn's heart. But can she trust him? What can a broken man like him offer a successful woman like her?

A Spring Retreat

She's gritty, he's determined. Who will back down first?

When spirited islander Beth McGregor learns of plans to build a road through the family farm, she sets out to stop it. But she's thrown off course by the charming and handsome project manager. Sparks fly, sending Beth into a spiral of confusion. Guys are fine as friends. Nothing else.

Murray Henderson has finally found a place to retreat from the past with what seems like a straightforward job. But he hasn't reckoned on the stubbornness of the locals, especially the hot-headed and attractive Beth.

As they battle together over the proposed road, attraction blooms. Murray strives to discover the real Beth; what secrets lie behind the tough façade? Can a regular farm girl like her measure up to Murray's impeccable standards, and perhaps find something she didn't know she was looking for?

A Summer Sanctuary

She's about to discover the one place he wants to keep

secret

Five years ago, Island girl Kirsten McGregor broke the company rules. Now, she has the keys to the Hidden Mull tour bus and is ready to take on the task of running the business. But another tour has arrived. The competition is bad enough but when she recognises the rival tour operator, her plans are upended.

Former jet pilot Fraser Bell has made his share of mistakes. What better place to hide and regroup than the place he grew to love as a boy? With great enthusiasm, he launches into his new tour business, until old-flame Kirsten shows up and sends his world plummeting.

Kirsten may know all the island's secrets, but what she can't work out is Fraser. With tension simmering, Kirsten and Fraser's attraction increases. What if they both made a mistake before? Is one of them about to make an even bigger one now?

An Autumn Hideaway

She went looking for someone, but it wasn't him.

After a string of disappointments for chirpy city girl Autumn, discovering her notoriously unstable mother has run off again is the last straw. When Autumn learns her mother's last known whereabouts was a remote Scottish Island, she makes the rash decision to go searching for her.

Taciturn islander Richard has his reasons for choosing the remote Isle of Mull as home. He's on a deadline and doesn't need any complications or company. But everything changes after a chance encounter with Autumn.

Autumn chips away at Richard's reserve until his carefully constructed walls start to crumble. But Autumn's just a passing visitor and Richard has no plans to leave. Will they realise, before it's too late, that what they've been searching for isn't necessarily what's missing?

A Christmas Bluff

She's about to trespass all over his Christmas.

Artist and photographer Georgia Rose has spent two carefree years on the Isle of Mull and is looking forward to a quiet Christmas... Until she discovers her family is about to descend upon her, along with her past.

Aloof aristocrat Archie Crichton-Leith has let out his island mansion to a large party from the mainland. They're expecting a castle for Christmas, not an outdated old pile, and he's in trouble.

When Georgia turns up with an irresistible smile and an offer he can't refuse, he's wary, but he needs her help.

As Georgia weaves her festive charms around the house, they start to work on Archie too. And the spell extends both ways. But falling in love was never part of the deal. Can the magic outlast Christmas when he's been conned before and she has a secret that could ruin everything?

A Flight of Fancy

She's masquerading as her twin, pretending to be his

girlfriend, while really just being herself.

After years of being cooped up by her movie star family, Taylor Rousse is desperate to escape. Having a Hollywood actress as a twin is about all Taylor can say for herself, but when she's let down by her sister for the umpteenth time, she decides now is the time for action.

Pilot Magnus Hansen is heading back to his family home on the Isle of Mull for his brother's wedding and he's not looking forward to showing up single. The eldest of three brothers shouldn't be the last married – no matter how often he tells himself he's not the marrying type.

On his way, Magnus crashes into a former fling. She's a Hollywood star looking for an escape and they strike a deal: he's her ticket to a week of peace; she's his new date. Except Taylor isn't who he thinks she is. When she and Magnus start to fall for each other, their double deception threatens to blow up in their faces and shatter everything that might have been.

A Hidden Gem

She has a secret past. He has an uncertain future.

Together, can they unlock them both?

After being framed for embezzlement by her ex, career-driven Rebekah needs a break to nurse her broken heart and wounded soul. When her grandmother dies, leaving her a precious necklace and a mysterious note, she sets out to unravel a family secret that's been hidden for over sixty years.

Blair's lived all his life on the Isle of Mull. He's everybody's friend – with or without the benefits – but at night he goes home alone. When Rebekah arrives, he's instantly attracted to her, but she's way out of his league. He needs to keep a stopper on his feelings or risk losing her friendship.

As Rebekah's quest continues, she's rocked by unexpected feelings for her new friend. Can she trust her heart as much as she trusts Blair? And can he be more than just a friend? Perhaps the truth isn't the only thing waiting to be found.

A Striking Result

She's about to tackle everything he's trying to hide.

When unlucky-in-love Carys McTeague is offered the job of caring for an injured footballer, she goes for it even though it's far removed from the world she's used to.

Scottish football hero Troy Copeland is at the centre of a media storm after a serious accident left him with career-threatening injuries and his fiancée dumped him for a teammate. With a little persuasion from Carys, he flees to the remote Isle of Mull to escape and recuperate.

On Mull, Carys reconnects with someone unexpected from her past and starts to fall in love with the island – and Troy. But nothing lasts forever. Carys has been abandoned more than once and as soon as Troy's recovered, he'll leave like everyone else.

Troy's smitten by Carys but has a career to preserve. Will he realise he's been chasing the wrong goal before he loses the love of his life?

A Perfect Discovery

To find love, they need to dig deep.

Kind-hearted archaeologist Rhona Lamond returns home to the Isle of Mull after her precious research is stolen, feeling lost and frustrated. When an island project comes up, it tugs at Rhona's soul and she's desperate to take it on. But there's a major problem.

Property developer Calum Matheson has a longstanding feud with the Lamond family. After a plot of land he owns is discovered to be a site of historical importance, his plans are thrown into disarray and building work put on hold.

Calum doesn't think things can get any worse, until archaeologist Rhona turns up. Not only is she a Lamond, but she's all grown up, and even stubbornly unromantic Calum can't fail to notice her – or the effect she has on him.

Their attraction ignites but how can they overcome years of hate between their families? Both must decide what's more important, family or love.

A Festive Surprise

She can't abide Christmas. He's not sure what it's all

about. Together they're in for a festive surprise.

Ambitious software developer Holly may have a festive name but the connection ends there. She despises the holiday season and decides to flee to the remote island of Mull in a bid to escape from it.

Syrian refugee Farid has made a new home in Scotland but he's lonely. Understanding Nessie and Irn Bru is one thing, but when glittery reindeer and tinsel hit the shelves, he's completely bemused. Determined to understand a new culture, he asks his new neighbour to educate him on all things Christmas.

When Holly reluctantly agrees, he realises there's more to her hatred of mince pies and mulled wine than meets the eye. Farid makes it his mission to inject some joy into Hollys' life but falling for her is an unexpected gift that was never on his list.

As their attraction sparkles, can Christmas work its magic on Holly and Farid, or will their spark fizzle out with the end of December?

Printed in Great Britain
by Amazon